A MIRANDA QUINN LEGAL TWIST | BOOK 3

Miranda Fights

Gail Ward Olmsted

Black Rose Writing | Texas

This is a work of fiction. Names, characters, businesses, places, events, and incidents are either the products of the author's imagination or used in a fictitious manner. Any resemblance to actual persons, living or dead, or actual events is purely coincidental.

ISBN: 978-1-68513-521-8
PUBLISHED BY BLACK ROSE WRITING
www.blackrosewriting.com

Printed in the United States of America
Suggested Retail Price (SRP) $21.95

Miranda Fights is printed in Palatino Linotype

*As a planet-friendly publisher, Black Rose Writing does its best to eliminate unnecessary waste to reduce paper usage and energy costs, while never compromising the reading experience. As a result, the final word count vs. page count may not meet common expectations.

Don't miss the rest of Miranda's stories!

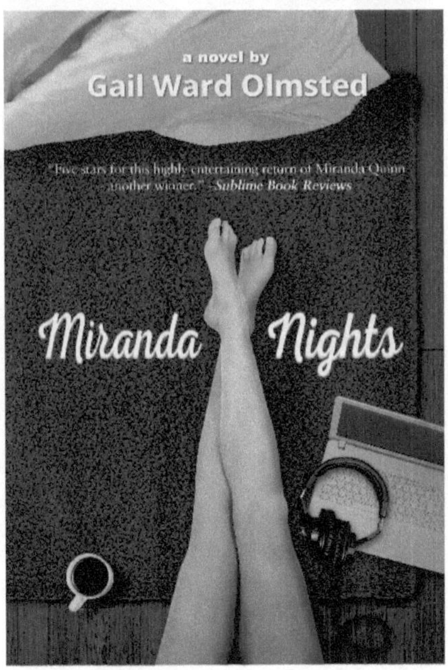

Thank you

To my loving family and dear friends for understanding when my fictional life takes precedence over my real one.

To my readers for your support and encouragement.

To my niece Kim Early and her wife Sarah Kalka for aiding in my understanding of the efforts of the Connecticut Department of Children and Families and more importantly, for the work you both do every day to protect our most vulnerable citizens.

To my neighbor and friend Charlie Adcock for answering my questions about police work, procedures, and the conducting of investigations.

To my editor, the fabulous Jennifer 'Jenny Q' Quinlan for your skill and patience in helping me craft a better story.

To my fellow Black Rose authors, the best and most supportive writing community I could ever imagine; you inspire me every single day.

To the staff of Black Rose Writing, especially Reagan Rothe, for making my books accessible to a vast audience and for working tirelessly to promote the work of your authors.

Gail

Miranda Fights is dedicated to eight strong, amazing women:
my daughter, Hayley,
and my nieces Aimee, Barbara, Jenny, Kim,
Sarah, Suzanne, and Witchuda.

I love you!

Miranda Fights

PROLOGUE

He looked up in surprise when she entered his office. He prided himself on maintaining an open-door policy, but maybe they could knock first?

"What's up?" he asked, and she parked herself on one of the chairs facing his desk without being invited. Where were the manners? Were young people today being raised by wolves? Since most of the clients they served were "unhoused" (they were discouraged from using the term *homeless* anymore), he realized he couldn't expect much in the way of basic etiquette. She was slouching, deep in thought, and he wanted to say, "*You* came to see *me*," but decided to practice a bit of patience. Finally, she spoke up.

"So, it's kinda weird," she began, her voice cracked, dry, possibly from lack of use. "I haven't seen Lyndsey all week. I usually meet her for breakfast, but she's kinda disappeared, you know?"

Yes, he certainly knew. It was always something with these kids. Most were from right here in New London or one of the small towns on the Connecticut coastline, but you could never guess who would show up for the programs or meals each day. It was typical of the juvenile justice system's revolving door. The at-risk youth and young adults they served would find different housing or go back to live with their families or couch surf at a friend's. Or end up in a hospital or the morgue. It was always something.

"Well, that happens often," he said. "I'm sure she found a new place to live, or she went back home to, um . . ."

"Norwich," she supplied, and he nodded as if he had known that little factoid all along. He knew the girl in question but had no idea where she came from. Didn't he already have enough on his plate? Was he honestly expected to remember their birthdays and childhood pets' names as well?

"Have you left a note for her on the wall?" he asked, referring to the large whiteboard in the lobby. It was cluttered with dozens of notes, phone numbers, and graffiti, and the girls relied on it to stay in touch with their friends. He would have preferred a nice piece of artwork or even some posters in its place, but no one had asked his opinion.

"Yeah, I've left messages telling her I wanted to meet, but she hasn't responded. Are you sure you haven't seen her?" Her plump face was etched with worry, and for a second, he felt a twinge of guilt. But it passed quickly, as it always did.

He looked at the report on his desk and pretended to find a typo needing to be corrected. He drew a small circle in the margin, nodding as if giving her question some serious thought. "No, but if I do, I'll let her know you're looking for her, okay? Now if there's nothing else . . ." He stood, and she did as well, but she paused in the doorway.

"It's weird cuz she was looking for a job. She quit working at the Point at the end of the season. And I found her something, but they won't keep it open much longer, you know?"

He nodded in response. "Of course," he assured her. "Well, it's nice of you to look out for your friend, but I need to fix this report and get it out today, so . . ."

She made eye contact with him for the first time since barging in, and he saw how red-rimmed her eyes were. Poor kid. Poor, stupid kid.

"Thanks," she said and turned to leave. "See you at dinner."

He turned back to his report, glaring at the circle he had drawn. Now he would have to reprint the damn thing. He stood and stretched, thinking about the last time he had seen Lyndsey four days earlier. Her tear-stained face had been blotchy, and her overgrown bangs covered her eyes, her eyeglasses left behind. The Rohypnol had knocked her on her ass. That's how they liked them, perfect for transporting. Three hours in the back of a van and she would wake up in New York City, ready to start a whole new life. An opportunity to meet men who would pay handsomely for an hour or two of her time, not to mention all the drugs she could handle. She had come to him looking for a job, and he had found one for her. He prided himself on his willingness to help others. Above and beyond; that was his motto.

He left his office, locked his door, and strolled down the hallway to the lobby. As he approached the wall, he spotted a message scrawled in red marker.

Lynds

Where u at? Breakfast tomorrow 9am. Got u a job. C

After glancing around to make certain no one was watching, he grabbed the dog-eared eraser and removed any traces of the message. Granted, the board was vast, but it was still sought-after space, and it wasn't like "Lynds" would ever see it. No, she was going to be working too hard to even remember her old friends. Another little birdie had flown the coop.

CHAPTER 1

I stared at my husband, unable to comprehend what he was saying. I understood the words, but I couldn't believe *he* was speaking them.

"Quinn, you can't say you never saw this coming," he said, sounding more than a little defensive.

"Seriously, Eric? Because those were the exact same words I was about to say. What the hell? London?" I slumped back into my seat on the couch, still in shock. Following a nice dinner at home, my husband of four years had told me we needed to talk. But not about new patio furniture or an upcoming vacation. No, he had wanted to tell me about a once-in-a-lifetime opportunity to lead a major company expansion. In freaking London.

He spoke more slowly now, and I tried to keep myself from focusing on his tone, which was a little condescending. "Remember I told you last year how I had met Cleveland Amory, the founder of Parametric, that British architectural firm, and how he was thinking of retiring or maybe looking to take on a partner?" Eric studied me closely, waiting for my response.

I nodded slowly. Sure, I remembered. But I had filed it away in the far recesses of my brain in the "never in a million years" folder, and that had been it. Occasionally, over the past year, Eric would say something like, "Can you imagine spending the holidays in London?" but honestly, it had never been more than the most casual of comments. And suddenly, it was a reality. Or at least a proposed reality.

I switched into lawyer mode, channeling my years as a prosecutor. I had been "Quinn for the Win," damn it, and had faced far more intimidating adversaries in the courtroom nearly every day. The sexy-as-hell architect pacing before me couldn't pose a real threat. Could he?

"What about our new home?" I asked with a sweeping gesture. We had barely broken the place in.

"We can rent it out for a year and circle back to it then," he responded quickly.

"What about Pop and Sally?" My dad and stepmom were getting up there in years, and . . .

"It's a six-hour flight," he reminded me.

"What about Tracey?" I asked. She was my best friend, and we spoke every day and saw each other all the time.

"It's a six-hour flight," he repeated. Argh. He had all the answers. What about . . . ?

"My job." I enjoyed working for legal aid and got a real sense of satisfaction helping others.

"You could hire on with our firm as a legal consultant or lecture part-time at one of the excellent universities or just relax and enjoy yourself. We could travel. Go to Paris for the weekend. Doesn't that sound great?" His green eyes shone with excitement as he pulled me into a hug.

"Tell me you'll at least think about it, okay?" he asked. I nodded and told him I would.

"It would be an amazing life, babe," he assured me.

"It already is," I reminded him sadly.

###

The next morning, I was about to step into the shower when my phone started to buzz. I had the day off from my job at the legal aid office, so it had to be Tracey. I lunged for the phone. Her calls were always welcome.

"Good morning," I sang out.

"Miranda? It's Rose."

"Hey, Rose, what's up?" I asked, a feeling of dread welling inside me. Rose was the administrative assistant at the legal aid office. She scheduled lawyers' depositions, court appearances, and client consultations. This was *not* a social call.

"It's strange is what it is. They brought in a young girl on a petty larceny charge, and she won't talk to anyone but you."

"Me? What are you saying? She asked for me by name?"

"That's what it sounds like. Can you see her? Her arraignment is scheduled for 10:00 a.m." *Crap.* It was already 8:45. I'd had a bit of a late start this morning thanks to my sexy husband, but I was not complaining.

"Well, I guess I could make it. What's her name?"

"Wait, I've got it here. It's, um, ack, don't you hate it when you can't read your own writing? It's Gallagher. Lennon Gallagher. She says you knew her mom, Charlene, in high school. Does that name ring a bell?"

I sat on the side of the bed, gripping the phone to my ear. Did I remember Charlene Gallagher? Oh, you bet I did. The last time I had seen her was twenty years ago in a courtroom. She had screamed at me as they escorted her off to jail. I remembered it like it was yesterday. "You owe me, Randi Quinn. You owe me big-time." I did owe her, and apparently it was time to pay up.

"I'll be there," I said and ended the call.

CHAPTER 2

Twenty minutes later, I was driving through the surface roads of Old Lyme, on the coastline of Connecticut. It was a picturesque town of roughly 7600 folks, and it was where all my memories, both happy and sad, had taken place. My parents and I had lived in a ranch-style house not too far from the beach. All these years later, the town was still home to me. I knew enough to keep to the speed limit, even though I really needed every spare minute this morning. It was a safe, family-focused town, and the local cops were tough on anyone driving too fast. Even someone like me, whose dad had been on the force for decades until he retired seven years ago. Other than my college years and a short time living with my ex in nearby Mystic, I had called this town my home. It was warm and welcoming, and even with the beach-going crowds in the summer months, it was convenient and easy to get around in. Not to mention the fact that nearly all my favorite people in the world lived nearby. I had turned down job opportunities in the past that would have required me to live elsewhere. Now there was a possibility that I wouldn't be here much longer, depending on what we decided about London. But that was a problem for another day. Today, I needed to get to court.

I had kicked off my legal career as an assistant state's attorney for the New London District after graduating from law school. I had loved the work despite the long hours and rather meager pay and was clearly the "heir apparent" to take over when state's attorney Rick Cooper moved up. Then I had been assigned the Terry Kane rape case, and that was the beginning of the end of my time working for the State. A crucial witness under my watch disappeared without a trace, and the case fell apart. My office needed a scapegoat, and suddenly I was on the outside looking in. When a serial rapist, even an alleged one, goes free, someone ends up taking the blame. I never thought I would be back in the courtroom again, but here I was six years later, juggling a sizeable caseload as a legal aid attorney. You just never knew.

I pulled into the packed staff parking lot at the New London Courthouse at 9:45 and waited as the car before me exited a space reserved for judges and attorneys. I grabbed my bag and bolted up the wide staircase and through the revolving doors into the lobby. There was a line of people waiting to go through the security checkpoint, but the crowd was not moving. I heard someone say the belt had jammed, and there was a lot of grumbling from those eager to have their day in court. Or maybe not so eager. Either way, we were at a standstill.

Then I heard my name being called and looked up. It was Frank, one of the court officers, and he was waving me through to the front of the line. I received glares and barely muffled sounds of disgust from those I passed, but I kept my head down, murmuring "I'm sorry" and "Excuse me" at regular intervals until I made it to the front.

"Why the special treatment?" I asked Frank, as he led me over to a small table. I opened my bag for inspection while he explained they were waiting for me in courtroom #7 and he had been asked to bring me there right away. I grabbed my jacket and followed him down the hallway. We entered the room to find . . . silence. No side conversations, no sounds of the gavel striking the block, nothing. Everyone in the room turned and watched as I made my way down the center aisle, the sound of my high heels echoing on the marble floor. What the hell was I walking into?

"Good luck," Frank called to me as he beat a hasty retreat out to the hallway. I took note of the empty seat where the judge would soon be presiding over the courtroom and caught the stare of the prosecuting attorney, who sat at the table to the right. He looked young enough to be, well, younger than anyone I recalled from when I worked there. I nodded briefly in his direction and headed to the defense side of the room. Still felt strange to me, but here I was, ready to seek justice for my client.

As I watched, a thin, dark-haired girl was led out into the courtroom, escorted by two guards. Even if I hadn't been expecting Charlene's daughter, I would have known her anywhere. She was shuffling along, and I realized not only was she handcuffed, but her ankles were bound as well. On a shoplifting charge? I was about to express my displeasure at my client's extreme treatment when one of the clerks approached me. I recognized him immediately.

"Tony, what's going on? Why is she in manacles?"

"Your client has already gotten herself into some trouble this morning," he said with a frown. "They brought her out early to stand up for her charges, but she didn't want the attorney they assigned. She made a huge fuss, yelling that she only wanted to be represented by you. 'I want Randi Quinn,' she kept insisting, and she put up a fight when they tried to remove her from the courtroom. I guess that's when they called you in." What the hell? This day just kept getting better and better.

I sat at the table provided for the defense and began to lay out what I figured I would need for this hearing. My trusty Day-Timer, a pen, and a watch. I never actually wore a watch, but I liked to keep track of the time when I was in court, and constantly checking a phone was frowned upon by most judges. I studied Lennon Gallagher as she was led over to me, sandwiched between two burly guards in full perp-walk style. Seriously?

"Can we please remove the cuffs?" I asked the younger of the two guards. He looked unsure, casting a glance at my client, who was staring straight ahead, paying no mind to the proceedings.

"She will not be a problem, I promise you," I said, and I thought I saw a hint of a smile on the young girl's face. God, she looked like her mother at that age. Same spiky dark hair, straight nose, olive complexion, and big dark brown eyes that seemed too large for her narrow face. It was like looking at an old photo.

"She'd better not be," he finally said. "The judge will have my ass if she acts up." He unlocked the handcuffs, and she immediately rubbed at her delicate wrists, already red and marked by a short time in cuffs. "Stand still," he commanded, which seemed totally unnecessary as Lennon had barely moved a muscle. The guard bent and unlocked the manacle keeping her ankles together. She flashed a grin at me as she flexed her legs in an exaggerated movement of relief.

"That's better," she said in a loud whisper. "Thanks."

I nodded in response. "Who's the judge?" I asked the guard.

"Russell," he said as he moved to stand several feet away from us.

Oh crap. Leona Russell was the toughest judge on rotation in the county. I had stood before her years earlier as an assistant state's attorney and could recall how many times I had witnessed her reign of terror as she exercised the considerable degree of power she wielded in the courtroom. She had to be nearing retirement by now, so maybe she had eased up a bit, I hoped. Either way, she would be arriving any minute, and I needed to confer with my client. I had to set some ground rules—and fast. I turned to Lennon and spoke quickly, in a low voice.

"Don't say a word to anyone," I warned her. "I do the talking. You got that?" She glanced at me briefly before nodding. I opened the folder Frank had given me. I saw this was the first time she had appeared before the court and felt somewhat relieved. Unless she had charges from when she was a minor, this should be straightforward enough. Today's charges were larceny and resisting arrest. I needed more information and couldn't take the time to read the whole report.

"Why did you resist arrest?" I asked her.

She blinked at me before answering. "The store clerk got handsy with me. He put his hand down my pants."

I was shocked. "He groped you?"

"Right there in the frozen food aisle. Can you believe it? What a perv."

I was confused. "What am I missing here? Are you telling me a grocery store clerk approached you and stuck his hand down your pants?" I asked, and she nodded. I waited for some sort of explanation. My patience paid off.

"Probably because he saw me shove a package of frozen lobster down there," she said with a shrug. "Still, rude, yeah?"

I could feel the beginning of a tension headache starting to simmer. Why had I answered the phone on my day off? What had I ever done to deserve this type of hell? Oh right, I ruined the girl's mother's life twenty-five years ago. That was probably it. *My bad.*

"What happened after he discovered the lobster?" I asked, and she told me how it had fallen through the leg of her baggy jeans and landed on the floor several feet from where she stood. He had brought her into the back room and called the police, who arrived less than ten minutes later to arrest her.

"So you see, I didn't actually have the allegedly stolen lobster in my possession," she said with a touch of cheek. Barely a smirk, but still. I needed to make certain Judge Russell never saw even a hint of the smartass standing before me. Like mother, like daughter.

"That doesn't explain why you resisted arrest," I said, and she shrugged again.

"The cop looked like he was going to stick his hand down my pants too, and I thought one old pedo was more than enough for one day, so yeah, I guess you could say I struggled a bit."

"Why did you steal the lobster?" I asked. "Allegedly?"

The picture of wide-eyed innocence, she shrugged. "It was sixty-five dollars. That's crazy expensive. I make minimum wage and a tiny share of the nights' tips. I can't afford to spend that much on frozen seafood." She rolled her eyes as if to communicate, *it's a crazy world, but I have to live in it.*

"It's also considered larceny in the sixth degree. When the value of items stolen is five hundred dollars or less, it's sometimes referred to as petty theft, but it's a class C misdemeanor. It could result in a three-month jail sentence and a maximum fine of five hundred dollars," I told her. For a second or two, she appeared worried, losing what seemed to be her trademark look of studied indifference.

Good. That was my job, among many. To scare her straight.

CHAPTER 3

"Your honor, I would ask the charges against my client be reduced to a single count of criminal mischief and, as she has no criminal record, that the charge be withdrawn." I held my breath as I waited for her response. I had defended Lennon's actions as more of a prank, with no real expectation of leaving the premises without paying for the item. I had stressed how the unfortunate incident was totally not in keeping with her history of steady employment and lack of priors.

The judge studied me closely for a moment before her face relaxed into a smile. "I remember you, Ms. Quinn. It's good to have you in my courtroom again. And I agree with you, Counselor, but I would like to remind your client that shoplifting even a pack of gum can have serious consequences, and I would not like to see her in my courtroom again. Is that clear, Miss Gallagher?"

I glanced over at the waif-like teenager who stood by my side and nodded for her to respond.

"Yes, ma'am. Your honor. You will not see me again," she said, sounding respectful as well as properly chastened. "I promise," she added.

"In that case, the charges against the defendant, Lennon Gallagher, are withdrawn." With a bang of her gavel, the judge called her next case.

"I'll pick you up back at the station," I called out, surprising both of us. Lennon recovered quickly and nodded before being led back the way she had come in. Where had that offer come from? I wondered.

I gathered my paperwork and shoved everything into the burgundy vegan leather satchel I carried, unlike the more formal black leather briefcase I had used as an assistant state's attorney. In my new role, no one expected me to dress as formally as I used to, and that was fine with me. I still liked my high heels for court, but cargo pants and faded vintage T-shirts were my clothing of choice whenever possible. I walked outside to my car and drove to the police station. I was looking forward to talking with Lennon. I wanted to hear more about her as well as her mother.

I waited while she changed into her street clothes, and when she returned, they processed her quickly and she was officially released. As she walked toward me, I saw how painfully thin she was and how her tattered army jacket hung on her. I was about to ask what her plans were when she spoke up.

"Thank you, Randi," she said. "I really appreciate everything you've done for me." I wasn't used to my younger clients calling me by my first name, let alone my nickname, but it's probably the name her mother had referred to me by, minus the swear words and other expletives that would have preceded it.

"I'm glad it all worked out," I told her. "But you need to promise me you won't steal any more food—or anything else for that matter. I can get you a list of the soup kitchens in the area as well as shelters that will feed you for free, even if you're not staying there. I don't want to see you go hungry, but trust me, you got off easy today." I shook my head in wonder at the apparent change in the judge. She had softened up quite a bit.

"Judge Russell is a reasonable woman with grandkids your age. I can't guarantee you'll be this fortunate next time. You got me?"

Lennon nodded so vigorously that her spiky dark hair bobbed up and down. "I promise. This was a one-off. I wanted to have something nice for my friend's birthday. You only turn eighteen once, you know?" Yeah, I knew. I had celebrated my own 18th with my best friend, Tracey, and Lennon's mother, Charlene. The three of us had been inseparable.

I nodded in agreement, pausing for a moment before making a suggestion. "Are you hungry? We could stop for a bite, and I can drop you off somewhere afterward. What do you think?"

She shrugged, but I could see a spark of interest in her eyes. Curiosity? Hunger? "Yeah, I guess so," she said in a noncommittal tone. "I mean, if you're gonna eat, I could join you if you wanted me to."

"Let's go," I said, and there was a comfortable silence between us as we left the building and zigzagged through the parking lot toward my car. In deference to the fact that I was a lawyer working for legal aid, my car was a bare-bones four-door sedan. Totally unassuming. Also, I had zero interest in cars and would probably drive this for several more years, regardless of where I worked—unless it was London. That was another argument I could throw back at Eric, I realized. I had no freaking idea how to drive on the left!

"I thought it would be nicer somehow," Lennon remarked as she settled into the front passenger seat. "I mean, no offense or nothing, but you know . . . you're like a fancy lawyer and all that." She looked around with curiosity. I thought she was waiting for me to respond with a "you should see my other car" comment, but I just smiled at her.

"It gets me from point A to point B," I told her. "And that's all I really need. I'm pretty . . . basic, I guess you would say." Hmmm. And hungry. My thoughts of grabbing a quick sandwich two blocks down the street at Due in Court, the coffee shop favored by lawyers and their clients alike, suddenly seemed unsatisfactory. It was a gorgeous day, and I decided we could splurge. I needed to hear more from this young woman. After all these years, I had the opportunity to learn more about my high school friend. If Charlene wouldn't talk to me, maybe Lennon would.

"I know you like lobster," I said with the hint of a smirk. "How do you feel about crab?" I asked and got a wide smile in response.

"I'm totally in favor of it," Lennon assured me. I started my basic-mobile and headed to the waterfront. Traffic was light as we approached the area, and I snagged princess parking in front of Delaney's, which, in my humble opinion, served the best seafood in the region. My taste in cars was admittedly underdeveloped, but when it came to food, I had my standards.

"Have you been here before?" I asked Lennon, who was busy checking out the passing boats.

"No, but it sure smells great," she said. I took an appreciative sniff of the scents of Old Bay seasoning and fried seafood and had to agree with her.

"Table for two," I said as I approached the hostess, and she gathered menus and led us to a small table tucked into the corner. It offered a sweeping view of Long Island Sound, and I thanked her. The dining room was less than half occupied, but I knew we had beaten the rush. In a half hour, the place would be packed.

"Can I check your coats?" she asked, and I shook my head as I saw Lennon frown in response. I would bet most of her life's possessions could be found in the pockets and folds of her jacket. "Your server will be right with you," the hostess said after depositing huge menus on the table in front of us.

Lennon grabbed one and started to rifle through the pages, her eyes wide as she scanned the choices. I started to have misgivings about the appropriateness of the restaurant but couldn't think of an exit strategy.

"The lunch specials are on the back," I suggested gently, and Lennon looked relieved as she reviewed the slightly more reasonably priced options. "I'm having a cup of lobster bisque and an order of crab cakes. But everything is terrific. Order whatever you like. It's my treat."

As soon as she put down the menu, our server approached us. "Can I start you with some drinks?" she asked. "A glass of wine or," noticing Lennon's youthful appearance, she added, "or a ginger ale?"

"I'll have a seltzer with lime," I said, and Lennon asked for a Coke. "And we're ready to order," I added. I gave mine and wasn't surprised when I heard Lennon say, "I'll have the same."

"And some sweet potato fries to share," I suggested, and the menus were whisked away. I looked around the restaurant, which was starting to fill up with the usual lunch crowd. "I'm glad we got here when we did," I said, and Lennon nodded. As I had only met her this morning, I wondered what I had been thinking by inviting her to lunch. I studied her as she perused the drinks menu propped up between the salt and pepper shakers. From her file, I knew she was eighteen and born here in New London. I remembered hearing my old pal had given birth to a daughter, and here she was.

Lennon's large, expressive eyes were dark, like her choppy pixie-cut. She looked younger than her years, at least until she spoke. Her voice was low and gravelly, and although she didn't reek of tobacco, it sounded as if she had already smoked a pack this very morning. I could only guess at the pain and suffering she had experienced in her young life. Charlene had been in and out of jail for the past twenty-five years. It was a miracle her daughter had not gotten herself into trouble of her own until now. Our drinks arrived along with a platter of sweet potato fries and a variety of dipping sauces, including ketchup, always my condiment of choice.

"Dig in," I suggested and scooped some of the fries onto the small plate in front of me. I sampled one and sighed contentedly. Crispy and piping hot, just the way I liked them. I smiled to myself as Lennon copied my movements exactly.

I looked up in surprise when she asked, "Do you do this a lot?" Eat lunch? Pour ketchup on my food . . . or . . .

"Take my clients out to lunch?" I asked, and she nodded as she snagged a few more fries for her plate. "No, not really. Actually, not ever."

"So," she said after washing down her fries with a gulp of soda. "Why does my mom think you owe her? She is freaking obsessed with you, man. What's the deal between you two?"

I patted my lips dry with my napkin and sat back. This young woman certainly knew how to get right to the point. But it would not be an easy answer. My past relationship with Charlene Gallagher was, well, complicated.

CHAPTER 4

"Do you want the extended version or the CliffsNotes?" I asked. Lennon made a show of looking at an imaginary watch.

"I have nowhere else to be, Counselor. As long as the fries keep coming and this place offers free refills, you have my undivided attention," she drawled.

I couldn't hold back a laugh. "You remind me of your mother." Charlene had been snarky and full of mischief. Despite her troubled family life, she was always upbeat and fun to be around. Until the fun ran out and things went badly for her.

"Gee," Lennon said. "That's so awesome. I remind my lawyer of my deadbeat jailbird mother. I'm tickled pink."

I winced. Charlene's life had been a shitstorm of legal woes, substance abuse, and periods of homelessness since our years together in high school. I had tried to be there for her as a friend, then as an aspiring lawyer, but she had shut me out of her life completely. Although I hadn't seen her in years, it was a small town and people liked to talk. Charlene and her entire family had always given people plenty to talk about.

"I meant back in high school," I said. "When she was about your age." Before the drugs and the jail sentences. Ugh, was this the right time to ask? "How is she doing?" The server approached with a tray, and seconds later we both had large steaming cups of creamy bisque in front of us with a drizzle of sherry dotting the top. It smelled heavenly. I thought my question had been forgotten as I watched Lennon dig into her lunch. Her movements were restrained, as if she were dying to slurp the soup quickly but realized not only were we in public, but it was also piping hot. After a few minutes of silence, she grabbed a cellophane packet of oyster crackers from the table and upended them into her cup.

"What happened between you two?" she asked again. "Lovers' quarrel?"

I sat back in my seat and looked at my lunch companion, my latest client. The daughter of a girl I had been friends with for several years. A girl I had traded secrets with, confessed my fears to. We had sneaked liquor from our parents, smoked cigarettes behind the gymnasium, and even, I hated to admit it, shoplifted candy bars and makeup from the five-and-dime. Together with my best friend, Tracey, the three of us had been inseparable from the time Charlene and her family moved to Old Lyme when we were twelve years old. How could I explain to her daughter all that had happened since then? I pushed my soup aside and began.

"We were friends, your mom and I. And Tracey D'Amici too. We met your mom when her family moved here from Hartford, and the three of us hung out a lot. Ours was not a huge class, but it was a typical high school, you know? We had the jocks and the nerds, the drama geeks, and the stoners . . ."

"Let me guess," said Lennon. "My mom was a stoner and you were a nerd."

I bristled at her faulty characterization. "Wrong on both counts," I said sternly. "Are you going to let me tell the story or not?"

She nodded and continued to slurp at her soup. "Yes, ma'am," she mumbled.

"As I was saying, we had all the cliques, but for some of us, like your mom, Tracey, and me . . . we didn't really fit into any of them. We were mostly good girls, I guess. Not wildly popular, but not outcasts either. And your mom was *not* a stoner, Lennon. You need to believe me. We went to some of the parties and all, but your mom wasn't any wilder than the rest of us. We just tried to survive. Plus, my dad was a cop in town, so everyone thought I was a narc." Lennon had been listening attentively, scraping away to get the last bits of lobster, but looked at me when I paused.

"So, it was after the accident. That's when she got hooked on drugs?" Her eyes were wide, guileless.

I nodded slowly. "I don't know how much you know exactly. It was the summer after we graduated. I was getting ready to go to UCONN, and Tracey was registered for courses at the community college. She always wanted to go into childcare, and when—" I stopped when I saw Lennon frowning at me. "Okay, so it was late summer, and there was a party at the beach. Your mom was working at the resort that summer bussing tables, so she said she would meet me and Tracey after her shift. There were a lot of us that night. It was to be the final blowout of the summer. We had a bonfire going, and there was music. I was dancing—we all were—and there was a keg of beer, some joints being passed around . . ."

Wow, this was getting uncomfortable. I was an officer of the court and had just admitted to my client how I had been a witness to both underage drinking and illegal drug use, not to mention a non-permitted bonfire on a public beach. Lennon's steely gaze bore into me, and I continued. "Tracey's boyfriend, Dale, showed up, and they went for a walk on the beach." To have sex, I didn't add. They had been hooking up for a year at that point. "I was waiting for your mom, thinking she should have gotten there by then. I was dancing with a group of other kids when a guy named Tim joined us. He was a good dancer and started to spin me around, and we were laughing and hugging, and he kissed me. It was all in good fun, you know?"

Lennon's eyes narrowed. "But Tim was my mom's boyfriend, right?"

"No. I mean, I knew she had liked him for a while earlier in the year, but I don't think he knew. It's not like they ever dated. It was just a crush, and I honestly thought it was over. She hadn't mentioned his name in ages. Seriously, it was nothing." At least that's what I had thought at the time. Our crab cakes arrived with another platter of fries. Lennon glanced at the food with interest, but she wanted information even more.

"And let me guess: My mom showed up, right? And caught the two of you?"

I groaned, silently recalling the scene Charlene had made when she came across Tim and me slow dancing. She had screamed at me, calling me a traitor, a slut, and a fake friend. He tried to intervene, but that made it worse. Someone passed her a joint and told her to chill out. She paced around, puffing furiously on the joint, and grabbed an open bottle of Jack Daniel's. She took a few long gulps and announced she was leaving. "I'm done with all you, especially you, Randi Quinn," she called out as she stumbled toward the parking lot. I tried to chase after her, but she pushed me away and I landed on my ass in the sand. By the time I got up, I could see her driving away. Fast. And clearly out of control. Her beat-up hatchback offered zero protection when she wrapped it around a telephone pole less than a mile down the road. She wasn't wearing a seatbelt and was thrown from the car. The medics rushed her to the hospital where they started to work on her. It had seemed hopeless.

I shared a slightly edited version of the evening with Lennon, who nodded frequently. It would appear my version was mostly consistent with what she had been told. I wiped at my damp eyes with a napkin, recalling the fear Tracey, Dale, and I had felt as we'd huddled together in the waiting room. It had been a long, horrible night, and more than once I had been certain my friend had not survived the crash.

"Your mom was a fighter, Lennon. She rallied and began the long, slow road to recovery." A process marred by courtroom appearances and her newfound addiction to the pain meds she had been prescribed. She had totaled her car, but thankfully no one else had been hurt. As it was her first offense, her driver's license had been suspended and she had been given community service.

"We tried to rally around her, but by the time she was released from the hospital, I was already living an hour away, settled into one of the freshman dormitories at the University of Connecticut. Tracey kept trying to visit her but generally was turned away by Mrs. Gallagher—um, your grandmother—saying Charlene was sleeping or needed her rest. By the time I saw your mom again, she was, well, in a bad way." I had been shocked at her appearance the first time I had seen her over Christmas break. She was dancing with some guy at this local bar we used to frequent. Always thin, she had grown positively gaunt, her pale skin stretched over her bones and her eyes like dark holes staring out of her wizened face. I had tried to talk to her, but she had told me to "fuck off" and once more called me a false friend and a slut. She was still walking with some difficulty, but the alcohol she had consumed seemed to loosen her up. I left soon after, the sounds of her laughter and jeers following me closely. I had tried to get in touch with her a few times over the next several months, but she never took my calls.

"The next time I saw her was several years later. I was taking a law simulation class to boost my application to law school for the following year. I was at the New London Courthouse helping to prepare a pre-trial motion for one of the associates, and Char—your mother—was brought in. She was . . ." Tears welled once more in my eyes as I recalled watching my former friend being escorted into the courtroom. She had been wearing the type of orange jumpsuit favored by most prisons, and she'd looked as if she had aged thirty years. How was it possible she had only been twenty-three years old?

"What did she say?" Lennon asked, her eyes cloudy with grief.

I shook my head as I recalled the anger, the sheer fury Charlene had unleashed upon me that morning. She had told me it was all my fault. If I hadn't been such a slut, she wouldn't have driven off like she had. Crashed her car. Gotten involved with drugs. Ruined her life. "She said I owed her. Owed her big-time."

Lennon nodded. "Yup, that's pretty much what she's been telling me for years. 'Course, she's a pathological liar, and you can't believe anything she says," she added with a shrug.

I took a bite of my crab cake, chewed slowly, and swallowed with some difficulty, my appetite now completely vanished. "I heard she'd had a daughter. I have always wondered about you." Lennon had been devouring her crab cakes, and I pushed my plate in her direction. She looked surprised but dug right in.

"These are the best fuck—I mean the best crab cakes I have ever had," she said, her mouth full and her eyes bright. "Mom used to work at the Point; you know that place, yeah? She brought home leftovers every night after her shift. Those were some seriously decent fried shrimp, but these crab cakes are epic."

I smiled, delighted to see she was enjoying her lunch. Maybe coming here hadn't been the worst idea after all. I knew next to nothing about her, so I asked about her childhood. Between mouthfuls of crab and fries washed down by swallows of soda, she shared how she had been born during one of Char's extended periods between incarcerations. She had only the shakiest of memories of her early years but confirmed that by the time she entered kindergarten, her mother was once more serving time in the York Correctional Institution for Women in nearby Niantic.

"My aunt Kelly used to bring me to see her. I guess I cried a lot cuz I wanted her to come home with us, so she stopped bringing me after a while." Another shrug, followed by a shake of her head. "Kelly was kind of a headcase herself, but she was the only one who could take me, so . . ." Her voice trailed off, and I could only imagine which of her terrible memories she was recalling.

"I remember Kelly. She was a few years behind us in school," I added, picturing a younger girl with Charlene's sharp features and long black hair. "It's so good she could take care of you."

Lennon rolled her eyes in response. "No one would confuse what Kelly did with actually taking care of me, but it kept me out of the system for a while, so that made my mom happy, I guess." She told me how Charlene had been in and out of prison for the past ten years on possession charges or parole violations. "She's locked up right now," she said. "I have no idea when or if she's getting out." Her tone was matter-of-fact, as if she had shared her feelings about the next day's weather, but her eyes were sad, her mouth downturned, grief marring her delicate features. I decided against taking her impossibly small hand in mine. I wanted to comfort her, but everything about this young woman positively screamed "stay away."

"I lost my mom when I was about your age," I told her, and she frowned.

"But you had your dad, the cop," she reminded me, and I nodded, picturing Pop, who had been by my side though all my personal and professional highs and lows, who had walked me down the aisle when I married Eric four years ago, and who had found love for a second time with a sassy and energetic divorcee named Sally. Lennon had clearly not been so lucky in her own short life.

"You don't have to worry about me," she said, dabbing at her mouth with a napkin. "I'm doing fine, or at least I was until I decided to score some lobster," she added with a sheepish grin. "I got my GED, and I'm thinking of taking some courses at the community college. I got a job with steady hours. Shit pay, but what can you expect, right? I'm bussing tables at the Point. And washing dishes too," she said with a touch of pride. "It was good enough for Mom, and it's, um, like home, I guess. They feed you before shift, and there's usually leftovers after the dinner crowd, so I'm not starving either." She glanced down at the two empty plates before her. "But these crab cakes were better than anything they serve. Do you think I could get dessert? I have this sweet tooth and . . ."

"Say no more," I told her and flagged down our server. Minutes later, Lennon was making short work of a large brownie sundae and I was enjoying a much-needed cup of coffee. "Where are you living?" I asked, digging in my bag for the notebook I carried everywhere.

"I'm in a group home," Lennon told me and rattled off an address that sounded familiar. She shared how there were eight girls in residence, two to a room, and a live-in "den mother" of sorts named Alan. "It's okay, I guess. I've lived in worse, that's for sure. The curfew is ridiculous. 10:00 p.m. on weekdays, 11:00 on weekends. I mean, c'mon. I work the dinner shift. I can barely make it in the door before he locks it. It's stressful," she added, and I made a mental note to check on getting her an extension on work nights. I understood why there were rules in place, but there should be some leeway in certain situations. But for now . . .

A quick glance at my watch confirmed we had been here for more than two hours, and the restaurant had all but cleared out. Certain our server was eager to head home or at least take a break before the dinner shift began, I waved her over and handed her my credit card. My lunch date was watching me closely. When I signed the receipt and added a healthy gratuity, she let out a low whistle.

"They let you charge lunches like that?" she asked, a note of suspicion in her voice. I was confused at first until I realized she assumed I was charging our meal to the legal aid office. As if. We relied on grants and donations to keep the lights turned on, and there was nothing left over for frills like lunches.

"This is on me. We barely discussed your case, and I wouldn't dream of trying to seek reimbursement," I said, hiding a grin as I imagined the reaction I would garner if I tried. "Your mom was important to me, and I've enjoyed the opportunity to meet you."

Lennon looked only partially convinced before rewarding me with a trademark shrug and a crooked smile.

"Rich people are nuts," she said. "But thanks. I mean, for this morning and for all of this." Her arm made a sweeping movement over our relatively empty tabletop. We made our way through the deserted dining room out to the street. I began to walk toward my car. Realizing Lennon was not following behind me, I turned to her.

"Can I drop you at home?" I asked, and she shook her head.

"No, I've got a couple things to do before I need to be at work. I'll catch a bus back home to change my clothes." Her tone was evasive, but I couldn't imagine grilling her here on the sidewalk. "Thanks again," she called out and, with a wave, set off down the sidewalk, her steps certain and her pace brisk. I watched her as she turned a corner and disappeared from my sight. That's when I realized I had not asked her the question that had been bugging me for hours. *Damn.*

CHAPTER 5

"What the hell did she steal a pound of frozen lobster for?" I asked Tracey as I drove toward home a few minutes later. She laughed in response. I had shared an abbreviated account of meeting Lennon in court and brought her up to date on our high school friend's lost years, ending with the question that had been gnawing at me. "She said it was something special, for a friend's eighteenth birthday celebration, but what can you actually *do* with a pound of lobster?"

"Lobster stew, lobster rolls, lobster tacos—yum, now I'm craving lobster," replied Tracey. "Lobster quesa—"

"I know what you can do with lobster, Forrest Gump. But a teenaged girl living in a group home? I don't think she's even allowed a hotplate in her room. It doesn't make sense."

Tracey's tone was dismissive. "First off, it was his pal Bubba who had all the menu suggestions, and b) it's a luxury. Something special, you know? Who's to say? And besides, the real crime is Safeway had the nerve to charge sixty-five dollars in the first place." Tracey hailed from one of the first families in Old Lyme. Her people had been fishing off the Connecticut coastline for generations. I would let her have this one.

"Anywho," I said. "What's happening in your world these days?" I had been monopolizing the entire conversation thus far.

"Status quo and delightfully so," she responded. "The boys are doing great, and Dale and I are enjoying our part-time empty nester status."

I smiled at the image of those two lovebirds. Other than a rough patch a couple of years ago, the two of them were so well matched, truly in sync. "I wanna be like you when I grow up," I told my friend. I could only hope my marriage to Eric would continue to thrive like theirs had. So far, so good. I literally counted my blessings every day.

"Look at the two of us, all happy and shit," Tracey said. "Oh crap, I left Ruth alone with eight kids for far too long. We gotta get hands washed and snacks served before parents start to arrive for pickup. Gotta go. Byeeee."

Tracey ran a thriving home daycare business. Where she found the energy to chase around a room full of little rugrats was beyond me. Ever since her twin sons had started college last year, she had talked about cutting back, but that had not happened yet. Her husband's construction business was doing well, and they were financially secure for the first time in more than a decade. It was wonderful to share in the happy life they had built for themselves.

I pulled into our driveway and parked behind Eric's truck. I was delighted he had gotten home early. He had been spending a good amount of time a couple of hours away in Danbury, where they were working on several high-end commercial projects. As I got out of my car, I grinned at the sight of my handsome husband walking toward me with open arms. I leaned in and let myself get swept up in his warm embrace. This man was an absolute delight. How had I gotten so lucky? I sniffed appreciatively. Citrus and something woodsy. Last year's stocking stuffer, maybe?

"You smell great," I mumbled into his shoulder and took another whiff. And clean laundry too.

"I aim to please," he assured me. "The little woman likes to treat me to all the latest scents."

"I do love to buy you pretty things." I pulled back to study his dear face, so familiar and so handsome. I had never really had a type before, but Eric Hansen, with his light brown hair with not a strand of gray and his bright green eyes, was clearly "it" for me. "You're home early," I said as we made our way to the open front door.

"I was hoping we could talk some more," he replied, and my heart sank. I had two choices. I could make up an excuse as to why I was unable to talk right now. An author signing at the library I didn't want to miss. Or maybe Pop needed me for something important. Or I could flat out refuse to talk, just because. There was a third choice I realized as I busied myself with taking off my jacket, hanging it up, and greeting our gorgeous tiger cat, Hobie. We could talk.

"All right, let's talk," I agreed, and Eric's face, which could only have been described as tense, lit up in relief.

"Thanks, Quinn. I really appreciate it."

"Let's not get ahead of ourselves," I cautioned him. "I only agreed to talk."

He nodded. "I understand. So why don't you change, and we can go for a walk on the beach. I ordered Thai to arrive at 7:00. Gives us plenty of time."

I kissed his cheek before heading to our bedroom. "Give me five," I said and started unbuttoning my shirt. Normally, he would have made a snarky comment, like he would take a lot more than five minutes or whatever, but he just stood there nodding. *Oh crap.* Despite my years as a successful prosecutor, I avoided confrontation in my personal life as much as possible. This was way outside my comfort zone.

I pulled on a pair of baggy jeans and a ratty sweatshirt. If my life was going to be ripped apart, at least I would be comfortable. I slipped my feet into an ancient pair of Keds and loped back down the hall, twisting my hair into the messiest of buns as I went. You got this, I told myself, but even I didn't believe me.

"That was quick," Eric said as I joined him by the front door. I didn't bother with a "that's what she said" retort because there was nothing humorous about any of this. "Okay, Hobie, you're in charge," he announced to our fabulous feline perched on the top level of his cat palace. I wondered how much it would cost to ship the bulky custom-made cat tree to London. I couldn't see Hobie living there any more than I could imagine myself. I followed Eric out the door and closed it behind me. We were having this conversation right now.

In my inimitable fashion, I had managed to stuff the whole situation so far back into my subconscious I had barely given it a thought since last night. And now we were back at it. Walking along the beach while the waves lapped at our bare feet and soaked the legs of our jeans. I brought up the same concerns as I had last night, and Eric countered with the same arguments. My concern about driving went nowhere. A combination of public transportation and a private car service would negate the need for me to learn how to drive on the *wrong* side of the road. For a kick-ass lawyer in my day, my defense was weak and highly emotional, while Eric's position was rock solid. The move would be financially lucrative, potentially life-changing with guaranteed early retirement and more financial security than either of us could ever have imagined. And now to add even more fuel to his already solid position, additional details were available. According to Eric, the firm would buy us a flat near Hyde Park, a most desirable neighborhood. They would pay any fees or charges for me to get my license to practice law in England, if that was what I chose to do. There was a company jet available to us if we wanted to come back to the States to visit or if we fancied a weekend away in the Canary Islands or perhaps Tenerife. I had no clue where these places were and questioned aloud why we would want to go to either one.

"What's in freaking Tanneriff?" I asked, purposely mispronouncing the name. Eric got upset with me, telling me I was being deliberately obtuse. That we could just as easily go to Ireland or Boston or Bermuda, conveniently naming three of my favorite places. I shut down as I generally did when I felt cornered, and we walked back home in silence.

CHAPTER 6

Shortly after we returned home, our dinner was delivered, but neither of us had much of an appetite. I stored all the leftovers in the fridge, wiped the counters, and turned off the kitchen lights. I wandered into the family room and pointed the remote at the TV, flipping around for something to hold my interest. Eric begged off, claiming he had an early morning. He kissed the top of my head and lumbered off to grab a shower before bed while I sat on the couch trying to figure out a solution to this very real dilemma.

If I were ever asked, I would probably describe myself as fairly adventurous, but the reality of my life would make that claim a false one. I went to college and law school at the University of Connecticut. A good school and easier on the budget than many other options. And oh yeah, only an hour from where I grew up. Moving forward, most of my professional life had taken place in nearby New London, and the two chances I'd had to live and work in New York, I'd turned down. More or less.

I loved our new home. Eric had put his heart and soul into designing an amazing space for the two of us and Hobie. We were so close to the ocean, my favorite place in the world. The thought of not being able to walk on the beach nearly every day year-round was horrific. What did England have that could top this? Okay, it was the same Atlantic Ocean, but who went to London and came back raving about the beaches? No one, that's who, and don't even get me started on the weather. All that rain? I had everything I needed right here, I told myself. And everyone. Pop was in his early seventies, Sally several years younger, but still. The time would come when one or both would need me, and where would I be? London? Only a six-hour flight, but still. Probably less if we used the corporate jet. Was that who I was—a corporate jet-setter? Not an image I'd ever had for myself. And my stepbrother's kids were close by, and it was a hoot watching them grow up. Being part of a bigger extended family was a wonderful experience, especially after years of it being just Pop and me. Plus, Eric's brother lived nearby, and of course Tracey, Dale, and the twins. The idea we could uproot ourselves and live in one of the largest cities in the world surrounded by total strangers . . . I just couldn't see it, nor could I imagine living separately in a commuter marriage. Never, ever.

But this is Eric, I thought. The man who gave up a lucrative career to live here in Old Lyme with me, only to be invited back into his newly expanding firm less than a year later. It had all worked out well, but when he'd left initially, he'd had no way of knowing what the future held. But he did have faith, both in me and in the world, and here we were, a few years later, considering yet another big change. He had sacrificed for me and supported my career moves as I transitioned from my failed TV show back to dedicating myself full-time to my legal advice blog to a year as a late-night radio talk show host spewing legal information from the studio he'd built for me in the basement of our new home. And currently, as an associate at a legal aid office in New London, where I worked part-time for peanuts. When would I be the one offering full-fledged support for his dreams? If not now, when? Hobie had curled beside me and clearly resisted when I had to move him so I could stand.

"Sorry, Hobes." I hurried to our room and nudged my sleeping husband awake. I hated to do it, but this couldn't wait until the morning.

"Eric," I whispered in his ear. "Wake up. I need to tell you something."

In the moonlight, his face took on a glow, illuminating his bright eyes, which he was now rubbing into some semblance of wakefulness. "What's up, Quinn?" he mumbled. "You okay?"

"I'm just ducky, guv'nor," I chirped in probably the world's worst Cockney accent ever. "Or at least I will be when we move across the pond," I added. His face broke into the loveliest of smiles.

"Aww, babe, you're gonna love it. I promise you," he said, pulling me into a warm and sleepy embrace. I relaxed against him, certain of only one thing. I would figure out a way to make this man's dreams come true no matter what it took. After all, he'd already done the same for me nearly every day since we'd met.

CHAPTER 7

I woke the next day feeling lighter, less stressed than I'd been lately. Resolving the "London situation" no doubt contributed to my mood. Before he'd left this morning, I had made Eric promise not to tell anyone about our plans, except, of course, for his partners. I did not look forward to telling my family and friends about our impending move, nor did I want to give my notice at work. There would be plenty of time after we had a timetable in place. But me being me, I decided to force everything way back in my brain to be retrieved and picked apart later. For today, I needed to get my butt into the office and focus on doing some good for the at-risk youth in the areas we served. I quickly showered and dressed before I drank a cup of the coffee Eric had made earlier. Racing back into the kitchen, I grabbed an apple I would probably not eat from a bowl on the counter and gave Hobie a quick snuggle before I left the house.

As I backed out of the driveway, my apple rolled off the passenger seat and onto the floor, where it lodged itself under the seat. Oh well, at least I'd had good intentions. I had a love-hate relationship with fruit, apparently. I bought it, displayed it, and unless Eric ate it, I generally tossed it. Except for watermelon, which I could eat daily year-round. I bet they don't even sell watermelon in London, I thought. I turned on the radio and was delighted to hear the soothing and familiar voice of my friend and former colleague Dr. Chris Westerhaus. When I had been on the air with Sterling Broadcasting a few years back, I had gotten chummy with some of my colleagues. Jeff, the sports guy, was a lot of fun, as were the twin sisters who discussed antiques with their devoted followers. But I had bonded most closely with Dr. Chris, a behavioral psychologist whose daily radio show, *Haus Calls with Dr. Chris*, regularly drew fifteen million listeners each week. My show, *Miranda Nights*, had done well in the ratings, but *Haus Calls* had been wildly successful for nearly ten years. Chris was direct, kind, and knowledgeable. His callers ranged from angsty teens to feuding exes. I had first met him at one of the meet and greets that management liked to throw several times a year. Since then, whenever Chris spotted me from across the room, he would scoot over and we would hug and catch up and trade industry gossip like schoolgirls. At a holiday party Eric and I attended, we spent the evening with Chris and his wife, Susan, a delightful woman who owned a feminist bookstore in the East Village. We had dinner with them whenever we spent time in the city.

After I let it be known I did not wish to extend my contract past the first year, I quickly fell out of favor with the top brass at Sterling, as well as most of the talent. I was "on my way out" and not worthy of anyone's time. But Chris had supported me through the last few months as the promotion for my show had dwindled along with my fan base. *"Illegitimi non carborundum,"* he would remind me during our weekly phone calls. "Don't let the bastards wear you down."

Now I listened to him responding to a young woman concerned about her meddling in-laws. His advice was sensible and straightforward. The kind of help you might expect from a caring friend, provided the friend had a PhD with thirty years of clinical experience and was the highest-rated talk show host in the US. I wondered what he would have to say about our plans to move to London and decided I would give him a call later in the day.

Before I knew it, I was pulling into the lot alongside Coastal Legal Aid Services, my work home for the past two years.

"Good morning," I called out to Rose, who was sitting at the reception desk with a customary scowl on her pretty face. I received a grunt in response, and I hesitated for a moment, not sure if I was in the mood for the doomsday prophecies that she frequently spouted. If it wasn't the economy, it was global warming or terrorism or simply that someone had parked over the white line of her favorite parking space. No, not today, I decided and turned down the hallway to my office, second door on the left. I let myself in and stored my tote on the credenza behind my desk before I went in search of coffee. Despite the relatively shabby furnishings we had inherited from a car dealership that had gone bankrupt a few years earlier, our breakroom featured a state-of-the-art coffee maker. Fancy a cappuccino or a low froth latte? This machine could make it for you, provided it was operated by a seasoned barista, that is. As a confirmed non-reader of instruction manuals, I could only imagine what it could do, but I was content to consume a couple of cups of regular drip brew each day I spent in the office. After a few attempts and way too many pushed buttons, I monitored the progress of my drink, spitting and sputtering into my "See you later, litigator" mug. Never let it be said lawyers didn't have a sense of humor, because some of us really did.

I carefully made my way to my office, balancing a full-to-the-brim mug of steaming liquid. As I placed it on the coaster on my desk, I heard a noise behind me. I turned in time to see my co-worker Joe Evans brandishing a tray of some sort of brown nuggets. Not donut holes. *Damn.* Meatballs at 8:30 in the morning? I greeted him, and he made his way to my desk.

"Hungry?" he asked, offering me the plate of what I now saw were not meatballs, but possibly . . .

"Pumpkin spice balls," he announced proudly. "Freshly made, gluten-free, dairy-free, and paleo friendly." *Hmmm.* I would have preferred the apple currently stuck under the passenger seat, but I nodded enthusiastically. Kind of.

"Ooooh, yum," I mumbled and, using the napkin he held out, selected one of the balls.

"Take two; they're small," he said with a grin. Not on your life, I thought.

"Oh no, I'm trying to watch what I . . . And besides, there are a dozen people here, and everyone will want to try them."

Joe shook his head. "Nope, you're the last one." I glanced again at the platter, noting there were only a few empty spaces, indicating most of my co-workers had refused the little nuggets of seasonal goodness.

"Nothing like a pumpkin spice ball with my morning coffee," I said. He beamed at me, and when the phone on my desk rang, he held up a hand.

"I'll let you go," he said with a wave. "I'll leave these in the breakroom, so if you change your mind . . ."

I gave a stupid thumbs-up gesture and grabbed the phone.

"Miranda Quinn," I said into the receiver and received a deep-throated chuckle in response.

"I thought you needed rescuing," my co-worker and good friend Sandi said, and I grinned.

"You're a lifesaver," I told her.

"Word to the wise, do not eat Joe's balls, whatever you do. They are even nastier than they look," she said, and I swore I wouldn't. "We still on for lunch today?" Sandi and I regularly ate lunch together on the days we were both in the office.

"Sounds great. Noon?" I looked at my desk pad calendar, trying to decipher the scribbled dates and times. "Um, no. How's 12:15? I have someone scheduled at 11:30." Riley Jackson was one of the teens I had been counseling in my spare time as a volunteer for the Center for Children and Youth Advocacy.

Sandi agreed and we ended the call. I had a few hours to get a whole crapload of work completed before Riley arrived. Armed with a plan, I started on the stack of paperwork that was the status quo with a state-run agency. Our paralegal, a hardworking young man starting law school next fall, had organized most of the reports I needed to review, and I made good progress on today's pile. When I sat back in my chair and gave a satisfying stretch, I realized it was already 11:45. Riley was late, and I was surprised she hadn't called to give me a heads-up. I left my office and headed to the reception desk.

"Any calls for me?" I asked Rose, who looked up from her computer screen.

"No, Miranda. Were you expecting a call?"

"I had an 11:30 appointment with one of the girls from my group, and she's late. I expected she would have called to let me know or to reschedule." I got a "what can you do" shrug in return, so I announced I would be in my office for another twenty minutes or so before going to lunch. I sat behind my desk for a bit and pushed papers around, unable to concentrate. Finally deciding to call it, I locked my office, made a quick stop in the restroom, and presented myself in Sandi's doorway.

"Ready when you are," I announced.

We left the office and headed toward the diner occupying the corner spot of our strip mall. It was a bustling place and hands-down boasted the highest traffic of the current tenants. A vape shop, a pawn shop, and a check-cashing center rounded out the roster. A real go-to destination for all.

We entered the large open space, highly redolent with all the smells and sounds you might expect from a greasy-spoon diner—sizzling burgers, slightly burned toast, and strong coffee. Just a little slice of heaven. We hustled over to the only vacant booth and got settled while the harried server collected the dishes and debris left by our predecessors and wiped down the Formica tabletop.

"Menus?" she barked at us, and we quickly shook our heads. We knew the choices by heart and pretty much ordered the same meals every time.

"We're ready to order," Sandi said, and a pen and pad made a quick appearance.

"I'll have the tuna melt on rye, no tomato, and a Diet Coke."

Our server nodded her approval before shifting slightly toward me.

"What's the soup of the day?" I asked, garnering a scowl in return.

"Split pea, chicken noodle, and cream of tomato," came her hurried response. Clearly, I was not the first of her customers to ask that question today.

"Tomato, please, and a grilled cheese on sourdough if you have it . . . or um, whatever bread you do have," I said in response to her flash of annoyance. "And water," I called out to her retreating back. "Yikes, who pissed her off today?" I wondered aloud.

Sandi grinned in response. I really enjoyed the company of my co-worker and was glad to have a friendly face in the office to confide in and speak off the record with. We worked with countless citizens in the middle of life-altering challenges, such as domestic abuse, child custody disputes, and unlawful evictions, and some of the cases ended badly. Although I could talk to Eric or Tracey or even my dad, having a trusted ally in the trenches with me made a world of difference.

"What are you up to these days?" I asked. "How's Mikey?" Her weathered face broke into the widest of grins at the sound of her seven-year-old grandson's name.

"He's doing so well," she gushed, her brown eyes twinkling. "He's made friends at his new school, and this past weekend we painted his room. He wanted fire-engine red, but I somehow convinced him a robin's-egg blue was a safer choice." She gave a fake scowl and held up her right hand, which was dotted with speckles of blue and—wait, was that red paint? "We compromised on a red racing stripe," she added, shaking her head. "That boy, I swear."

Sandi had won custody of her grandson this past summer after years of court battles. Her son had died in a car wreck when his boy was only two, and her daughter-in-law had gone off the rails. Years of drinking and drugs had landed her in rehab on more than one occasion, causing her son to enter the system as a foster child. I had taken over the case when Sandi decided to seek sole custody, and Michael had finally been awarded to her care a few months ago.

"He's a lucky kid," I told my friend, who was trying to blink back tears and smiling gratefully.

"How was your 11:30?" she asked as she took a sip of her drink, which had just appeared. No sign of my water.

I frowned in response. "She was a no-show. No call, nothing."

Sandi shook her head. "She'll turn up," she assured me, but I wasn't so sure. I couldn't be certain, as our client base tended to be less than stable, but it felt like there were several girls who had stopped coming around in the past few months. Jobs, relationships, moving out of the area—that was all a part of it, but in a handful of cases it seemed totally unexpected.

Our food came, still no water, and we dug in to our lunches. As we ate, I told Sandi about my meeting with Lennon the day before and how I had been close with her mother once upon a time.

She nodded in recognition. "I remember your friend," she told me, and my ears perked up in interest. "I tried to help her when she lost custody of her daughter years back. Heartbreaking." She pushed her now empty plate to the side.

"All this talk of losing kids has me feeling like dessert is in order. Want to join me? My treat," she added, but I held up a hand in protest.

"You go right ahead. Next week is Halloween, and I am trying to save all those extra calories for the big night." Eric and I had started the practice of sitting in camp chairs in our driveway, handing out candy to the neighborhood ghouls and goblins. One piece of candy for the kids, one for me. And that's how it went all night. "Eric keeps telling me to buy candy I don't like so I'm not as tempted, but seriously, there's hardly a brand out there that doesn't hold my interest."

Sandi shook her head fondly at me and waved our server down to place an order for their signature dessert, bread pudding. I stayed silent, figuring my quest for water was a lost cause.

"I need to get Michael to decide on a costume," she complained good-naturedly. "First it was a ninja warrior, then he decided to be Spider-Man, and the other day, he told me he'd changed his mind and wanted to be a member of the Paw Patrol. Can you imagine?"

"Whatever he decides, be sure to take lots of pictures," I reminded her, and she smiled happily. It couldn't be easy for her, raising the little guy on her own, but I had no doubt my sweet friend was up to the task.

We chatted for a bit about office updates, personnel changes, and our caseloads as Sandi picked at her dessert before asking for the check. "My turn," I assured her as I counted out bills and added in a generous tip despite the lackluster service. We made our way back to the office in companionable silence, and my mind wandered back to the morning's missed appointment. What had happened to Riley?

I rifled through a short stack of pink message slips on my desk, but there was nothing from her. I logged in to my computer and brought up the database containing our clients' contact information. I went right to the *J*'s and found a phone number for Riley. Most of our clients had cellphones, often burners with a preset number of minutes to be used each month. I quickly dialed the number, and seconds later I heard a recorded message informing me the number I had dialed was no longer in service. Had she gotten a new phone and neglected to update her number? I told myself there was no use stewing over her skipped appointment, and I got back to work. I returned the phone calls I had missed, leaving messages for every one of my callers. It was no wonder to me why progress was so slow with our case files. Too much time was wasted every day leaving messages and waiting for callbacks. Despite a reliance on voicemail and texting, the game of phone tag was still rampant within the justice system. I opened the online office calendar that we all had access to and grabbed the files I would need for the next two days in court. Acting on impulse, I pulled Riley's file as well and shoved the whole stack in my bag.

Figuring I had what I needed, I locked up and walked to the reception desk to let Rose know I was leaving for the day. Along the way, I poked my head into the break room, where I saw a mostly full plate of Joe's pumpkin spice balls. Poor guy had probably slaved over the damn things. I snuck in and grabbed several in a paper towel. I would toss them once I got home, but at least he would believe someone had enjoyed them. But then would he just bring more?

I walked out to my car, which was parked near the end of the mostly deserted lot. The diner was already closed for the day, and it was too late for check cashing and too early for weed, maybe?

I sat in my unlocked car for a moment before I did what I had known I would all along. I grabbed Riley's file, checked the address of the group home, and plugged it into my GPS. It was only a few minutes out of my way, and if I got lucky, I would be able to chat briefly with her, to check in. If she wanted my help, she would need to come to my office. This was merely a courtesy call, I told myself. A wellness check, as it were.

CHAPTER 8

Ten minutes later, I located a parking space directly in front of Bradford House. It was one of the independent living transitional group homes in our district, and although I had never visited, I knew it to be larger than the others we worked with. It was designed to house sixteen to twenty girls, and instead of an on-site residential supervisor, Bradford House was managed by a regional director who lived on-site during the week and several staff members who rotated shifts. I left my bag in the car, locked up, and headed to the front door. It was a large and rather imposing entrance, ornate woodwork outlining the double oak doors. I tried the knob, but of course it was locked. I saw a discreetly placed doorbell and pushed it, immediately hearing a muted ringing from inside the house. I waited for a moment before trying again, and this time I heard approaching footsteps. Seconds later, the door swung open, revealing a slim, redheaded male about my height. I guessed him to be about thirty, give or take a few years. His look was guarded, but he smiled pleasantly.

"Can I help you?" he asked, and I thought I detected a hint of an accent. Brooklyn, maybe?

I smiled back at him. "I'm Miranda Quinn with legal aid, and I was hoping to speak with one of your residents." When I got no immediate response, I hurried on. "She was supposed to meet with me today to talk about more permanent housing. She never showed and didn't call to cancel either, so I thought . . ." I spread my arms in a "and here I am" gesture.

His smile deepened. "Kids today. Am I right?" He shook his head good-naturedly, but this was no joke. If these "kids" didn't show for appointments, court appearances, and job interviews, the consequences could be dire.

"I'm looking for Riley Jackson, Mr. . . .?" I said, and he nodded in recognition as he extended his hand to me.

"Where are my manners?" he deadpanned. "I'm Jordan Myers, the Regional Director here at Bradford House." We shook hands, but he made no move to invite me inside. "You'll have to excuse me, Ms. Quinn. It's our housekeeper's day off, one of my supervisors called out, and I'm trying to make up one of the rooms. We are expecting a new arrival this evening as we had an unexpected vacancy."

"That sounds exciting, but I'm wondering if you've seen Riley? It's important that she—"

Jordan's tone shifted, and he looked grim. "Well, it's a shame you came all this way looking for Riley. She left us over the weekend. Packed her things and moved out, I'm afraid." He shook his head, and I knew if he continued with a "Kids today, am I right?" comment, I would lose my shit.

I cut him off, nearly sputtering with frustration. "Why wasn't my office notified?" I asked. "This is her legal address, assigned by the court. She can't just leave."

He shook his head again. "Ms. Jackson is eighteen years of age, an adult in the eyes of the law. I had no legal recourse to stop her from leaving, especially when she had such a wonderful opportunity land in her lap. I wouldn't have stopped her even if I could."

"What opportunity?" I asked, no doubt sounding as suspicious as I felt. I lived in the real world, as did most of our clients. Riley had aged out of foster care earlier in the year and had signed a post-majority form for services. As she had already turned eighteen, it was strictly voluntary, but still. These kids didn't win the lottery when it came to securing jobs or permanent places to live. Those who worked hard might eventually find themselves in a desirable situation, but none of the young people I ever worked with could be described as lucky.

He chuckled, clearly picturing the young woman living a charmed life. "Riley was contacted by a long-lost relative. Seems there was a bit of family money left for her, so she headed for Burlington, in Vermont, to be reunited with her family. Isn't that terrific?"

"She had no family," I countered. At least none she ever mentioned in all her sessions with me. "I don't really understand any of this."

Jordan shrugged. "It was a cousin, I believe, from her mother's side. Apparently, Riley had no idea of the woman's existence. But she tracked Riley down and reached out to her. And now they are all together, one big happy family."

I still had questions. So many questions.

"How did she get to Vermont?" I asked. Jordan seemed embarrassed as he looked down at the blindingly white Nikes on his feet.

"I wasn't supposed to do it, and I know it's against regulations, but I got her a ride. A buddy of mine was heading that way the next day, so I chipped in some gas money. Out of my own pocket, of course. Nothing in the Bradford House budget for that." I didn't respond, so he hurried on. "Anyway, she packed up and the next morning she was gone."

I shook my head. It was all too convenient, and everything had happened so quickly. I was as optimistic as the next person, but opportunities like this one were unicorns. I had no reason to doubt this young man's explanation, but I did. It felt rehearsed, and as a former prosecutor, I could generally spot an overly practiced response. Something was off, I just knew it.

"I'm sorry," Jordan said. "It seems like you were close. If it's any consolation, she is enjoying time with her newfound family. Her cousin sounds terrific, and he has a lovely wife and two children, so it's been quite the homecoming, as you can probably imagine. If she calls again, I'll ask her to give you a ring. How does that sound?"

I nodded halfheartedly, a niggling something in my gut. I produced a business card from my pocket and handed it to him. "Please give her my number and ask her to call me anytime. She must have gotten a new number, and if you could get it for me—for the file, of course—I would be grateful."

"Of course," he replied smoothly. "Now, if you'll excuse me, that bed won't make itself, so . . ."

"Is the vacant room Riley's?" I asked. When he nodded, I continued quickly. "Would I be able to see her room, check it out? Maybe she left something behind that would—"

Jordan cut me off, his tone firm and his smile long gone. "You'll have to take my word for it, Ms. Quinn. I went through that room from top to bottom this afternoon, not a single surface I didn't dust, mop, or disinfect. There is literally no sign Riley ever lived there. Enjoy your evening," he added, and before I knew it, I was once again facing a solid wood door.

I returned to my car, puzzling over . . . well, I didn't know exactly what. If what he told me was true, Riley would have a fresh start with family to support her. I should be glad, but the fact she hadn't reached out or sent a text with a forwarding address or her new phone number— nothing? She had literally disappeared into thin air, and I remembered all too well what that felt like. The case that had ended my career with the district attorney's office had relied upon the testimony of an important witness, a young woman named Becky Lewis. When she had gone missing, I had lost everything, and a serial rapist had been set free.

I drove home lost in thought, thinking about Becky and Lennon and Riley and all the young women I'd worked with and tried to help over the years. Becky's was truly a success story. She had broken free of the path she had been on in her teens and was now a loving mother to a delightful five-year-old named Jesse. She was a paralegal working part-time and, oh yeah, full-time live-in girlfriend to Eric's nephew, Skip. The three of them were making a life together in a suburb of Miami. I was certain that my in-laws, Eric's brother, John and his wife, Tricia, would never fully forgive me for introducing their son to Becky and seeing him move two thousand miles away, but anyone who saw the two of them together could see how devoted they were to each other and to Jesse.

Maybe Lennon could have a success story too. I wondered if she knew Riley. I would have to remember to ask her. I pulled into my driveway, noting the absence of Eric's truck. I could take a shower, start dinner, and try to get myself in a more positive frame of mind before he came home. He knew I took my job seriously, but it bothered him to see me upset over a client. And if I tried to deny it, he would assume I was having second thoughts about moving to London. And I was, of course . . . second, third, and fourth thoughts if I'm being honest. But I had given my word, so it was essentially a done deal. It was Eric's turn to shine and mine to bask in the glory with him.

After a much-needed shower, I threw on my comfiest sweats along with an *Out of Time* R.E.M. T-shirt. Twenty minutes later, Eric found me dissecting a rotisserie chicken and sauteing onions and peppers for tacos.

"Honey, I'm home," he called as he approached me, arms out for a hug. Not for the first time, I reflected on the amount of joy he brought to my life. How had I ever gotten so lucky? "Smells good," he murmured into my ear, "and the food does too." I held on for a moment longer before releasing him.

"Hey, handsome," I said, turning my attention back to the sizzling pan. "You hungry?"

"I could eat," he said, sniffing the air appreciatively. "What can I do to help?"

"I have this under control, but our fur baby might want to be fed." As if on cue, Hobie strode into the kitchen. Before I could stop him, he jumped onto the counter and made a beeline toward the pile of shredded chicken on the cutting board.

"No, Hobie," I protested. "That's not what good boys do."

Eric scooped him up and snatched a handful of chicken. He deposited both on the feeding mat by the door. As we watched Hobie attack his food, Eric shook his head at me.

"It's so cute how you pretend he doesn't stroll around on the countertops whenever he pleases when it's just the two of you."

I feigned surprise. "*Moi?* Let our boy up on the counters where I prepare our daily meals? Slice our daily bread? Think again, my friend."

"I stand behind what I said," he told me with a grin. "I'm going to hop in the shower, but I'll be quick . . . unless you want to join me, that is. And I can still be quick."

"I just showered, and this feast is not going to cook itself. Go get cleaned up, and when you come back . . . ." I kissed my fingertips to my lips. "Dinner will be served." As soon as I heard the bathroom door close, I turned to Hobie. "Dude, what the hell? Remember our rule about how we behave when Dad's home or we have company?" He wound his way around my legs, purring loudly, his way of reminding me a small scoop of shredded chicken had been merely an appetizer. I opened a can of whitefish pâté and scooped half out on his plate before I topped off his water bowl. Then I got to work chopping tomatoes and shredding a small block of cheddar cheese. I was removing the tortillas I had warmed in the oven as my beaming husband returned. We assembled our tacos, and despite my forgetting the all-important fresh chopped cilantro, they were delicious.

By 8:00, we had straightened up the kitchen and stored away the makings for another meal. I turned to Eric. "TV, bed, hot tub, or walk on the beach?"

He threw up his hands. "All of the above? I hate to say bed because it's early, and I know you never want to fool around after eating Mexican food. A walk sounds good, but honestly I'm too beat. TV or hot tub, I guess."

"TV in bed," I decided, and we went to find something to watch together. An hour later, I woke with a start to find Eric sleeping soundly beside me and a commercial for Red Lobster on the TV. I pointed the remote at the set a split second before the image of a platter of fried shrimp filled the screen. Damn, now I wanted shrimp. I lay next to my husband and tried to think sleepy thoughts. But images of shrimp led to lobster, which got me thinking of Lennon, then of Riley living the "good life" in Vermont with her long-lost cousin and his family. But wait, hadn't Jordan said the cousin was a woman? I probably heard him wrong I decided as I rolled onto my side. I would need to get more information and an updated address to close out Riley's file. Maybe she'll reach out on her own, I thought as I let myself fall back to asleep.

CHAPTER 9

Lennon was humming as she tackled the mountain of pots and pans at the end of a busy night at the Point. It had been a good day; actually, the last few days had been pretty good. She was looking forward to Sunday, the start of her official weekend. Her usual routine consisted of a group breakfast at home, going for a walk, napping, and reading before pulling herself together, showering, and donning the least wrinkled of her white button-downs, a pair of black pants, and arriving at work by 4:30 p.m. But on Sundays and Mondays, she was free to lounge around or hang out with her friends once she had completed her daily chores, as indicated by the ever-changing weekly schedule at the home. Sometimes they would catch a movie or share a pizza before returning to the living room to play cards, watch TV, or just talk well into the wee hours.

But this week was different because on Monday, Lennon was going to see her mother at the York Correctional Institution. When she was a little girl, her aunt or her grandmother had brought her to visit every single week. As she got older, Lennon's visits had become more sporadic as it had been an ongoing challenge to arrive during visiting hours without skipping school. Weekend visiting hours were always mobbed, and more than once there had been so long of a wait to enter due to a strict occupancy code, that time with her mother was reduced to ten to fifteen minutes tops. At least that's what she had started to tell herself and to explain to Charlene during their weekly phone calls. Charlene wouldn't get mad or anything, just usually grow silent, leaving Lennon to apologize repeatedly and try to jolly her out of the funk she would fall into. Making her feel guilty; *that* was her mother's superpower.

Her aunt Kelly used to remind Lennon of how she got hysterical when visiting hours ended and Charlene was escorted back to her cell. She couldn't imagine getting upset over something as commonplace as watching her orange-jumpsuited mother being led away by guards. She had been doing it for most of her life. Freaking Kelly, who could never be counted on to remember a car seat for little Lennon, requiring she lay on the floor in the car's backseat the whole round trip from New London. She always fell asleep on the drive to the prison and would wake, all fuzzy and confused, when Kelly announced they had arrived at their "final destination," always spoken in a mock-foreboding tone. After a visit that seemed to drag on forever, she would watch her mother leave again, just as she was starting to get comfortable with this thin, old-before-her-time woman who argued with her sister and essentially ignored Lennon until it was time to leave. Then she would swoop her up, moaning and keening about how much she loved her precious baby, her darling little angel. The guards would warn her against any physical contact, and Charlene would sob and hold her even tighter. Finally, the guards would pull her away and escort her back to her cell. Charlene would wave and blow kisses, and Lennon, who craved any sort of physical contact, would apparently start to cry, and wouldn't stop until Kelly had given her a smack on the behind, warning her she would really give her something to cry about before dragging her to the parking lot.

On the way home, her aunt would stop at a drive-through, usually McDonald's, but sometimes Wendy's, which was Lennon's favorite. They would eat burgers and fries and slurp chocolate shakes before continuing home. Lennon learned to hold on to the grease-stained bags the food came in. They were the ideal receptacle to throw up in, something frequently brought on by nerves at seeing her mother, combined with the rich, heavy food, and topped off by carsickness caused by lying on the floor of the backseat.

Lennon knew all too well the source of her issues with food, trust, and physical closeness. It all traced back to being abandoned by her mother and those dreadful trips to visit her in prison. Was it any wonder why she had created every sort of excuse or rationalization for missing a week or two or three?

But this upcoming visit would be different. In a weird way, she was looking forward to spending some time with Charlene. She figured her mother would be proud of how she had gotten to meet that fancy lawyer and let her know Charlene Gallagher still had a bone to pick with her. If she were being honest, Lennon found it hard to believe the lawyer had gone to school with Charlene and they had been besties. Lennon thought of her mother as ancient, and if you were trying to describe what a meth head or burned-out junkie looked like, you would describe Charlene to a T, right down to her pockmarked skin, soulless eyes, and chewed-to-the-quick, grubby fingernails. She had gone gray early on, and despite the availability of a daily shower, her chin-length hair hung around her sallow face in limp strands. By contrast, the lawyer had glossy brown hair, clear green eyes, and a fair complexion with signs of crows' feet just starting to make an appearance. But apparently, they *were* the same age and had been quite close until a boy Charlene had a crush on set his sights on Randi.

Lennon knew she would need to tone down her description of Randi Quinn when telling her mother of their recent encounter. She knew Charlene would press her for details.

"How'd she look? Older, yeah? Thick across the middle? Gray hair?" She would be looking for an affirmative response to all these questions, but the truth was nowhere close. And Charlene would know if she was lying. Then she would be pissed with her daughter, as if Lennon were somehow to blame for any of it. Maybe she should hold off sharing the news about the meeting until the last few minutes of their visit, eliminating the opportunity to be grilled relentlessly. The more she thought about it, the less she now looked forward to visiting. Goddamn Charlene. Everything always had to be so fricking complicated. Most mothers would freak about the fact their daughter had gotten picked up for stealing lobster, but not Charlene. She would ignore the shoplifting charges and head straight for the heart of the matter, the only thing that really counted in her pickled brain. Was Randi Quinn still the same beanpole she had been in high school with zero tits and a flat ass or what?

Ugh, Lennon thought as she gave the worn linoleum countertop one final wipe with her dishtowel. How had she gone from looking forward to seeing Charlene all the way to dreading it? She found her jacket and punched her time card and made for the back door. The cold, crisp air was a delightful change from the stuffy kitchen with its smells of grease and burned coffee. She strolled across the parking lot before adopting a more determined approach, walking quickly on the sidewalk toward home. One hand held her keys in a manner meant to stab anyone who even dared to look at her funny. Getting mugged or attacked was *not* on her to-do list tonight. She picked up the pace, eyes scanning every doorway and alley along the mostly deserted street. What would it be like to live in some fancy suburban neighborhood or a glam high-rise with a doorman? she wondered. Not happening, she thought grimly. Not in this lifetime.

CHAPTER 10

"I might have to go visit her in jail, you know?" I watched Eric to gauge his reaction but found him staring blankly at me. "What?" I asked him.

"You'll have to be a bit more specific, my love. Which of your jailbird buddies are you referring to? Are you assisting in a prison break, and if so, do you require the services of a reliable getaway driver?"

"You're a laugh riot," I said. "Charlene, of course. I told you about her. How we were so close before her life fell apart?"

He nodded vigorously in return. "Oh yeah, now I remember. Mother of lobster girl. So no break-in and no driver. Got it. But why do you need to visit her?"

I shrugged and set my coffee mug on the counter. "I don't know. I guess I feel kind of responsible. It was a lot back then. Everything went to hell, just like that. And now my life is pretty great and hers has been a total shitshow."

"Pretty great, huh? It looks to me like you are living the dream, Quinn. A meaningful career, a nice house, a cat who worships the ground you walk on. Oh yeah, and a sexy-as-fuck husband who lives to serve you and satisfy your every desire." He approached me from behind, wrapping his arms around my middle and nuzzling my neck. "I'm more or less your devoted love slave, in case you hadn't noticed."

"Hobie does *not* worship me," I protested weakly, his fresh-from-the-shower citrusy scent getting to me, as always. "But I really should go to jail."

"Who's going to jail?" asked Pop as he and Sally joined us in the kitchen. I made a mental note to start locking the front door during the day. A few more minutes and Pop would have gotten an eyeful if I'd let my husband have his way with me.

Eric recovered more quickly than I did. "You know, Dez, when we invite you over for Sunday brunch, it doesn't mean you have to hit the deli on the way over as well as the bakery," he said, eyeing the bags of food they had brought in.

"And the florist," Sally piped in, brandishing a lovely bouquet of my favorite orange tulips.

"You are so sweet." I gave my stepmother a big squeeze and took the flowers from her. "Let me get these in water," I said and went in search of a vase.

"Who's going to jail?" Pop repeated, and I busied myself at the sink, adding water to the vase and jamming the stems in, two at a time. This was a sore subject between my dad and me; one going all the way back to when I was in high school.

"It's, um, Charlene, Pop. Charlene Gallagher." My eyes darted to his before I turned my focus back to the flowers. Just long enough to see the storm clouds gathering over his head. To say my dad was not a fan of Charlene or any of the Gallaghers was an understatement.

"I thought they locked her up," said Pop. "Don't tell me. Overcrowding at York and they had to let her go. That's what's wrong with this—"

I cut in before his rant began in earnest. "No, Pop. She's still locked up." I held up the vase. "These are so gorgeous. Thank you, guys." Sally beamed, but my father was not ready to let it go so easily.

"So why are you going to visit her?" he asked suspiciously. "What's the sudden interest in the goddamn Gallagher clan?" To be fair, the Gallaghers had been a thorn in his side for decades. As a cop charged with keeping the good folks of Old Lyme safe and sound, all the shenanigans committed by Charlene's extended family had made it a challenge. For years, it was a safe bet that at least half of the arrests made and citations written in our little town were Gallagher-related. DUIs, petty theft, loitering, domestic disturbances—you name it, Charlene's family was probably responsible. Despite her descent into a life of crime as an adult, Charlene had been a well-behaved teenager, which was the only reason I had been allowed to hang out with her.

"I didn't say I was going, Pop. I said I was thinking about going. There's a case I'm involved with. It's Charlene's daughter, Lennon. No biggie. She got into a little scrape. Kids today, am I right?" I threw up my hands, hoping for a sign of support from Eric or Sally, but they had left the kitchen and were strolling around the patio. From where I stood, it looked like Eric was pointing out the various types of ferns and plants artfully arranged in large terra cotta pots. An Eric-thing for sure. I had finally ended my plant killing spree several years earlier, but not before a vast number of green leafy souls were needlessly slaughtered. I have even killed a cactus or two in my time. I'm not proud of my record of death and destruction, and I have no desire to sacrifice yet another plant for the cause.

"Well, the apple sure didn't fall far . . ." he continued, but I had tuned him out. I had been warning him about the whole "grumpy old man" trap for a while now. He was usually easygoing, but the name Gallagher had set him off today.

"How about some juice?" I suggested. "Or would you like a cup of coffee?"

Pop frowned. "I better have juice, I guess. The doc has been on me to cut back on caffeine." At my worried look, he held up his hands in surrender. "Don't you start on me too," he warned. "I get enough nagging from Sal on that front. She wants me to switch to decaf."

I shuddered in mock horror. Glad to be finished talking about the Gallaghers, I nodded vigorously.

"I mean, what's the point? Am I right?" Decaffeinated—as if! "Nobody should have to live like that," I assured him and poured him a glass of orange juice before we went outside to enjoy some delightful late autumn sunshine.

An hour later, while Pop and Eric headed to the garage to discuss either the engine of some motorized thingy or the plight of whatever team had been eliminated from the playoffs, Sally and I were clearing the table and wrapping the leftovers. I had prepared a French toast casserole and a panful of turkey sausages. Despite everyone eating their share, the addition of Fortuna's famous sausage bread and a basketful of their decadent lemon poppyseed muffins had cut into the consumption of the fare I had provided. I would press as many of the leftovers on my folks as I could. Despite my best intentions to not waste food, I confess to needing to make a weekly sweep of the discarded containers sitting far too long in the fridge.

"How's he doing?" I asked Sally. Pop had been strangely silent during the meal, and his appetite had been less than robust. "He seems off, you know? And please don't tell me he's just fixated on my friend from high school. I don't feel like I am really reaching him lately."

Sally straightened up from loading plates into the dishwasher. "I don't know what to tell you, sweet girl. He has been a bit of a Grumpy Gus recently. There's something . . . but I think he wants to talk to you himself."

My hackles raised, I turned to her. "Oh my God, is he sick? Is that it? Is it . . . ?" I couldn't say the C word. "Sal, please . . ."

She came over and threw her arms around me. For a tiny woman, she had the grip of a grizzly bear but in a sweet-smelling, cozy way. "He's not sick, Randi. I promise you. Just give him a little time, okay?" I nodded and willed myself to calm down. For a split second, I almost asked if it had anything to do with our pending move to London. Had he heard about Eric's new career opportunity? I reasoned there was no way he could have, but he had eyes and ears on the ground from his years on the force. Still . . .

"Well, I guess he'll talk to me when he's ready," I said, and minutes later everything had been put away and the kitchen was spic and . . . well, fairly tidy. Just then, Eric and Pop came in through the garage door, still chatting away.

"I heard about your news," said Pop, and my stomach dropped. I thought we had decided to hold off saying anything about moving to London today. Why had Eric gone ahead and . . .

"Congratulations my girl."

"Don't keep me in suspense," Sally said. "What are we celebrating?" I flashed a worried look at Eric, who was grinning broadly. Help me out here, I begged him silently.

"I was telling your dad about how you were asked to give the keynote at the annual conference in January," he said smoothly, and I almost groaned in relief. I had been offered the dubious honor to speak at a gathering of legal aid lawyers from across New England in a few months. I smiled and tried to look thrilled.

"Lucky me," I said.

"Where's the conference?" asked Sally. "Someplace good, like the Bahamas or Disney World?" Sally and Pop had been talking about bringing their grandchildren to Florida, and she clearly had "the happiest place on earth" on her brain these days.

I chuckled at her obvious excitement. "I wish. It's in Hartford this year," I told her with a grin. We wild and crazy lawyers would be tearing it up in our nation's insurance capital. Big whoop.

"Well, that's still . . . Nope, sorry. I got nothin'," she said. "But if you want me to go dress shopping with you . . ." she added. Sally rarely missed an opportunity to buy a new dress. I knew I would probably find what I wanted in my very own closet, but I nodded in agreement.

They left for home a short while later, and I asked Eric about Pop. "Did he seem a bit off to you? I thought he was, I don't know . . . distracted or maybe distant. What do you think?"

"I think you are maybe feeling a bit guilty about keeping our move a secret from your old man and you might be projecting that on him." At my worried look, he added, "Or maybe it's the result of caffeine withdrawal. What do I know?"

I nodded slowly. "Yeah, I think you're probably right. Can you imagine if either of us tried to go cold turkey? It would not be pretty, my friend, not at all."

As we were both pretty much buzzing on caffeine, we decided to head for the beach. After a long walk in the nippy air, we headed for home and warmed up in bed. Aside from stresses about work, anxiety over our move to London, and new worries about Pop's behavior, all in all, it was a simply delightful day.

CHAPTER 11

Despite the difficult decisions I needed to make as a legal aid attorney, I really did enjoy my job. Offering free advice as well as legal representation to those who could not afford it was a wonderful way to give back to the community that had provided me with so much in my life. My dad had served as a small-town cop, and my mom had worked part-time at the grammar school I had attended, so it wasn't like the Quinn family was rolling in dough, but there was always plenty of food on the table, more than enough to share with friends, neighbors, and co-workers. Last-minute guests did not stop by for my mom's excellent cooking, by the way. Nora Quinn was a lovely woman and a gracious hostess, but cooking was not one of her strong suits. Both of my folks had come from humble beginnings and had learned to make do with relatively little. So an overcooked roast became the base for a satisfying stew or soup. Brownies that were raw in the middle tasted great served warm over store-bought ice cream, and, in a pinch, sandwiches, fruit, cheese, and crackers were always available. So yeah, I never went hungry, knew the value of a dollar, and saw the benefit of a hard day's work.

But many in our neck of the woods were not as fortunate. Landlord disputes were common, especially in the urban areas.

Although it could be challenging to evict families, especially those with younger kids, I had seen dozens of cases of wronged tenants working at minimum-wage jobs with minimal health benefits sick from mold, a lack of heat or hot water, you name it. If they withheld their rent money, the rooms got colder and the snow piled up at their doorways, only to melt and flood their kitchens when it turned warmer. They would pack up and move someplace only slightly less awful, allowing the scummy landlord to slap on a coat of paint and jack up the rent for some other unsuspecting family. I had put away some totally deplorable criminals in my years as an assistant state's attorney, but those slumlords were as despicable as any of them.

Unless I was in court representing my clients, I was generally chained to my desk, shuffling a fair amount of paper. Wrongful evictions, home foreclosures, and denied disability benefit claims were the most common cases in our office. And for several years in a row, there had been an uptick in situations involving domestic violence, which naturally went hand in hand with the nation's economic woes. *Hurt people hurt.* I had seen it on a bumper sticker, and while I didn't stick trendy sayings on my car, if I were to do so, it would be that one. Or maybe *The Closer You Get, the Slower I Drive.* I honestly couldn't decide.

Due to recent budget cuts, I had willingly given up my full-time status and the health benefits I was entitled to. Eric's insurance plan was better than anything available at our nonprofit, and I was glad to cut my hours back, allowing co-workers who needed the income to stay on full-time. I had requested to be allowed to serve as a volunteer counselor for the Center for Children and Youth Advocacy and hold both individual meetings and group sessions at the office on "my time," and no one had a problem with that. The center served youth currently experiencing or at risk for homelessness up to the age of twenty-one and offered counseling in the areas of domestic violence, both civil and criminal court-related issues, education, and employment. There were currently a dozen young women I worked with, roughly half living in one of the group homes in the area. We met on Monday mornings, and I looked forward to it each week. I would stop and get donuts or breakfast sandwiches as well as bottles of fruit juice, energy drinks, and flavored waters, relying on my pal Sandi to prepare a large pot of coffee before I arrived on-site.

On this Monday morning, I unloaded bags of sandwiches in the conference room and set up drinks for what I hoped would be an informative session about the importance of building and maintaining networks, both personal and professional. I met with most of the girls individually every couple of weeks, so I had a sense of what was going on in their lives. But it was always something special to watch them greet each other and swap stories of legal snafus, romantic relationships, job opportunities, and childcare woes. I normally gave them time to ease into things, get out their news, or rant a bit if needed while they ate and sipped their drinks.

I watched as Sandi entered with a carafe of coffee. I invited her to join us, but she waved me off and slipped out seconds before the first of the group arrived. Always chatty and generally upbeat, today's early arrivals seemed quieter, in less than good spirits. I greeted each young woman by name and invited them to help themselves. Drinks were chosen, sandwiches unwrapped, and soon there were seven members of my group sitting at the huge, scarred conference table. Noticing it was now fifteen minutes past the hour, I wondered aloud where the other women were.

Tasha, the oldest of the group at nineteen, looked around the room, shrugging her shoulders. "Dunno," she mumbled through a mouthful of bacon, egg, and cheese biscuit. "Caitlin is sick with the flu, and Sammy got called into work, but I have no clue what happened to the others."

I counted on my fingers. "So that still leaves Nicki and Ari and Riley." This was really odd. It was common for the occasional missed appointment for individual sessions with me, but it was nearly unheard of for this many members of our group to miss the weekly get-together.

"Ari is freaking out these days," said Cora as she got up to throw her trash in the receptacle and grab a Snapple. A lanky girl with purple frosted hair, she had a lengthy juvenile arrest record and had been court-ordered to live in a group home two years ago at the age of sixteen. She usually had more to say about the others in the group and less about her own issues, but everyone adapted to the program at their own pace. "She's getting her kid back, so she probably needed to hit up Target and go to the grocery store."

That made sense, but still. "Well, let's get started. Who has some good news to share?" I looked at the faces around the table but got mostly blank stares in return. What was up with everyone today? "Nothing? No one has anything positive to report?" At the end of the table, Sara Gonzales cleared her throat before speaking.

"Well, I'm not sure if it's relevant, but my landlord finally replaced the furnace, so I was pretty glad about that." Since she was the mother of a newborn, I could only imagine the relief she felt. I scribbled a note to myself to check her address and see if other issues had been reported.

"And just in time for the colder weather. But, Sara, next time let me know and we can get you some help. You shouldn't have to live without heat. And that goes for any of you. We're here to help you with those kinds of issues. But we can't unless—"

"I would like to have my puke-green wall-to-wall carpeting replaced with luxury vinyl plank flooring. Can you get right on that, Ms. Quinn?" asked Mai Lin from her seat next to Sara. Amid the cheers of support and "someone's been watching too much HGTV," I told her unless the carpeting posed a health or safety problem, she would need to learn to live with it.

"Besides, no one wants to be, what do they call it, a whistle-blower," said Cora, and most of the girls nodded in agreement. "The ones who complain or make a fuss," she added, "they get gone pronto." More nods.

I was confused. "What do you mean? *Who* gets gone?"

"It happens, Ms. Quinn," said Cora. "Girls who are seen as a problem or are always complaining . . ." She snapped her fingers. "Vanished," she added darkly.

It took me a second to realize she was serious. Looking around the room, I saw most of the girls wore a look of complacency, as if disappearing off the face of the earth was expected, a non-issue. "Who are we talking about here?" I asked and received an avalanche of responses.

I heard different names called out, including Lyndsey, Jade, Ivy, and Chloe. It seemed everyone knew of at least one girl who had gone missing.

Cora attempted to clarify the situation. "It's not like it's all the time, Ms. Quinn. It's not like girls are being snatched from their beds or nothin'." A few girls shook their heads, clearly disagreeing with Cora's assessment. "But it's like, every once in a while, someone just stops coming around." I had thought about that very same occurrence the other day while I was having lunch with Sandi. They just stopped coming around.

Tasha nodded emphatically. "Yeah, and like Cora said, it's always the smart ones or the ones who mouth off a lot. It's like someone wants to shut them up." A roar of dissent followed with girls claiming, "So and so wasn't all that smart," and "What about this one?" or "That one?" The resounding sentiment? "It's not fair"—an understatement if I'd ever heard one.

"Girls, one at a time, please," I begged them.

"It's not fair," said Mai, sounding tired and frustrated. "Social workers, parole officers, bosses, landlords . . . Why does everyone expect us to be quiet and obedient and shit? Can't we even have a say about our own lives?" Everyone nodded in agreement.

"I'll be right back," I announced and hurried to my office. I grabbed a stack of copier paper and a handful of pens, and as I was leaving, I found Joe standing in my doorway. "No time to talk," I said as I rushed past him.

"Your minions are restless today," he called out to me. *Argh.*

"They're not my minions," I called over my shoulder as I let myself back into the now quiet conference room. Joe had teasingly started referring to the group as "Miranda's Minions," thinking it would catch on with the rest of the staff, but as far as I knew he was the only one who used that moniker. He really was kind of a tool. A savvy attorney, but still a tool.

I looked around at the mostly silent women. Everyone seemed to be lost in thought, with only a couple whispering together. I passed out sheets of paper and pens.

"I need your help," I announced. "I want you to think about these young women you say are missing. Write as much as you can about them. Use a separate page if you can think of more than one. Anything—full names, nicknames, their age, general description, last known address, where they might have been working, hobbies or interests, names of friends, anything you can think of." A couple started writing furiously, while others appeared to be trying to recall what they knew. "C'mon," I urged them. "You were all throwing out names before. Start with a name and think about the person. Where did you last see them? When?" I saw a few more were now scribbling away. To give them some time without me breathing down their necks, I poured myself another coffee and walked over to the large window overlooking the parking lot of our little strip mall location. Nothing much to see out there. I snuck a quick peak over my shoulder and saw all seven women deep in concentration and writing furiously. How much was there to say, and how many missing girls were there? It appeared I was about to find out.

Bursting with curiosity mixed with the feeling something big and horrible was about to rear its ugly head, I returned to my seat. After a few minutes, one by one they stopped writing, collected their belongings, and wordlessly dropped their "assignment" on the table in front of me. A few grabbed an extra sandwich on their way out along with a juice or water bottle. "G'bye, Ms. Quinn," I heard several times. "See you next week." The door closed on the final girl to leave, and I stared at the pile of papers in front of me. Our time was up, but my work had only just begun. What the hell had we uncovered here today? Who or what was making these girls "get gone"?

CHAPTER 12

Lennon had taken a rideshare into the center of Niantic and walked the rest of the way to the women's prison. She wasn't certain if it was to save a few bucks or just the embarrassment of admitting to the driver that her mother was locked up. But the air was bracing, and it felt good to be out of the city—if you could really call New London a city. Growing up with a mother in and out of jail or court-ordered rehab had been a constant cause of shame despite being surrounded by others in similar situations. She hadn't let it truly define her, but she could hardly ignore the impact it had on every aspect of her life. She buzzed to be let in and hurried through the door as soon as it opened. The smell in this place never really changed, she thought as she joined the short line of family members here to visit their daughter, sister, mother, or wife. A dreadful, stultifying combination of body odor, fear, tobacco and weed combined with whatever tasty culinary delights the inmates had been served that day. Something beefy, maybe? Lennon shuddered and tried to slow her breathing.

She emptied her pockets into the plastic bowl provided: a handful of loose change, a used tissue, a cracked vinyl wallet containing several well-worn bills, her state-issued ID, a SNAP card, and her house key. She added her flip phone at the last minute and watched closely as most of her worldly belongings passed through the metal screening. She started to make her way through the archway but was told she needed to remove her coat. Shivering in a threadbare T-shirt, she waited until she got the all-clear from the guard before thrusting her arms back into the sleeves of her tattered jacket and stuffing everything back in her pockets. Fuck, was that a hole in her left pocket? Maybe she could score a few pieces of tape from the home. What she really needed to do was part with a few of her hard-earned dollars and visit the Goodwill soon. It was nearly the end of October, and the days of below-freezing temps were right around the corner. Her last warm coat had been stolen from the common area on the first floor of her group home, but at least the thief had held off until mid-March. Good times, she thought bitterly and made her way to a table for two in the far corner of the large visitor's room.

A few minutes later, Charlene was led in and Lennon was taken aback, as usual, at her appearance. Although it hadn't been that long since she had seen her mother, she was shocked at how thin she had gotten.

"Well, look at you," Charlene said cheerfully as she approached. "Quick one," she whispered, and Lennon leaned in for a brief hug. Before the guard could call out, "No touching," Charlene had taken a seat across from her, leaning in expectantly.

"Didja meet with her?" she asked, her eyes bright in her sallow face. "Kelly said when you got popped, you asked for her. Just like I always taught you. But she never told me what happened next."

Lennon shook her head in disbelief. Leave it to her family's morbid fascination with all things criminal to get the word to her mother in prison that she had been picked up for shoplifting. She wondered how Kelly had heard about it. "I'm fine, by the way. If you're interested, that is. Work's good, and they're giving me plenty of hours, so there's that." Her mother was eyeing her with a frown on her face. "I'm just sayin'," she added. "I *am* your daughter . . ."

"Well, that's just ducky. You're fine, I'm fine. Blah, blah, blah. I want to know what happened with Randi Quinn, *daughter*. What did she have to say for herself after all these years?" Hurt that her mother was more concerned with an old frenemy than her own flesh and blood, Lennon forgot what she had told herself and instead went for the jugular. She couldn't seem to stop herself. All her good intentions evaporated, just like that. Charlene always could get to her. *Damn.*

"Oh, she was fabulous, amazing, really. Smart as can be and real pretty. Her hair is real nice, and she was wearing this real businessy suit. Classy, I would say, and man, is she ever a good lawyer. She really knows her stuff." She stole a quick glance at her mother and felt an instant stab of guilt. She looked so sad, wrecked, actually. She knew better than to let her mother push her buttons like that. "But I mean, she did her job, you know? No biggie. Working at legal aid, she probably makes not much more than I do at the Point," she said matter-of-factly. Her mother shrugged, all the wind depleted from her sails. Aw crap, thought Lennon. "She asked about you," she said gently. "Said you were one of her closest friends and real popular in high school." Charlene brightened and broke into her best "shucks, little ol' me" grin.

"Yeah, back in the day I was all that and a bag of chips," Charlene said wistfully. "She remembered me, yeah?"

Lennon nodded vigorously. "Of course she did. It was all 'me and Charlene this' and 'me and Charlene that' . . ." Her mother was now looking suspicious, and Lennon realized she had probably been laying it on too thick.

"How long of a meeting did y'all have?" Charlene asked with a frown. "All this chitter chatter took place in the courtroom?"

Lennon remembered just in time that she had vowed not to tell her mother about the fancy lunch and the lengthy conversation. "Well, yeah, I mean, she was pretty chatty, I guess. Maybe she was nervous meeting me, seeing as how she owes you big-time and all."

Charlene nodded shrewdly. "Yeah, she was a real motormouth in high school. Guess she hasn't changed. Bet she's filled out some. I seen her on the TV a few years back. She was gonna host this big-ass talk show, and if I'm being honest, she looked a little, I don't know, chunky, I guess. Like maybe she had let herself go a bit." She made eye contact with Lennon again, practically begging her to agree.

The best Lennon could do was waffle a bit. "Yeah, I dunno. I mean, she's old and stuff, so whatever, but what's going on with you?" Lennon asked, feigning interest in the comings and goings of the women in cell block G. The names would occasionally change due to any number of variables, including early releases, moves to solitary, and the like, but the situations rarely did. Someone received divorce papers, another was having problems with her kids, and still another had overdosed, but "it was accidental, Lennon. She wouldn't leave all of us without saying goodbye" her mother always insisted. Yeah, because no one had ever heard of a thoughtless junkie.

Lennon knew she had shared all that was needed to satisfy her mother's curiosity, so instead of racking her brain to come up with newsy tidbits of her own, she sat quietly, a smile pasted on her face, and listened, occasionally interjecting a "wow" or a "seriously?" The guard called out a reminder that visiting hours would be ending in just five minutes, and to Lennon's surprise, Charlene stood quickly, ready to make her exit. No hugs, no tears? As much as she dreaded the usual dramatics, Lennon felt mildly disappointed.

"Things to see, people to do," Charlene announced cheerfully. "I won't mention any names, but *someone* is up for parole," she winked, "and that someone needs to get ready for bunk check." She blew a kiss at her daughter and sashayed across the room toward the exit. Lennon stared at her mother's retreating back, shocked at her news. Charlene was up for parole? Instead of going on and on about the women in her ward, they could have discussed this very important turn of events. What in the hell was she up to now?

As Lennon walked across the parking lot, she realized the wind had kicked up and her tattered jacket offered little protection from the cold. *Screw this nonsense.* She logged into the rideshare app, and several minutes later Roger, driving a red Ford Escape, pulled into the lot. She got in the back and buckled her seatbelt.

"Boyfriend?" he asked, motioning toward the prison. Sexist prick, thought Lennon. And a dumbass to boot. Everyone knew York was strictly a women's facility.

"Early release," she said, puffing out her chest, and he grinned nervously.

"Cool, cool," he said, and there was blessed silence all the way back to New London.

CHAPTER 13

I left the office shortly after my group session broke up and everyone had taken off. While driving, I placed a hands-free call to the Old Lyme Police Department. A couple of years earlier, I had worked with a detective on the force when Tracey's son had gotten caught up in a sexting scandal. Detective Dennis Reynaldo had been rather curt with me as I was the unofficial attorney working with the Ryan family, and even I knew I could be a bit of a pain in the ass, but he was tuned in to the goings-on of the Connecticut shore communities. Although he would not have jurisdiction in New London, he might be able to offer me some valuable perspective.

The desk sergeant answered, a nearing-retirement crony of my dad's. "OLPD, Sergeant Williams speaking."

"Hey, Mike, it's Randi Quinn."

"Randi, it's been too long. How's the family? How's Dez? Still on his honeymoon?" It had been four years since Pop and Sally had gotten hitched, but they *were* still acting like newlyweds.

"Yes, he is," I agreed. "Say, is Detective Reynaldo around? I was hoping to touch base with him on something."

"Yeah, he's here," he said. "Want me to put you through?"

"Yes, please. Thanks. I'll let Pop know you were asking after him."

"You got it, Randi. Here you go."

There was a moment of silence, then: "Dennis Reynaldo," came his crisp, deep voice.

"Hi, Dennis," I said. "It's Miranda Quinn. How are you doing?"

"I'm fine, thank you," came his reply. "How can I help you?" A bit less frosty than the last time we had talked, but no warm and fuzzy vibes either.

I explained about my Monday morning sessions with the young women who were viewed to be at risk or in the middle of any number of official court proceedings. I told him of my concerns about the missing girls whose names had been shared with me. I tried to stick with the facts and ended with, "I realize you don't handle New London, but I was hoping maybe you could check into it for me? If I gave you some names, maybe you could see if there have been any reports filed with missing persons?" Silence on his end. After another moment, I continued. "What do you think?" I asked and waited again for his response.

"There has been some chatter about some girls who have gone missing. I don't recall any of the names offhand, but yes, there is something going on. Nothing here in Old Lyme, however, and I don't even know if the cases are all related or not." I tried not to read too much into his tone, but he sounded intrigued.

"I am happy to meet with you and share what I know. What works for you?"

He cleared his throat, and I heard some clicking on his keyboard. Maybe he was checking his schedule?

"How's tomorrow morning? 8:30? Can you meet me here at the station?"

I tried to visualize my own schedule for tomorrow. Provided I was on the road by 9:00, I would arrive at the courthouse in plenty of time for my first case, which I was fairly certain was at 10:00.

"How's 8:15?" I countered. "I'll bring pastries, okay?" He agreed and ended the call.

By the time I arrived home, I had already made a to-do list in my head. Seconds after walking in the door, I started to transcribe my thoughts into writing. Gone were the days when I could recall with almost perfect clarity what I needed to do each day. Now I relied on jotting down a hastily scribbled list or sending myself a text message with reminders. As I leaned over the kitchen counter, my buddy jumped up and pushed his nose into my cheek. Never sure if it was "I missed you" or "Feed me, woman," I generally assumed it was the latter. I splashed some cold water in his bowl and topped off his kibble supply, and he hopped down to enjoy a midday snack.

"You're easy," I told him as I made my way to our bedroom to change into sweats and an *Even Flow* Pearl Jam T-shirt. I grabbed a water and headed downstairs to my studio/office. While I had been the on-air host of *Miranda Nights*, I had recorded live, right from here. It had been enjoyable at first, but a few months after the show premiered, I'd had to deal with a stalkery fan whose behavior had grown increasingly violent. Daniel McMurphy was a cop who I'd convicted when I was a prosecutor, and his years in jail had only escalated his anger and resentment toward me. He had broken in, nearly burned down our home, and had catnapped my poor Hobie. He was currently serving fifteen years with no possibility of parole, and I knew he posed no further threat, but after all that, my enthusiasm for being an on-air celebrity waned, and I'd notified the executive board I was not interested in renewing my contract. It was a stupidly large amount of money, but I'd walked away without a single regret. I had to admit I missed seeing the billboards and bus signs advertising the show, always featuring a likeness of yours truly, looking all wise and full of advice guaranteed to alter the very trajectory of listeners' lives for the better. But now the studio was my home office, with most of the recording equipment packed away out of sight. I planned to resurrect my blog and podcast one day, but for now, three days at the office, courtroom appearances, and the group and solo sessions with my Monday crew were about all I could handle. Knowing his live show would have ended a couple of hours earlier, I placed a call to Chris, but it went straight to voicemail. I decided not to leave a message, but I made a note to call him again. We needed to catch up and soon.

I unearthed the jumbled stack of papers from this morning's session and spread them out around me. I sorted them by girl's first names, and even that proved challenging. Some of the accounts were well into a second paragraph before the individual's name was listed. Once I had them organized, I tried to make sense of the information I was seeing. There were four Chloes, two Jades, and one each of Lyndsey, Lyndsay (probably the same girl?), Ivy, Maria, Jess, Jessie (same?), and a couple of pages with no identified first names. I read through those two and made a tentative match with the first one as Chloe (brown hair, overweight) and the second as Lyndsey/Lyndsay (dark hair, pale, with freckles and eyeglasses). There was no mention of Riley Jackson. I started my own sheet on her, jotting down what I already knew and adding info from her file.

Since five of the seven girls today had identified Chloe as one of the missing, I thought I could make the most headway with her. I grabbed a highlighter and started noting information on the various pages. After twenty minutes, this was what I knew.

Chloe
Last name Andrews or Anderson
Between 17 and 19 years old

Born in Stonington, CT, probably
Straight brown hair, shoulder-length, brown eyes or hazel?
Chunky? Curvy?
Lived at Bradford House for between 6 months and a year
Hung around with Lyndsay/Lyndsey, Emily and Jayce (f/m?)
Got her GED
Worked at Dunkin' in New London (closest to downtown) for 6 months to a year
Always on her phone, watched cat videos, and never missed an episode of The Bachelor
Swore she was a vegetarian but always requested pepperoni if anyone was ordering pizza
Last seen heading to work or in the group lounge at Bradford House or going to her room

It made sense everyone had last seen her at different times or in different locations. This was plenty to go on as far as I was concerned. I looked at the clock on the wall: 2:15. It would be hours before Eric got home. Plenty of time to drive to the Dunkin' location and ask about Chloe. I could always go back to the Bradford House, but I didn't relish being patronized by the arrogant Mr. Myers. Dunkin' it is, I decided. I called out a goodbye to Hobie, grabbed my bag and my keys, and headed toward I-95. With any luck, I would be able to talk to a co-worker of Chloe's or even a supervisor and fill in some of the missing information.

CHAPTER 14

Thirty minutes later, I walked into the donut shop. While the parking lot was relatively empty, the small space was buzzing with teens and preteens. Must be the after-school crowd. I waited in a line snaking around the lobby, moving slowly. I took it all in—the smell of coffee and donuts, the sounds of f-bombs being dropped and students bragging about how wasted they were or had been or planned to get. They seemed impossibly young to me despite an almost universal sort of blasé manner, like they'd already seen and done it all. I tried to recall how Tracey, Charlene, and I had behaved in high school. Probably equally immature, but more, I don't know, giddy? Certainly way less cool.

"Can I help you?" the young man behind the counter asked with a yawn. Seemed like he needed a mug of what they were selling.

I gave him my best smile. "Hello, um, Max," I greeted him. "Busy here today, huh?"

He looked at me like I was a gnat or something equally annoying. "Yeah, thanks for noticing. What can I get you?"

"I'll take a large black coffee and some information, please."

He narrowed his eyes at me. "About?"

"One of your co-workers. Chloe Anders . . . maybe?"

"Why are you asking about Chloe?" he asked, studying me closely.

"I'm an attorney, and I'm trying to locate Miss Anders . . . or is it Andrews?"

Max scoffed. "Not for nothin', lady, but you don't look like a lawyer. And even if you did, how come you don't know your client's name?"

I glanced at my ratty sweatpants and T-shirt. *Crap.* "I'm working from home today, and I never said Chloe was my client. So do you know her?"

He looked thoughtful for a moment before nodding. "Yeah, Chloe Anderson. She used to work here. Fat chick, brown hair? I hardly ever worked with her cuz she was mostly on the morning shift."

Yes! I now had her full name, which was more than when I arrived. But wait, she *used* to work here? Max rang up my order. "Total is $4.15. Cash or credit?"

I dug around and found a five-dollar bill, which I handed to him. He gave me back my change, and I dropped it in the well-marked TIP JAR along with a couple dollar bills.

"Next in line," he called out, and I decided to ask another question while I still had a sliver of his attention.

"Excuse me, is your manager available?" I asked.

Without skipping a beat, he called out, "Lena, got a customer for you," followed by, "Next in line." I moved away and waited in another line to pick up my order. A minute later, I was making my way through the crowd carrying a large cup of coffee. A petite Black woman about my age approached me.

"I'm Lena Torres. You wanted to see me?" she asked.

"Yes, thank you," I said and explained I was a legal aid attorney and was trying to get some information on a young woman who worked there.

"You don't look like an attorney," she said skeptically, checking out my outfit and messy hair.

"Yeah, I get that a lot," I told her with a smile. Out of the corner of my eye, I saw three kids vacate a booth and I motioned toward it. "Could we sit and talk?"

She eyed my coffee and nodded. "Gimme a minute." She walked back toward the counter.

I slid into the booth seconds before it was claimed by a group of bored-looking teenaged girls. I gave them a tight smile, not wanting to look too pleased at my victory, and they slithered away. Seconds later, Lena returned carrying her own cup of coffee. She slipped into the seat opposite me and took a short sip.

"Goddamn, that's hot," she complained, patting at her upper lip with a paper napkin.

I chuckled. "Yeah, you would think after that lawsuit filed against McDonald's, they would—" At her blank stare, I hurried to explain. "You know the one: an elderly woman got a coffee at the drive-through, and she put the cup between her legs and it spilled. It was like 190 degrees." Nothing? "She received a huge settlement." I shook my head in amazement. "Can you even?"

Lena's eyes went from neutral to steely gray in seconds. "That's why you came here?" she asked. "You're filing a lawsuit?" She started to stand, and I tried to stop her by explaining quickly.

"No, there's no lawsuit. I promise you. I'm a huge fan of hot coffee. Love the stuff. But I'm with the courts. I'm here to ask you about one of your employees. Chloe Anderson. It's important I speak with her. Can you help me?"

Lena sat back down, staring at me with open hostility. "What do you want with that poor girl? Haven't you people put her through enough?"

I was now thoroughly confused. "I'm trying to help girls like Chloe. I understand she's gone missing. Her friends are worried and want to know where she is. Has she been showing up for work this past week?"

Lena shook her head. "Chloe gave her notice last week. She emailed me, said she'd come into some money from a long-lost aunt, I think it was. Said she was going to go back home to her family."

Money from a long-lost relative? Her family, such as it was, lived right here in New London. Of that much, I was certain. Where had she gone? Trying to tamp down the rising panic I was experiencing, I asked, "Where is that? Her family, I mean."

Lena looked unsure for a moment before responding. "Vermont. Yes, I'm sure she said it was Vermont."

Vermont? What were the odds? Two girls in and out of foster care for most of their lives, living at the Bradford House. Both had been contacted by long-lost family members and both had moved to Vermont with the expectation of a financial windfall within a week of each other. I had never been a believer in coincidences, but even if I was, this situation stank to high heaven. I tried to compose myself to learn more.

"I'm sorry, but one more quick question, please?" I got the briefest of nods and hurried on. "You referred to Chloe as that 'poor girl.' What did you mean by that?"

Lena Torres drew herself up to her full height and looked down at me, her dark eyes blazing. "That girl has been in and out of foster homes since she was in diapers. She told me she'd been beaten and assaulted and near starved in some of those places, but you folks couldn't be bothered to find her someplace safe." She shook her head in disgust. "I'm not blaming you, but the system is broke. These kids ain't safe," she added and walked away.

I called out a "thank you" for her time, pitched my lukewarm coffee in the trash, and hurried out to my car. I needed to talk to Jordan Myers immediately. My heart pumping, I drove toward the Bradford House, playing her words over and over in my head. *The system is broke. These kids ain't safe.* But I was part of the system, and keeping kids safe was my job.

###

I found street parking and bounded up the steps to the stately Victorian house that sixteen of our most vulnerable citizens called home. I pounded on the door, which was finally opened by a tiny woman in a blue uniform. She kept the safety chain on, and I yelled through the narrow opening.

"I need to see Jordan Myers. It's important. It's critical we talk right away."

I could only see a sliver of her face as she tried to explain in broken English. "Mr. Jordan, he's not here. He had to go to New York. Beezness. Important beezness."

What the actual fuck was going on here? I slipped my card through the opening, and our hands touched ever so briefly. "Please give Mr. Jordan my card. Tell him to call me as soon as possible. Tell him it concerns two of his residents. Riley Jackson and Chloe Anderson. Can you remember that?"

Her voice was soft, almost tearful as she responded. "Ah, *si*, Miss Chloe and Miss Riley. Such good girls. Brave girls."

I felt a surge of something. Hope, maybe? "Do you know what happened to them? Do you know where they went?"

I felt more than I could see the woman shaking her head. "No, I'm sorry. They are just gone." Before I could ask her to explain, the door closed and I was once again on the outside, trying in vain to look in.

CHAPTER 15

"For the first time ever, I wish you were a dog," I told Hobie, who looked totally unfazed by my shocking admission. He rolled over in the top tier of his cat hotel/climbing tree and allowed me to scratch his furry spotted belly. "I don't really wish you were a dog," I whispered, "but I have all this pent-up energy and your dad's not home, so I can't jump his bones, and Tracey is busy with her damn small fry, and it's too late in the day to go visit Pop since they eat dinner even earlier than you do. If you were a dog, I could throw a ball in the backyard and you could catch it." Hobie gave a long yawn, allowing me to see every one of his tiny sharp teeth. "Never mind," I told him as I stalked away. "But wait until next time you want to snuggle with me at the ass crack of dawn."

I considered cooking something for dinner, but Eric had told me he was working late, so I knew I would end up with a bowl of cereal and a banana, or maybe I would skip the banana. I stripped down to my skivvies and contemplated a hot shower, but at the last minute I decided to go out to the patio and climb into the hot tub.

A minute later, I sank gratefully into the steaming water, leaned back, and closed my eyes. I willed my brain to slow down and tried like hell to "be here now," and all that sort of Zen stuff, but it was no use. My mind went straight to worrying about Riley and Chloe and Lindsay/Lyndsey and the other girls my group said were missing. I began to work out exactly how to present the information I had compiled to Detective Reynaldo in the morning. I knew that just like an opening statement in the courtroom, I would have to grab his attention right off the bat with startling facts and figures or risk losing his interest completely. I was lost in thought when I heard my name being called. I sat up quickly and saw my neighbor Louise Donnelan striding across the lawn toward me. A six-foot-tall border of arborvitae separated our backyards with an opening large enough to allow Louise and Jasper, her Cairn Terrier, to drop by at random hours.

"Hey neighbor," she called out, and as I watched, she crossed the patio and plopped into a chair a few feet from where I sat. Wishing I had taken the extra minute to change into a swimsuit instead of the ratty underwear I had on, I tried to adopt a friendly tone.

"Hi, Lou. You're looking good." An understatement for sure. Her long glossy hair swung below her shoulders, and in her skinny jeans and light pink crewneck sweater, she could pass for a woman roughly half her age. I knew she was several years older than me, and I wondered briefly if she'd had work done.

"You as well," she countered, and I could just imagine the sight I made with my messy bun, faded bra with a loose strap, and my face damp with sweat and steam.

"I would ask you to join me, but you look like you are on your way somewhere."

"You kill me," she said with a throaty chuckle. "Always with the jokes."

Yes folks, I'm a laugh riot.

"How's Carl?" I asked and got another chuckle in response.

"Oh, you know Carl," she said and threw up her hands as if to say, "Who can keep up with Carl?" and I smiled. Actually, I barely knew him and could count on both hands the number of times he and I had exchanged more than a few words in the four years since we had moved in. But he had helped in the search for Hobie a few years ago when Daniel McMurphy had stolen him, so extra points in the plus column for Carl, that was for certain.

"Tell him I said hello," I said, and Louise nodded.

"Oh, you bet. And speaking of good-looking hubbies, where's your fella keeping himself these days? I haven't seen him in forever."

Man, I wanted to like her, I really did. But she always spoke of Eric like they shared some sort of bond or connection, and it made me feel something. Not jealous, just not all that comfortable. I couldn't totally let down my guard around her, which was difficult to admit for a woman sitting in her underwear with sweat dripping from every pore.

"Eric is doing great. He's looking at a promotion—" I began before stopping myself. That was all I needed, to tell her about the move to London. The way in which Louise gossiped about other neighbors made it clear to me she would talk about us if I ever gave her something to talk about. No, she and Carl would find out a day or two before the moving vans showed up. But would we move everything? Or leave the house fully furnished for a long-term rental? Someone sitting in my hot tub or sleeping in my bed? Not for the first time that day, I wondered why the hell I had been so quick to agree to the move.

"Earth to Randi," Louise called out, and I blinked at her, trying to focus my attention. "Well, that's cool about Eric. Just remind him from me that all work and no play . . ."

"Oh, he makes time to play," I told her, trying not to sound defensive. "Plenty of time to play."

She was about to respond when Carl's voice could be heard. Sort of a yodel followed by, "Lou, I'm home. Tell me Jasper is with you."

"Oh dang. I left him a note saying I was coming over to visit, and I let Jasper out to do his business, but forgot to call him back in. Gotta go," she said with a quick wave, and I watched her hurry back to the opening in the row of trees and wiggle her way through into her own backyard. She was a bit of a flake but had proven herself to be a reliable friend on several occasions over the years. If we weren't moving across the pond, perhaps I might have suggested a get-together, but it was probably pointless after all this time. And that was fine with me.

A few minutes later, I stepped out of the water and wrapped myself in a big towel. The air had gotten much cooler in the past half hour, and I rushed back into the house shivering with cold. Maybe a can of soup instead of a bowl of cereal, I decided and went to our bedroom to change into something warm and dry. I should probably use this free time to look for some boxes and begin the process of deciding what to take to London, but who was I kidding? Tomorrow was another day.

CHAPTER 16

The next morning, I pulled into visitor parking at the Old Lyme PD. Coming here brought back so many good memories for me. Every time I walked through the doors and into the dated and cramped lobby, I felt a sense of pride and nostalgia as well. Pop and his colleagues had worked tirelessly to keep our town safe. Today, I hoped I could convince Detective Reynaldo to take me seriously and investigate the disappearance of the girls on my list.

"Randi," a voice called out, and I was quickly wrapped up in a hug by a bear of a man. My pal Mike.

"Good morning to you," I responded. "I'm here for—"

"He's waiting for you," Mike told me, and I entered the first door on the right. It opened into a small conference room with a scarred wooden table and a trio of metal folding chairs. As I entered, Detective Dennis Reynaldo stood to greet me, his hand outstretched and his smile wide.

"Ms. Quinn," he said, his deep baritone warm and welcoming. "Thank you for coming in."

I was the one who had asked for the meeting, but whatever. "Hi, Dennis. It's good to see you. But please, it's Miranda."

He nodded his agreement and offered me a seat. I sank into one of the two unoccupied chairs and unbuttoned my blazer.

"Can I get you a coffee? Water?" he asked. Oh crap, hadn't I offered to bring coffee or donuts?

"I'm good, but thank you. I know how busy you must be, and I'm due in court soon," I explained. I had over-caffeinated at home, knowing from prior experience how dreadful the coffee they served here was.

"Of course. What do you have for me?" he asked, watching closely as I spread out the contents of my folder. After warming up last night, I had spent a couple of hours identifying several of the partial names of the missing young women before reviewing my notes and writing a quick summary of what I had learned. Now I reiterated how I had established the support group over a year ago and described the young women I met with weekly. Since the beginning, there had been a total of sixty-five participants with some only showing up a handful of times and most attending weekly for a few months. My goal had been to keep the group at around twelve, as any more and it was too easy for the quiet ones to get lost in the shuffle. Not to mention the size of our conference table was a deterrent to adding more women to the group. But there was always room for a guest or drop-in. Most of the women attended regularly for two to three months until work and family commitments made attendance more challenging. I told him the attendance had been unusually low yesterday and how my question about those who were missing had prompted a barrage of rumors and speculation.

"I have been able to identify the following women as missing: Chloe Anderson, Riley Jackson, and Lyndsey Wilson. All three were in residence at the Bradford House, but that may or may not be relevant as there are more girls there than at any of the other homes. According to Ms. Anderson's former supervisor and Ms. Jackson's residential director, both women were recently contacted by long-lost family members and both reportedly left for Vermont to seek their fortunes without a word to their friends. I am not yet aware if Ms. Wilson has provided a similar sort of explanation to anyone. Additionally, the following are young women who may be missing, pending further investigation, based upon reports from my group." I read off several more names and the addresses of the homes where they were assigned and sat back. "What do you think?" I asked, hoping I had provided enough to spark the detective's interest. From the little I knew, he was not one to engage in a wild goose chase. I waited.

Clearing his throat, he leaned forward, his eyes bright with interest. "I think you would make a good detective, Miranda. Tell me more about the two with the long-lost family members and the money."

"Yes," I said, nodding vigorously. "Apparently, Riley has a cousin of unknown gender, and Chloe has an aunt, I believe. Same weak-ass story explaining their disappearances. And both living in Vermont? I mean, what are the odds?"

Deep in thought, Dennis stroked his chin, and in the silence that followed, I wondered how long ago he had shaved his beard. Clearly, he was not someone given to idle chatter. After another moment, he spoke up.

"We need to talk with my colleagues in New London. This is valuable information that needs to be shared."

I was amazed at the speed with which he had considered my information and was choosing to act on it. "That's great, Dennis. When can we make this happen?"

He pressed a few buttons on his phone. I heard it ringing on the other end before a woman's voice answered, although I couldn't make out her name.

"Good morning, it's Dennis. Remember that situation we were talking about last night? I'm discussing it with her now, and it seems like solid intel." He glanced at me briefly. "Yeah, Quinn. That Quinn, yes. But I think she's on to something. Could be big." He waited while she responded, and I tried to imagine what he'd meant by "that Quinn." The failed TV host, the late-night know-it-all, or the former ADA with the moniker "Quinn for the Win"? All of the above?

Dennis was nodding and motioned to me. "How's 3:00 p.m. tomorrow? Does that work?"

I thumbed through my calendar and found I once again was due at court in the morning but had no scheduled appointments in the afternoon. "I'll be there," I assured Dennis and confirmed the meeting would take place at the New London Police Department. He nodded as he ended the call. Time to hit the road, I decided.

"I've got to get to court," I announced, and, gathering my notes, I shoved the folder into my bag. "Thank you so much. See you tomorrow."

I waved over my shoulder at Mike as I zipped past.

"Say hello to Dez for me," came his reply.

I drove through the surface streets of my town, finally pressing the gas pedal once I got onto the highway. I tuned in to soak up some of the positive vibes from Dr. Chris. As usual, he did not disappoint as he spelled out the ground rules of making a blended family work.

I pulled into the parking lot next to the courthouse and for once moved quickly through security. I hurried into the courtroom marked with a large #3 and walked into . . . nothing. No seated judge, no prosecutor, and no court officers. What the hell? I rushed out into the hallway, nearly running into a clerk whose face seemed familiar.

"Excuse me, but I have a hearing scheduled for this courtroom right about . . . now," I said, confirming the time with the large wall clock. When I had checked earlier, this was the assigned room, but changes were often made at the last minute, and it was likely I'd missed a text alert. It certainly wouldn't be the first time.

She shook her head, studying her clipboard closely. "Quinn?" she asked, and I nodded. "Looks like your girl is missing," she told me with a disapproving shake of her head.

Another girl is missing? "What are you saying?" I asked, trying and probably failing to appear calm.

She looked up from her clipboard. "Your client, a Ms. Shawna Walker, was a no-show this morning. They are supposed to report a half hour prior to their scheduled time in front of the judge. She didn't report or call in, so there's a warrant out for her arrest." She spoke as if she were explaining something quite complex to someone quite slow.

I really didn't appreciate her tone, both condescending and cynical at the same time, as if clients like mine made a habit of skipping out on their responsibilities. She wasn't completely wrong, but still. "I understand the protocol," I snapped. "But when you said 'missing,' I was surprised." Was Shawna Walker now "missing" as well?

"Sorry, It's been a crazy morning," she said apologetically. With a half wave, she and her trusty clipboard were off. I sagged against the wall, feeling much more than just the concern I had been carrying around since yesterday's session. I was officially scared shitless. I left the courthouse, and as I walked through the lot to my car, I dialed Reynaldo. When I got his voicemail, I told him there might be another missing girl. I supplied her name and said I would see him tomorrow. Digging through my court files, I confirmed Shawna had never lived at the Bradford House. As I tried to determine which was more pressing, a visit to Bradford House to call on Jordan Myers or a search to try and locate Shawna, my phone buzzed. What fresh hell was this? I wondered, looking at an unknown number on my screen.

"This is Miranda," I announced tersely.

A brief silence, then: "Randi? It's Lennon Gallagher. I need to see you. It's important. Please."

Gone was the slightly mocking voice of the girl I had met only a few days ago. She sounded scared, really scared.

"Are you in a safe space, Lennon?" I asked, and she said she was. An idea came to me. "How close are you to the Shoreline restaurant on Front Street?"

"I can be there in ten minutes," she assured me and ended the call. Decision made, I buckled up, paid the exorbitant fee for less than thirty minutes of parking, and headed to the diner where one of my "minions" worked. Granted, Nicki had only missed a single group session, but it wouldn't hurt to check on her. I had asked Rose to contact her, but so far there was no word. I would meet with Lennon, and once whatever was brewing got handled, I would ask about Nicki and then try to get hold of Shawna. If this kept up, I would need a spreadsheet to keep everyone straight. I hoped like hell I was already seeing the whole iceberg, not just the tip.

CHAPTER 17

I slid into a booth opposite Lennon and tried to hide my shock at her appearance: the dark under-eye circles, her choppy hair looking like she had combed it with an electric mixer, and her baggy gray sweatshirt. The New London High School mascot, a bulldog, was emblazoned across the front.

"I'm glad you called me. What's going on?" I asked.

She stared at me blankly, before speaking. "Were you going to order something?" she asked, looking both hungry and hopeful. I was certain she hadn't called me for the sole purpose of scoring a free lunch, but I knew whatever was going on with her, it would be easier to discuss while we ate together.

"What can I get you?" I asked, and she shrugged.

"I don't care. Whatever you're having. Um, thanks, Randi."

I nodded and made my way to the counter. I studied the menu in front of me and placed an order for two chicken sandwiches—one grilled and one fried—an order of curly fries, a Coke, and a Diet Coke. As I paid, I asked casually, "Is Nicki Santiago working today?"

The young man looked around the nearly empty restaurant and shrugged. "Doesn't look like it," he said. "Is there something I can help you with?" His tone clearly communicated he hoped there was not.

I shrugged in return, maintaining a look of casual indifference. "No, I'm good. But do you remember when you last saw her?"

He narrowed his eyes slightly, studying me. In my full-on lawyer garb today, he would probably believe me if I told him what I did for a living. But then he relaxed.

"Nah, but it's probably been a few days. The more I think about it, I'm pretty sure they've already canned her ass. But hey, your order's ready," he said, gesturing to the loaded tray in front of me.

"Thanks," I said. "Was she sick, do you know?"

He grinned at me. "No way. She told one of the dishwashers she was heading to Vermont with her family or somethin'. Freakin' fall foliage, if you ask me. Pretty lame, huh?"

I nodded mutely and, lifting the tray with both hands, made my way back to Lennon. *Lame?* Yeah, not so much. When I set the tray of food down, Lennon started, looking panicked. Had she been sleeping? Was she high? Neither, I realized. She really was scared.

"What's going on?" I asked as I divided up the food.

She shoved a handful of fries into her mouth and took a long swig of her drink, her eyes darting around the restaurant. After she swallowed, she spoke up.

"Something is wrong, Randi. Someone is messing with us."

Messing with us? "Who is *us*, Lennon?" I waited as she carefully unwrapped her sandwich, reminding me of the way Sally unwrapped her gifts at Christmas. I was about to ask if she planned on saving the grease-stained paper when she looked at me, her eyes wide and her expression grim.

"Us. All of us girls in the group homes around here." She spoke softly, as if she didn't want anyone to hear her. Maybe not even me. It was as if saying something this horrible out loud made it even more real.

"Tell me what's going on," I begged. "You can tell me anything, you know that, don't you? Anything you say to me is confidential."

Lennon shook her head sadly. "It's not that simple. I don't honestly know. Maybe I'm paranoid. Comes from being raised by a pathological, lying junkie, I guess."

"How about you let me be the judge, okay? What do you mean by 'messing with'? Give me an example."

Her eyes were as dark as night as she scowled at me. "Disappearing, that's what I mean. Someone or something is making us disappear." She took a large bite of her sandwich and chewed reflexively.

A wave of panic flooded my brain, and I stared at her, horrified. "Do you have names?"

Lennon nodded slowly. "Yeah. I mean I have some names. Like my friend Tyler. I haven't seen her in days. We were real tight, you know? And like that, poof, she's gone. Disappeared. Her bed's not been slept in; her phone's disconnected."

"What about work? Where was she working?" I tried to keep the desperation out of my voice, not wanting to freak her out any further. "Have you checked there?"

She shook her head, looking offended. "Well, duh, Sherlock. Of course. That was the first place I looked." Based upon the current situation, I could ignore her sarcasm for now.

"Where?" I asked again. Was there a pattern I was missing?

"That dump motel on Capital. She's been cleaning rooms there for maybe six months. No one has seen her, and they said she never picked up her paycheck."

"When was this?" I asked, and Lennon appeared to be counting backward before she answered.

"It was last Wednesday. That's the day she blew me off. We were gonna go for a walk, maybe grab a coffee before I had to go to work. She always works 6:00 a.m. to 2:30. We were gonna hang out before I went in at 5:00. But she never showed. I remember I was pissed because I was running late, so I had to hurry to meet up with her. And then she didn't show."

"So what did you do?" I asked.

"I hung around for a while, figuring she was running late. I called, but it rang and rang, so I wandered over to the motel. I thought maybe she got some overtime or something. I asked one of the other maids, and she got all pissy. Said Tyler hadn't shown up for work. Made a lot of extra work for her and the others. I went back to my room, wrote in my journal for a while, and left for work. That's me . . . livin' the dream."

"And what's happened since then?" I asked.

She shrugged and drank more soda. "I've gone by her place a couple times, and no one has seen her. She was living at the home on Greenleaf. Her phone's been disconnected, and that's all I know." Greenleaf? That's also where Nicki Santiago was living.

I had grabbed my notebook, and now I started scribbling furiously, my lunch forgotten. "So it's almost a week?" I asked to confirm, and Lennon nodded. "What's her last name?"

Lennon rubbed at her eyes with her fists. "Tyler's her last name. It's Allie. Allison Tyler."

"Who else?" I asked. Knowledge of one missing girl, even a close friend, wouldn't have scared Lennon like this. She struck me as a tough kid who had learned from an early age how to bounce back and survive during difficult times. There had to be more for her be so upset.

She spoke slowly, once again almost whispering. "Lyndsey something. Wilson, yeah. She used to work at the Point as a waitress. We used to talk sometimes, and one day she didn't show up for work, and I never saw her again. I heard someone say she went to stay with family in Vermont, but she had told me she was from Long Island, so who knows?"

The thin line of dread I had been holding on to since Lennon's call now threatened to explode. I already had a sheet on Lyndsey and Lennon had just confirmed that, like Chloe and Riley, Lyndsey was linked to Vermont. "When was this?" I asked, writing *Lyndsey, the Point,* and *VT* on a fresh page. I looked up to find her staring at me. "When?" I pressed.

"It was still hot out, so maybe around Labor Day?" She narrowed her eyes at me. "You don't seem all that surprised, Randi. And the way you're taking notes is making me wonder how much of this you already knew."

I looked at her pale face and guarded eyes as I considered how to respond. I didn't want to scare her any more than she already was, but I couldn't tell her it was all her imagination either. I reminded myself I was her attorney and was honor-bound to give her good advice. I nodded slowly and met her gaze directly.

"You're right, Lennon. I'm not surprised. Worried, yes, and more than a little concerned about your safety and that of all the other girls. I'm sorry about your friend. Her name is new to me, but I already had Lyndsey's." I explained about my group and what I had discovered so far. Lennon nodded throughout my explanation and nibbled at her dwindling pile of curly fries. When I finished, she shook her head.

"There's more girls than that," she said emphatically, and I asked her for names. After she rattled off what she knew, I stared in horror at the growing list. Was this it, the iceberg?

Riley Jackson (Bradford House) Vermont?
Chloe Anderson (Bradford House) Vermont?
Lyndsey Wilson the Point (Bradford House) Vermont?
Nicki Santiago Shoreline Diner (Greenleaf Dr) Vermont?
Allison Tyler motel on Capital St (Greenleaf Dr)
Jade Morales (Pierpont Ave)
Ivy?? N/A
Cassie or Kassy?? (possibly Pierpont?)
Shawna Walker??? (Birch St)

"Fuck me," Lennon muttered. She shivered, looking like she was about to cry.

I took a picture of the list. "I'm going to send this to the detective in Old Lyme and share it at the meeting in New London tomorrow, okay?" I had no clue as to why I felt the need for Lennon's approval, but she nodded.

She was about to say something, then stopped herself.

"What is it?" I asked and sat back, prepared to listen. I had been working on listening to others before jumping in with a solution or answer. It was not easy at times like these.

"I'm not sure. I'm scared. I mean, what the fuck? But I'm also mad. Why us? What did we ever do to deserve this? I'm not trying to throw any shade here, but there's a lot of girls who are easy targets out there—they take drugs or drink too much, live on the streets, pick up randos to sleep someplace warm for one night—but this group, these names? We're not like that. I can't speak for everyone, but most of us work and live quiet lives. We help out at home, keep to our curfews, go to our meetings, and try to save a few bucks. I don't get it. It's not . . . fair," she ended, her voice catching on the last words.

No, it sure as hell was not fair. I watched as tears welled in her eyes, and, acting on impulse, I reached across the table and took her hands in mine. Her ice-cold, chapped red hands. She didn't pull away as I had imagined she might. We sat there looking at each other, both sad and scared and exhausted. I wanted to take her for a manicure, buy her some warm gloves, take her home and keep her well-fed and safe from harm. But I couldn't do any of those things. At least not all at once. But there was one thing I could do. I could do my damnedest to find out what was happening to these young women and bring them home.

"Would you want to stay with me for a few days? Just while we figure things out?" I asked.

She shook her head. "No way. I need to be where Tyler can find me. I'll be fine," she assured me, and I wanted to believe her.

My phone buzzed, and I saw I had an incoming text. It was from Shawna!

I am soooo sorry Ms. Q. I forgot court today. Can we reschd? Pleeze?

It was followed by the praying hands emoji and several hearts. I looked at Lennon, who was studying me closely.

"Good news," I told her, slashing a line through Shawna's name. "One mystery solved." Lennon nodded, clearly still upset. "I want to help. Whatever is going on, it's not right." There was not much I could do before tomorrow. But I could help Lennon today. The girl was sitting right in front of me, shivering from cold and fear. Retail therapy wasn't always the answer, but right now, it would have to suffice.

CHAPTER 18

I spoke briskly, as if our next steps had already been decided. "There is a terrific consignment shop a couple blocks from here. Let's head over. You need a warm coat and some gloves." She started to protest, and I interrupted her. I know, so much for listening. But sometimes you just knew what was needed in a certain situation. "I have a credit from selling a few outfits I no longer wear. And it expires at the end of the month, so you might as well use it." Okay, sometimes a little white lie was in order as well. I knew there was no end date on the store credit. "Use it or lose it," I said, and she smiled for the first time that morning.

"I guess it can't hurt to take a look," she said and shoved her arms into the sleeves of her army jacket. I scooped up our trash and deposited it in the nearby waste receptacle. As we walked to my car, I called the office and told Rose about Shawna.

"Get them to squash the arrest warrant," I said. "Then get her rescheduled with a new court date and text both of us the details." Rose agreed to get on it immediately, and I thanked her and ended the call. If Shawna wasn't cleared of the pending loitering charge she was facing, she would be evicted from her group home. But at least she hadn't disappeared!

My basic-mobile transported us to a shop where Tracey and I liked to browse on occasion. *You Wear It Well* was a nonprofit organization, and I really did drop off articles of clothing whenever the desire to purge my wardrobe struck. The next hour was very enjoyable as Lennon was an enthusiastic shopper and looked great in absolutely everything she tried on. I didn't want to go full-on *Pretty Woman* on her and hoped the fact the clothes were used and heavily discounted made it less so.

Camped out on an overstuffed armchair right across from the dressing room, I got to ooh and aah every time she came out wearing something new. Sharon, the salesclerk, got into the fun as well and brought out everything from cruise wear to prom dresses. To humor her, or perhaps to satisfy her own curiosity, Lennon paraded out wearing an emerald-green cocktail dress with spaghetti straps and a full skirt.

"Gorgeous, just gorgeous. Your daughter looks like a fairy princess," Sharon told me, and I saw Lennon visibly stiffen.

"Oh no, she's not my—" I began, but Lennon interrupted me.

"She's my parole officer," she told Sharon with a smirk, causing the woman to deflate like a popped balloon.

"All right, well, if you need me for anything, just, um, just . . ." and Sharon scurried away.

I shook my head at Lennon. "Was that really necessary?" I asked, earning me a wide grin in response before she disappeared behind the curtain.

"So whadayathink?" Lennon asked, returning from the dressing room with a white puffer-style jacket in one hand and the charcoal-gray parka she had tried on earlier in the other. I wanted to tell her to get both, but I decided to practice some restraint.

"They're both great on you," I said, studying the two coats closely. "But the gray one has a hood, and it's a little longer. It'll keep your butt warm when you're out walking or riding the bus. Plus you know . . . white?" I shook my head, recalling how once I'd worn a pair of white jeans to a cookout years ago. Once.

Lennon nodded her agreement and returned the jacket to the rack reserved for returns, hugging the parka close to her.

"I would get both pairs of jeans and the three sweaters as well," I said, motioning to the pile of clothes in her cubicle. "How are you fixed for T-shirts and underwear?" She pulled a face, and I remembered we were in a consignment store. "We'll stop and get some and socks too. There's a Target on the way back to your place."

"Do you have a credit there as well?" Lennon asked me and waited, daring me to lie.

"No, but these are necessities, and your mom was my friend, and I want you to keep warm. Until I can make sure you're completely safe, this is the best I've got. So don't be a brat, okay?"

Back to business, Lennon nodded. "Yes, ma'am. Can I look at the boots over there before we go?" she asked, motioning to the corner of the store dedicated to footwear. I said sure and stayed behind to collect the items we had agreed upon. At the last minute, I grabbed the green dress. It was marked fourteen dollars, certainly a fraction of the original price. I approached the register, where Sharon was finishing with another customer. She smiled when she saw me, then looked around for my parolee.

"I'm not her parole officer," I said softly. "I'm a family friend." I handed her the green dress from the top of the pile I was carrying. "Can you place this in the bottom of the bag? I want it to be a surprise." And she did, folding it carefully. While she finished ringing up the clothing we had selected, I watched Lennon approaching. She was grinning happily and swinging a pair of Doc Martens in her hand.

"Can I get these?" she asked, her eyes wide and hopeful. "I love them. They are so comfortable," she practically gushed, and I nodded. She handed the boots to Sharon, who added them to the total and placed them in a separate bag.

"That's $108.25," she said, and I told her I had a credit on my account and rattled off my phone number.

"Of course, Ms. Quinn," she said after looking me up in her system. "That brings the total to $39 even." I paid in cash and shoved the dollar bill in change into my bag. I wondered if Lennon had any cash on her but couldn't think of a way to bring it up delicately. We thanked Sharon and left the store. As we walked back to the car, I noticed Lennon was smiling and humming to herself. I wondered for a moment if she and Char had ever shopped together like this before deciding they probably had not. After stowing the bags in the backseat, Lennon buckled her seat belt, sat back, and sighed happily. I was feeling pretty good myself, I decided as I drove to the Target a few miles away. During a quick trip around the perimeter of the mega store, we selected gloves, mittens, several pairs of warm socks, three T-shirts, and an assortment of ridiculously tiny thongs, camis, and bras. I offered to pick up snacks or groceries while we were there, but Lennon shook her head.

"I've got it," she assured me.

I waited in line to pay and watched as Lennon chose a loaf of whole-grain bread, a jar of all-natural peanut butter, and a quart of oat milk. Without making eye contact with me, she hopped on a self-checkout register and paid for her transaction with a shiny blue card. I recognized the SNAP debit card used by lower-income individuals to purchase groceries from the dozens of times I had assisted clients in securing them. I waited as she bagged her purchases, and we left the store. Checking my phone, I saw I had missed calls from Dr. Chris and Rose. *Dang.*

I dropped Lennon off at her rooming house less than ten minutes later. As she leaned in to grab her bags, she spoke up. "I don't think you have anything to feel guilty about when it comes to my mom. She's been making bad decisions for twenty-five years. So if you're doing all this because you're a good person or whatever, thank you. But don't do it for her, okay?"

I nodded, not entirely sure of what had motivated me today. Just knowing it was the right thing to do, I figured.

"No worries, Lennon. It was fun," I assured her. "Please be careful and let me know if anything strange or worrisome occurs, okay? I'll be in touch and let you know how the meeting went."

She smiled gratefully at me and nodded in agreement. "Thanks, Randi," she said, and I watched her climb the stairs, cross the wide front porch, and let herself into the house with her key.

Stay safe, Lennon, I thought. *Please stay safe.*

I returned my missed calls from earlier, speaking briefly with Rose about a meeting later in the week and then calling Chris. Voicemail again.

"Tag, you're it," I told him. "You're gonna want to call me back. I have big news to share. Talk soon."

CHAPTER 19

Lennon was perched on her unmade twin bed, unpacking her new wardrobe. She already knew the skinny jeans would look great with the new boots and any of the sweaters. And wait a minute, what was this? The green dress? What the hell? Randi had bought her a fancy dress, perfect for all the glam holiday parties she would be invited to. As if! What a waste. Still, it was nice of her. She smiled, thinking about her lawyer. A new friend, maybe? An adult she could depend upon? We'll see about that, she thought. On impulse, she stood and held up the dress. Clasping it to her waist, she pirouetted around the room, stopping suddenly when there was a knock on the door followed by a male voice.

"Lennon, you in there?"

Crap, it was Alan, the creepy resident supervisor. He was a short, husky guy in his mid-twenties. She avoided him as much as she could.

"Yeah, what do you need?" she called out seconds before the door opened and he stepped into her room. He stared in surprise at the pile of clothing covering her bed and at the green dress she had been dancing with. His mouth twisted into a wide grin, showing tobacco-stained teeth.

"Been shopping?" he asked with raised eyebrows. "Or maybe shoplifting. Which is it, girl?"

"I didn't steal anything. They're used," she said flatly. "They were having a sale, and—"

Alan flashed another grin at her, more of a smirk. "I'm just razzing you, girl. I seen you getting dropped off just now and come rushing in with all these bags. Who's your fairy godmother?"

"She's a friend of my . . . a family friend. Just being generous to a charity case like me," she said with a shrug.

"Must be nice." He started to inspect some of the items, holding up a pair of jeans. "You'll look hot in these," he said with a gleam in his pale eyes. "Too bad we're not allowed to fraternize with the likes of you girls." He shook his head. "Or I'd be asking you to . . ."

Yeah, thought Lennon. It was against the rules. *That* was the reason she and Alan weren't dating. She had already grown tired of this cat-and-mouse game he liked to play. Although she was rarely the object of his misplaced affections, she had witnessed his teasing countless times with the other girls. "Was there something you wanted?" she asked, and he stared at her blankly for a moment before breaking into a grin.

"You forgot to sign in again," he said, wagging his finger at her, attempting and failing to adopt a stern tone. "You know the rules."

"Yeah, my bad," said Lennon. "My arms were full, and I wanted to dump all of this, then I was going to sign in and put this in the fridge," she added, locating the milk in her bag. Alan's eyes lit up.

"Well, look at you, bringing home the bacon and shit," he said with a chuckle. Having no clue what he was talking about, Lennon just nodded.

"There's always regular milk in there, but I'm lactose intol— I mean, I like oat milk. So sue me," she finished, feeling defensive and jumpy. Leave it to him to ruin her day. Despite missing Tyler and feeling fearful about whatever was going on, she'd had a terrific morning with Randi.

"Aren't you fancy?" he said with a wink. "I didn't know of your special dietary concerns. We shall strive to be more aware of your needs in the future." Perhaps sensing he was pushing the limits of a male supervisor loitering in a resident's room, he stood suddenly. "Sign in next time. Rules is rules." Preparing to leave, he reached over and grabbed the black fleece-lined gloves from the bed. "Did you pick these up special for my ma?" he asked, feigning a tone of delight. "She'll be tickled pink."

Lennon watched as he pocketed the gloves and left her room, leaving the door wide open. What a dirtbag, she thought. She slumped back on her bed, oat milk forgotten, and wondered what had happened to Tyler.

CHAPTER 20

A late morning phone call had Jay driving a few towns over to meet Gus, the guy who had originally approached him with a scheme to supplement his meager salary. It was soon after he had started as a regional manager for the company that owned and operated residential group homes throughout Connecticut. He'd been asked to a meeting to discuss his new position. So he went, chugged a couple of brews, and listened to what the guy had to say. It was basic economics: supply and demand. He would be well compensated for identifying young women looking to break into the hospitality field. Being in possession of an extremely flexible moral compass, he immediately agreed to the arrangement, especially after he learned how unsafe it was for girls to be living on the streets and how many of them would be raped, beaten, or killed out there on their own. The girls he selected would get a warm bed and three squares a day. And he could start his own rainy-day fund and possibly work for himself one day, supplying girls to some of the classier hotels for conventions and shit. No more pulling in a measly thirty-seven grand a year with two lousy weeks of PTO. Jay was pumped to be offered this opportunity, and things had been running smoothly until recently. Today's meeting was probably no big deal, he assured himself.

"You're late," Gus complained as Jay slid into the booth across from him. Jay shrugged, turning up his hands in a "What can you do?" expression.

"I got hung up and traffic sucks, so stop bustin' my balls, wouldja?" he said, earning him a smirk in response.

"Was it one of your little chickies who held you *up*?" Gus asked, a leer forming on his ruddy face.

"That's your style, bro, not mine," Jay protested. He looked at the empty plate in front of the other man. "You already ate?"

Gus nodded. "Yeah, I've been here long enough to clean my plate and get the waitress's digits." He licked his lips and pushed the menu over to Jay. "Order whatever you like, but Rosie's all mine," he said as a cute dark-haired server approached with her pen and pad ready. "Isn't that right, Rosie?"

She giggled. "Whatever you say, Gus. What can I get you?" she asked Jay. "We make the cherry pie nice and fresh. Goes great with a cup of coffee."

Jay considered his options for a moment before nodding. "Yeah, pie sounds good. But no coffee. Got any herbal tea?"

Gus snorted while Rosie scrunched up her pert freckled nose. "I'm not sure, but I'll check," she said before turning on her heel and sashaying toward the kitchen. Gus watched her closely, a wolfish grin on his face.

"I sure hate to see her leave, but I love to watch her go," he said with a deep-throated chuckle.

Jay looked around the empty dining room nervously. "So what's up? I can't stay too long. Plus it wouldn't be so great to be seen together . . . you know."

Gus chuckled again, pulling a dog-eared memo pad from the pocket of his shirt. "Man, you have got to learn to relax. Nothing bad is gonna happen. At least not to me," he added.

"Looks like someone needs a snack," Rosie cooed, pushing a slice of pie covered with a mound of whipped topping toward

Jay. "We ran out of cherry, but I managed to snag you the last piece of blueberry. Oh, and no herbal tea, I'm afraid."

She pronounced it "herb-al" and Jay had to fight to keep from correcting her. *The 'h' is silent,* he wanted to tell her. Who raised these morons? he wondered. He looked up, realizing Rosie had asked him a question. "What was that?" he asked.

"She wants to know what you want to drink, ass-wipe," Gus said. "Get him a Coke," he told Rosie. "And more coffee for me, darlin'."

Rosie headed back toward the kitchen as Gus started rifling through his pad. "Where were we? Oh yeah, that's right. You were gonna tell me why last week's delivery was one short, I believe," he said with a frown.

Jay felt his insides turn to liquid as he dropped his eyes to the plate in front of him. The purple juice from the berries was oozing out, causing the aerosol-formed topping to turn a hazy shade of pinkish blue. He had thought he was in the clear on last week's debacle.

"Um, well, remember how I told you there was a change in the schedule? How there were some questions raised, and I didn't want to cause any more suspicion?" Jay asked.

Gus shot daggers at him as Rosie approached with fresh coffee and a sweating glass of soda. He kept his silence while she fussed, arranging things, and gathering used napkins. As soon as she was out of sight, he leaned closer, snaked his hand under the table, and grabbed Jay by the testicles. Jay sucked in his breath, tears in his eyes, as Gus squeezed tighter.

"The only thing we don't want is to disappoint our friends in New York. And trust me, when we promise two and only deliver one, that is what they are. Disappointed. You feel me?"

Jay could only nod, slumping back in relief when Gus released his grip, now focusing his attention on the cup of coffee in front of him. He took a long sip and sat back, seemingly satisfied—with the coffee or his delivery of an important message, possibly both.

Sensing Gus was waiting for him to respond, Jay wiped at his eyes with a paper napkin and tried to find his voice. "It won't happen again, I swear."

The older man looked at him, somewhat amused. "All right, let's see if you can recall what they taught you in school. Here's a math problem for you. If the number is two every week, but last week was one short, what would this week's new number be?"

Jay groaned. What the hell? How was he going to find three? Gus's arm shot out quickly, and Jay instinctively cupped his privates, but the man was only reaching for the pitcher of cream.

Gus shook his head good-naturedly. "If I were you, I'd be figuring out how to get back in the saddle instead of sittin' around this dump with me and Rosie. Tell you what. You get outta here and get back to work, and I'll enjoy my coffee and your pie. Rosie's off in a half hour, so make yourself scarce, *capisce*?"

Jay did not need to be asked twice. He nodded and limped out of the diner. Where the hell would he find three girls this week? As he sank gingerly into the worn seat of his car, he mentally went through the names of possible options in his head. That Ari chick should have been gone last week, but he'd checked her out and found problems. Big fucking "rot in jail for the rest of your life" problems. Goddamn that idiot Alan. How come he hadn't known the bitch was getting her kid back, for chrissakes? Talk about a red freaking flag. Maybe that Lennon chick from over at Alan's place? Alan had told him she had a sugar momma, some do-good lawyer or social worker probably. Maybe it would be wise to cut that budding relationship off quickly and disappear her. Unless this woman started asking questions about her missing little friend? Hold on Lennon for now, he decided. There had to be some lower-risk girls he could snatch.

After he got home and took a shower, he could assess the damage inflicted by that neanderthal Gus before calling each of his contacts at the various houses around town. That was the deal, he reminded himself. The on-site staffers, whom he had hired for their discretion and lack of empathy, were the recruiters and were paid well for each girl they referred to him. His job was to vet the girls they came up with, choosing only those with little or no family in the vicinity and preferably with a drug or alcohol problem. If they also had a history of arrests for soliciting or loitering, that was a three-fer, a hat trick. Jay would get them drugged up and ready to travel the three or so hours to their new home in New York. The girl would start a new life, Gus's people were happy, and he was making bank. Win-win-win, he frequently told himself.

It used to be one or two girls a month, and that had been fine. Easy money, only hat tricks whenever possible, and no one was the wiser. But demand had increased, which on the one hand was pretty sweet, but people were starting to notice and questions were being raised. Disappear one or two girls, mostly runaways or junkies, and no one gave a shit. But Jay sensed the gravy train he had been riding for the past eight months was coming to an end. Another month or two and he would have to give up his position and lay low for a while. Move out of state, get a new ID, and take it easy while he searched around for a better high-paying gig. At least his safety deposit box at the bank was flush with cash. At a thousand dollars per girl, he had amassed enough to disappear for as long as he needed to.

He pulled into his reserved parking space behind the three-story residence, stepped out, and immediately doubled over in pain. Christ, that asshole had done a number on him. Maybe as a going-away present, Jay would drop a dime on him. If they dragged Gus in, the cops would be looking for the names of the big fish Gus took orders from, not someone like himself. It would serve the creep right. He limped up the wide steps of the porch and let himself inside. The back door was unlocked, which was against the rules. Dumbass bitches, he thought. Any lowlife could just walk right in here. He would need to send a reminder to his staff. Days like these made starting over sound like a real good plan.

CHAPTER 21

I arrived at the New London Police Department ten minutes prior to the meeting's 3:00 p.m. start time. I made my way across the parking lot and headed toward the main entrance. As I approached the desk, I spotted Dennis Reynaldo's lanky form. He was deep in conversation with a small blond woman dressed in civilian clothes. Not wanting to interrupt, I gave my name to the desk sergeant, who beamed in recognition.

"You're Dez Quinn's kid, yeah? Look at you, all grown up. I remember when you were just a little bit of a thing, following your dad around like a puppy."

As much as I did not appreciate being compared to a furry pet, I smiled broadly. It never got old, hearing how well my father was remembered by fellow cops and citizens, even other attorneys. Desmond Quinn had never reached the upper levels in his department, but he was a well-respected, honest cop, loved by all. Except, of course, those he had arrested or ticketed over his years of service.

"That's my dad," I said with a grin. At the sound of my voice, Dennis turned to look in my direction. He spoke quietly to the woman he had been talking to, who nodded, and he headed toward me, a curious look on his deeply tanned face.

"You've been busy," he said, only half teasing. I nodded and began digging in my bag.

"I really think we're on to something, Dennis. Last night, I couldn't sleep, and I started looking at the locations of the missing girls. At least the ones we know about." I straightened my crudely drawn map and began to point out the various group homes. "See here, Riley was living at the Bradford. Chloe and Lyndsey were as well. Nicki Santiago and Allison Tyler were from the house on Greenleaf, and Jade Morales was most recently living on Pierpont. And you want to know something else that's interesting? All these homes are owned by the same company."

"I thought these halfway houses were state-run," Dennis said with a frown.

"Everyone thinks that. But the state privatized most of the homes a few years back. Private agencies and corporations run them," I explained.

"So who owns these homes?" Dennis asked.

"Well, I hit a dead end on that. It's an offshore holding company. I couldn't find any more info on them, but the paralegal where I work is going to dig around."

Dennis's eyebrows drew together as he studied the map more closely. "You really have been busy. Let's get some copies to hand out. Can you ask your pal at the desk?"

"Sure thing." I headed back to the desk and glanced at the ID worn by the sergeant. "Paul, can you make three copies of this for me?" I waved the sheet in front of him, and he smiled as he took it from me.

"I'll deliver them to you in a flash," he promised and disappeared through the door. I walked with Dennis to a small, well-lit conference room, and we took seats across from each other. Looking for something to do, I unearthed a warm bottle of water from the bottom of my bag, twisted off the cap, and took a sip. *Bleh.* If water could be stale, mine was.

I looked up as we were joined by an older man and the woman Dennis had been talking with when I arrived. She approached me, holding out the copies of my map.

"I believe these belong to you," she said, and I nodded and took them from her. "You must be Miranda. Dennis has told me so much about you. I'm Jennifer Fields, lead investigator with the State Sex Crimes Division, based here in New London."

I shook the hand she held out to me. "Nice to meet you, Jennifer," I said. I turned to the burly guy who had arrived with her. "Hello, I'm Miranda Quinn, legal aid attorney and concerned citizen." I saw Dennis wince at my weak attempt at humor, but the man who held out his hand was grinning happily.

"Chief Ed Brody," he said, his iron grip at odds with his soft voice and kind eyes. "Your reputation precedes you, Ms. Quinn. And of course, I knew your father when he was on the force in Old Lyme. How is Dez doing?"

I quickly brought him up to speed with Pop's marriage, move to a condo, and his switch from deep-sea fishing to ocean cruising with Sally.

"Tell him I was asking for him, would you?"

I told him I would, just as Jennifer started the meeting.

"Thank you for being here today," she said. "Let's get started as we have a lot to discuss." She began by sharing some statistics, and the alarm I'd felt earlier began to simmer. The list of names I had started was only the tiniest tip of the iceberg that was the growing problem of girls missing from the Connecticut shore. Naturally, I had known sex trafficking was rampant nationwide, but had I really been that naive to think it wasn't an issue in my own backyard? Clearly, it was.

Jennifer handed out copies of a professionally done map of the Connecticut towns, from Bridgeport all the way to Stonington on the Rhode Island border. It was color-coded and drawn to scale. I cringed, burying the copies of my hand-drawn map, replete with a ring stain from my coffee cup.

Jennifer asked us to look at the legend, showing what the various types of shading meant. "I believe with the additional information Attorney Quinn has compiled, it is more than safe to say that New London should now be considered part of the red zone, joining Bridgeport and New Haven as critical areas of concern." Everyone nodded, although Chief Brody looked less than pleased to learn of his city's most recent distinction. Jennifer asked me to quickly summarize the information I had shared with Dennis.

"Certainly," I said. "I meet with a group of at-risk teen girls every week, and several of them informed me they were concerned that girls from the area had gone missing lately. There were several mentions of a long-lost relative, family money, and homes in Vermont. That was the story I heard from the missing girls' friends as well as from the residential manager, a Jordan Myers, from Bradford House. Detective Reynaldo and I were discussing the situation, and he suggested I share my findings with you. I believe he forwarded the list of names to you last night." I caught Dennis's eye, and he nodded his approval. Succinct and to the point.

"Thank you, Ms. Quinn. It's helpful as we try to get a handle on this problem. Let me share with everyone where we stand on the investigation so far." Jennifer proceeded to describe the interviews that had taken place and the ones being planned. The process of questioning the staff members at the residential homes in the area was in the planning stages, and next up came the daunting task of tracking down all the current residents as well as those who had lived in the homes in the past year. There were a couple hundred names on the list, and she described the process as both arduous and draining. "We are struggling to obtain the resources needed to contact the young women, and even if we do, not everyone is trained to handle the interviews in a sensitive manner. These are not just names of potential witnesses," she added, sounding both tired and irritated. "Many are victims and deserve to be treated with patience and respect." Chief Brody scowled at that, but Jennifer quickly explained that she'd meant no disrespect to the NLPD. "Everyone's stretched thin, but we have to remember the difficulties these young women have already faced."

Brody nodded and asked for ideas on how to bridge the gap in not only the number of personnel that could be utilized, but their training as well.

I spoke up quickly. "I am happy to meet with the officers who will be reaching out and provide them with some background that might help them as well as thoughts on how to conduct the interviews." Everyone nodded their agreement, and I continued. "Also, I have someone in mind who can assist with compiling the names and contact info of the current and past residents. If we take that burden off your plate, Chief, that would free your people to conduct interviews, not struggle through the quagmire of paperwork and red tape of the state's filing system." That got an enthusiastic response from all present, and the meeting broke up soon after.

I drove home feeling confident I could put together a training session to help officers in conducting the interviews with sensitivity and respect. Now I would need to develop a compelling argument to convince Rose to take on the daunting task and deliver the results I had just promised. And perhaps a bribe, something that fell somewhere between a box of donuts and a cruise.

CHAPTER 22

Lennon made her way through the half-deserted streets separating her seedy, mostly residential neighborhood and the high-priced, exclusive waterfront area where the Point was situated. She passed a few neighborhood bars, family-run bodegas, and a check-cashing joint with a line out the door. She made a mental note to remember to deposit some cash in Charlene's commissary, or she knew there'd be hell to pay. The one time her mother's account had a zero balance, for like a day and a half, she had not heard the end of it for weeks. She was painfully aware of the fact she bussed tables and washed dishes for minimum wage at the same restaurant where her mom used to earn loads of cash waiting tables in order that her mom, who had blown all those fabulous tips on drugs and booze, could smoke cigarettes and eat her weight in Reese's peanut butter cups in jail. Was that irony or what?

She thrust her hands in the deep pockets of her new parka and smiled, thinking of the nice day she had spent with Randi. Whether it was guilt for ruining Charlene's life or the fact Randi was just a super nice and generous person, she didn't really care. It had been fun and she was truly grateful for the new clothing. Although it wasn't cold enough to require wearing her new mittens, she had shoved them in her pockets to keep them safe from Alan's pervy hands. It would do no good to report him for taking her gloves; he would say they were a gift or it was a misunderstanding, and it would be her word against his. And she knew how he got back at girls who crossed him. Sonia, who had lived down the hall when Lennon had moved in, had reportedly spurned his advances, and complained to his supervisor. Less than a week later, a bag of crystal meth and a well-used pipe had been found among her things during a "routine" bed check, and she had been kicked out. Should she add Sonia's name to the list she and Randi had been compiling? Sonia was even more straitlaced than Lennon herself when it came to alcohol or drugs. As far as Lennon knew, no one had heard from her since she left. Could she be among the missing? She had always thought Alan to be dumb as a stump, but honestly, how difficult would it be to overpower one of the girls and . . . what? Rape them and leave them for dead or kill them and toss their bodies into the ocean? She watched too many true-crime shows, she decided as she hurried across the parking lot into the back entrance of the restaurant.

As she hung her coat carefully on a hook, she sniffed appreciatively. There was always something delicious on the stove for those who worked the dinner shift. Although not the aged steaks and fresh seafood enjoyed by the Point's patrons, the head chef always made sure the food was well-prepared and delicious. Tonight was chili, she saw, and a huge pan of cornbread to accompany it. She hurried over to the short line of co-workers eager to enjoy a free meal before work.

"Hey, Lennon," a young man in a white shirt and black tie greeted her with a smile. Seth!

She scooped a good-sized serving of chili into her bowl as she returned the smile. "Hey, Seth. How're you doing?" She made her way over to the large table, and he followed closely behind.

"Can I join you?" he asked, and she looked around at a table that could comfortably seat a dozen and nodded. There were only two waitstaff sitting at the far end of the table, and they were deep in conversation.

"Sure," she said, and he pulled up a chair next to her. She placed a napkin in her lap, painfully aware of his presence as she nibbled at her food. Although she was rarely alone at the table before her shift, Seth was, well, different. As far as she knew, he was a full-time college student who worked here mainly on the weekends. He was friendly and reliable, always willing to go the extra mile for customers and co-workers alike. She looked up in surprise, her spoon halfway to her mouth, as she realized he was talking to her.

"I'm sorry. What did you say? I was . . ."

"A million miles from here," Seth said. "I was asking if you wanted me to pass you the cornbread," he added, motioning to the steaming basket that had been placed near him. She nodded enthusiastically, and he grabbed a hunk before handing it to her. "Still warm," he said, and as Lennon watched, he slathered his piece with softened butter flavored with honey and took a huge bite. He looked like a little boy, she thought. Enjoying a treat, his chin glistening with butter. He looked at her quizzically.

"What's so funny?" he asked. "Do my nonexistent table manners amuse you? So now I'm a clown?" As soon as he had spoken, he shoved the remaining hunk of bread into his mouth and chewed happily, causing her to laugh out loud.

"You're really smooth," she told him, still giggling. "You come across all handsome and sophisticated, and then you act like . . . well, like you do."

He swallowed his food and studied her closely. "So you think I'm handsome, do you?" he asked, and she laughed again, nervous now. Had she just called him handsome?

She feigned an air of indifference as she cut her bread into tiny squares. There was no need to study his appearance. She had all but memorized his features since the first time they worked a shift together. Skin the color of melted caramel, large dark brown eyes with the longest lashes she had ever seen on a guy. His hair was shaped stylishly, clean shaven on the sides and fuller on top. His lips were full, and his teeth were straight and white. He was one fine specimen of a young man. And he was spending his dinner break talking to her!

"You're a'ight, I guess. Never really thought about it. Well, those dishes aren't going to wash themselves," she said, standing quickly, nearly knocking over her chair in her haste. Seth put a hand on her arm, and she stared, mesmerized at the sight of his hand on her pale, skinny arm.

"Before there are dishes to wash, diners have to finish their meals, and before that can happen, they need to place their orders with waiters, like me." He looked at the large clock on the wall. Lennon saw it was only a quarter to five, and the first seating wasn't for another fifteen minutes. Still . . .

"Tell me about yourself," he said and mopped up the remaining dabs of chili with another chunk of cornbread. "I don't know much about you," he added, studying her closely. "And I want to."

Lennon sat down as if on autopilot, staring at her feet. She never liked sharing information about her personal life. Ten seconds in and she was bound to be getting "the look." Sympathy, discomfort, guilt, horror, and shock were the usual reactions to even a whitewashed version of her fucked-up life. Emboldened by the sight of her new-to-her Doc Martens, she turned it back to Seth.

"You go first," she said, and he did. While she ate every bit of the chili and nibbled at the dozens of tiny cornbread pieces she had created, he told her he was the oldest of three children, his parents were Mary, a grade school teacher, and Frederick, a plumber, and he had grown up in nearby Groton. He was attending the University of Connecticut, about an hour away in the town of Storrs, on a wrestling scholarship and wanted to be a civil engineer. He ended by saying he watched Disney movies with his little sisters and his favorite food was pasta. She stared at him, marveling at how freaking normal his whole life sounded. How the fuck could she compete with that? He smiled but seemed puzzled by her lack of response.

"Angel-hair," he said and she looked at him, confused. "I was trying to save time," he told her. "I figured your next question would be what kind of pasta, and I decided to cut to the chase."

Lennon stood once more and pushed her chair back toward the table. "Sounds terrific, Seth. Gotta go and clock in now. Have a great night," she said and hurried toward the restroom. Her cheeks were burning with embarrassment as she pushed her way in and slid into the first vacant stall. She sat on the toilet seat and willed herself to not cry. Calm down, she told herself. Just because the cute guy you've been crushing on has been living the American Dream while you've been getting the shit kicked out of you doesn't mean . . . anything. She knew she had been rude and had shut down any chance of a friendship with someone who seemed like a great guy, but who the hell was she kidding? Her mom was a strung-out junkie who had spent more than half of her daughter's life incarcerated. But wait, there's more, she thought. No one knew who her father was, although some of the skeevy guys who Charlene had brought home over the years would have liked for her to sit on their laps and call them daddy. And who could forget the foster homes ranging from horrific to merely dreadful. And her aunt Kelly, who had left her sitting in a parked car in a biker bar parking lot more nights than she could count. And to top things off, her only friend had disappeared without a word and her pervy "den mother" was a loser who probably dissected frogs in his mother's basement and had stolen her brand-new gloves. Lennon blew her nose with a wad of toilet paper before she exited the stall and faced herself in the mirror overlooking the row of sinks. She looked as tired and wrung-out as she felt. It was going to be a long night.

She washed her hands thoroughly and dabbed at her damp face with a paper towel. Just go to work, she told herself. Bus the tables, wash the dishes, and hope none of the waitstaff stiffed her out of her share of the tips. What would Seth say to her as he handed her a few bills at the end of the evening? Not her problem, she decided.

She caught sight of the sign that always bugged her as she exited the bathroom. The one instructing all employees to wash their hands before returning to work. Even she knew that, for God's sake, and she had been raised with no guidance on anything. She grabbed a clean apron from the stack and tied it around her, feeling antsy and aching for a fight with someone, anyone. She clocked in at 4:59 and headed back into the kitchen, now milling with staff and servers. No sign of Seth, she noted with a sigh of relief. If she were lucky, she could avoid him all night long.

Ha, *if* she were lucky, what a joke. Lennon knew full well that she had never been lucky, not a single day in her life.

CHAPTER 23

Eric had cooked burgers on the grill while I threw together a salad for dinner. We caught each other up on our equally busy days while we ate and were discussing the merits of a quick walk on the beach when my phone started buzzing. It was Chris!

"I gotta take this," I told Eric and grabbed my phone. "Doc, how are you?"

"Miranda," he said. "It's good to hear your voice."

"I have been hearing yours nearly every day lately."

"I saw my numbers were up on the shoreline," he countered. "Have I solved any major life problems for you?"

"Game changers, each and every show," I assured him.

"How's Eric?" he asked.

I watched my husband out on the patio scrubbing the grill.

"He's great," I told Chris. "Is Susan still selling books in the Village?"

"Yes, and she's been pestering me about setting a date for you two to visit us on Long Island. The renovations are finally complete." In the three years I had known Chris, their "cottage" in the Hamptons had been in a constant state of repair. Out of curiosity, Eric had googled the address, and we had been able to inspect the sprawling estate from every angle.

"It might be difficult to plan anything in the short term," I told him. "Looks like we'll be living in . . . wait for it . . . London."

He immediately peppered me with questions, and I shared everything I knew.

"Sounds like an exciting opportunity for both of you," he said. "But I'm sensing some reservations on your end. What's your take, Miranda?" I never could hide anything from him.

"The usual. You know, missing my family, the distance, big-city living, having to learn the metric system . . . But don't worry, Doc. I'm a big girl. I'll figure it out."

"I know you will," he assured me. "But is Eric aware of your concerns?"

"Oh sure, we've talked about everything. But seriously? It's his turn. He's worked his whole life for this. It's too good to pass up. I'll be fine, really I will."

"So . . . Cleveland Amory, heh? That old dog is still on the hunt?"

"You know him?" Chris was a global celebrity, a broadcasting icon with friends in high places. But a British architect?

"His firm did some work on the Sterling offices a few years back. We met at the official groundbreaking ceremony. He's an interesting fellow," he said. "Well, Eric must be thrilled."

"So what's the latest with the broadcasting biz these days?" I asked, and he filled me in on all the office gossip and staff changes, who was losing their prime-time slot and who was sleeping with who.

"How glad are you to have gotten out when you did? Do you miss all the drama?" he teased.

"Plenty of drama here," I told him. "There may be a sex-trafficking ring operating out here. I'm working with the State Sex Crimes Unit to locate some missing girls."

"What? You lost me," Chris admitted. "Last time we talked, you were working on wrongful evictions and food stamps. Aren't you still a legal aid attorney?"

I told him about Charlene and Lennon, my volunteer work, and explained how we had identified possible links between missing girls and the group homes.

"I'm hoping we catch a break soon," I concluded. "If we can't catch the low-level players, it will be next to impossible to cut this off at the source. The ones in charge must have a lot of money and loads of clout. But somebody is bound to talk, right?"

We chatted for a few more minutes before Chris said he had somewhere he needed to be. "Dinner in the city before you depart," he told me. "Shoot me some dates, or Susan will ride my ass until you do."

I told him I would, and we said our goodbyes. I headed to our bedroom, where I found my husband sleeping soundly. It was 9:15. We were such early birds. How would we adjust to a fast-paced life in a city like London?

I brushed my teeth, stripped, and joined Eric in bed. It had been great to catch up with Chris tonight. He was such a good listener. I hoped we could spend an evening with him and Susan before we left for London.

CHAPTER 24

The sound of an angry man's voice woke Lennon early. She lay quietly, trying to decide if it was something Carmen was watching on her phone. Never a sound sleeper, Lennon was always on guard, listening or watching for signs of danger. From her mother's drug-fueled, middle-of-the-night tirades to the endless parade of lowlifes in and out of their lives, her life had been a ticking time-bomb, ready to explode at a moment's notice. She prided herself on always being vigilant. She looked over at Carmen's bed, which appeared to contain only a sleeping girl. No phone, no movie.

She pushed her way out of her warm bed and padded across the hardwood floor in a pair of her new wool socks. Despite the barrier they provided, she felt the cold, due to a combination of poor insulation and a furnace that wouldn't be turned on for a couple more weeks. Budget cuts were the possible culprit, but secretly she thought Alan was a sadistic SOB who cut expenses to make himself appear more effective as a supervisor. If he referred to this group home as a "tight ship" he was running one more time . . . *Asshole.* She unlocked the door and stuck her head out in the dark hallway. Someone was arguing in the foyer, and the sound traveled right up two flights. She looked at her phone: 5:35 a.m. What the hell could be so important?

She crouched down and inched closer to the mahogany banister. This must have been quite the grand home back in the day, with its high ceilings, wide-plank oak floors, and ornate molding. But years of neglect had left it looking shabby and worn. What was happening downstairs? She strained to hear what was being said. She recognized Alan's whiny voice first.

"I'm telling you. It wasn't my fault. How was I supposed to know she was looking to get her kid back last week?" Who was he talking about? One of the girls who lived here? She heard the unmistakable sound of a slap—had this other guy slapped Alan, and if so, why? She personally could rattle off a dozen reasons right off the bat, but what was this guy's beef with him?

"That's your job, dumbass," the other guy said, and something about his voice made Lennon's ears perk up. It wasn't just his angry words, it was . . . something else. Where had she heard it before? "Do you have any idea how much screw-ups like this cost us? No, of course you don't cuz you're a freaking idiot, that's why." Despite her strong dislike of her residential supervisor, she felt almost sorry for him.

"I'm sorry, Jay," Alan blubbered, and Lennon felt her whole body go numb. She knew a guy named Jay. Tyler had said she talked to him a couple of times about switching to Bradford House. It was closer to work for her, and her roommate at Greenleaf apparently never took a shower, so she had been motivated to make a move. Wait a minute. Lennon had met Jay one time when she and Tyler had gone out for a walk. A ginger, Tyler had called him. She had thought he was cute, but Lennon shuddered at the image of the lanky loser with the holier-than-thou attitude. Like he was God's gift. Was this the same guy threatening dumbass Alan?

Jay let out a hoot of laughter. "Sorry, pal, but that bus has left the station and I already tossed your sorry ass under it. I told my contact how I asked you to vet her and to find out what she had going on and how you swore to me she was cleared."

Alan stuttered in response as he tried to defend himself. "N-n-no, Jay, you g-got it all wrong. You never asked me about any of that. It wasn't our deal. I was only supposed to give you a name and a headshot, you know? You were the one who was gonna dig up any dirt, find out if there's any legal actions or family. Loose ends, you called them. You didn't want to mess with no girls with l-l-loose ends." It sounded to Lennon like Alan was struggling for breath. What was happening down below?

"O-k-k-k-kay, A-A-Alan. I'll tell you what. The heat is on, and mistakes like this ain't gonna fly. I can replace a pissant like you in a heartbeat, you feel me? Get your shit together, man, or you're done." Lennon could picture Alan sniveling in front of Jay. Nodding in agreement. Anything to save his sorry ass from more violence.

The front door slammed, and Lennon scrambled to get back in her room, closing the door softly behind her. Peering into her dark room, she could make out the sight of Carmen, who was standing, looking out the window toward the street.

"Who's that?" she asked, pointing to the man striding down the sidewalk. She turned on the bedside lamp, and as Lennon rushed to turn it off, she saw the man look up at their window in surprise. She had only caught the quickest of glimpses, but she knew he was the same guy she had met with Tyler.

"Get down," she begged Carmen, but it was too late. Lennon was certain Jay would have had just long enough to make out the stocky dark-skinned girl in the window. Had he seen her as well?

"Who was that guy, Len?" Carmen asked again, and Lennon swallowed hard. There was no way she could explain right then. She would call Randi in a couple of hours to figure things out.

"Some guy trying to sell Alan solar panels," she mumbled. "Go back to bed. It's freezing in here."

Carmen complied, and Lennon climbed into her own bed, the rumpled sheets no longer holding any of her body warmth. She shivered and punched her pillow into the least uncomfortable shape she could and lay there, trying to process what she had heard and briefly seen. Jay was like, in charge, of guys like Alan. Could he be running some kind of trafficking ring? And who was the other girl Jay was so pissed off about? Someone who'd gotten her kid back. She racked her brain trying to recall who she knew fitting that description. Suddenly, it came to her. Of course. He must have been referring to Ari, who used to live on the floor below her. She'd left with little or no fanfare over a week ago, and Lennon had assumed it was because she was aging out of the system. But someone had said she was getting custody of her little boy and the two of them were gonna live with her mom.

It was 5:55. Lennon would have to wait another hour or two before calling Randi. Trying to picture being somewhere warm, she closed her eyes and tried to slow her breathing. Maybe some place with Seth? Yeah, right. She rubbed her cold hands together briskly, trying to make as little noise as possible. The last thing she needed right now was a game of twenty questions with Carmen. Her phone buzzed with an incoming text. She read it, feeling happy at first. Then she read it again more closely and felt a chill, but not from the icy cold room. It was from an unknown number.

> Hey Lenin I am loving life up here in VT.
> You haf to come and visit. Talk soon.
> Hugs, Ally

CHAPTER 25

I could hardly make out what Lennon was trying to tell me. I had taken her call several minutes ago, and she was still sounding close to hysterical. Also, it was barely 6:15.

"Lennon," I said, speaking sharply. "Slow down. You're not making any sense." I heard "Allie" and "Jay" and "Ari," but it took several tries before I could get her to explain the reason for her call.

"Jay is behind all this, Randi. You've got to believe me. I heard him threatening Alan about some mix-up with a girl named Ari. He thinks Alan was supposed to check her out, you know?"

I shook my head, then brightened as my dear husband placed a steaming cup of coffee on my nightstand. "Bless you," I whispered to him as I sat up straight and took a tentative sip. "But you said you got a text and you thought it was good news, and now you don't. What am I miss—"

Lennon hurried to explain. "Yeah, see, that's what's so weird. I didn't recognize the number, but it's early, so I read it and it says, 'Hey Lennon,' But it's spelled wrong. Lenin, like the—"

"Former head of Soviet Russia," I guessed. "Okay, so what else?"

"It was all 'I'm having such a great time. Come visit me, blah blah. Love, Allie.'"

My confusion was reaching an all-time high even though I was now wide-awake and had consumed nearly half of the coffee. "Why is that not a good thing? I don't under—"

"It was signed Ally. A-L-L-Y. Not Tyler. I always knew her as Tyler. It makes no sense. And even if she did use her first name, it was A-L-L-I-E. So you tell me. How could my best friend not only spell my name wrong, but hers as well?"

Autocorrect? "I'll grant you it does sound suspicious," I began. I had to be careful not to spook her, but blowing smoke wasn't a good idea either. "Where are you now?" I asked, and Lennon told me she was sitting on a bench in the middle of Waterfront Park. I pictured her huddled in her pitiful army jacket before I remembered the new parka. Still, it sounded like a rather isolated place to be this early in the morning. "I want you to get to a coffee shop, a diner, anyplace bustling with people on their way to work. Find a seat, order a coffee or something to blend in. Text me the name of the place, and I'll come and find you. Got it?" So much for not letting her know I was panicking.

"Coffee shop. Order something. Lay low. I'm on it." Now I could hear background noise, and I guessed she was walking out of the deserted park. Good girl.

"Okay. I'm at Empire Bagels on um . . . Division Street, 777 Division. They are open, and I'm heading inside." From the sounds of hungry diners and impatient servers, I knew she was safe for a short while at least.

"Buy a bagel. Keep your head down and don't talk to anyone. I'll see you as soon as I can," I told her and ended the call. I dashed across the room, stopping only to pull on a pair of jeans I had discarded on the floor last night. I knew I would find a jacket to pull over my sleep shirt by the back door as well as a pair of rubber clogs.

"Keys, handbag," I mumbled to myself and raced into the kitchen to find Eric holding out my jacket and my satchel along with a travel mug of coffee.

"I overheard your end of the call, so the truck is warming up and the coffee is ready. Grab your shoes and let's go," he said. "I'm driving."

My teeth chattered as I pulled on my fleece, stepped into my clogs, and followed him out to the damp chill of a rainy predawn morning.

Eric double-parked in front of the bagel shop twenty-seven minutes later, and I ran inside. Lennon was sitting on one of the stools at the far end of the counter. She had clearly been watching for me since seconds later she made her way through the packed space and was standing right by my side. I gave her a quick smile and, taking her by the arm, propelled us both outside and into Eric's truck.

Crammed in between us, she looked at Eric and said, "Good morning. Can I interest you in part of a bagel?" She held up a third of a brown and shiny bagel, and Eric shook his head.

"No, I'm good. Also, I'm Eric," he added and offered a hand in greeting. Lennon gave him a half-assed high five before settling back in her seat. I decided to give her a chance to tell me what was going on before interrogating her. Once we were on the highway, I leaned in.

"You're safe now, and we're going to keep it that way," I told her, and she nodded and closed her eyes. "You said you knew him . . ." I tried to keep my tone casual.

Lennon's eyes flew open, and she studied me closely. "Who?" she asked with a wobble in her voice.

"The man who was arguing with Alan."

Her eyes narrowed, and she shook her head. "I'm not sure. It sounded like someone I've met before. But it was early, you know? And I was still half-asleep."

I knew that was a lie. Lennon was always alert when it came to raised voices and signs of a conflict. Her very survival had depended upon it. I was not going to let this go. We needed to identify the players if we were going to put a stop to their sick game. "If it wasn't Tyler, who could have sent you the text?" No response. "You said you saw Jay. Who's Jay, Lennon?"

I could feel her reaction immediately, crammed in as we were. Her whole body stiffened and her voice, usually low and gravelly, suddenly rose several octaves, coming across as a squeak. "I don't know. Maybe it wasn't him. I couldn't hear all that good." But she *had* seen him. Clear as day when she joined Carmen at their bedroom window and looked out to see the early morning visitor walking away from their house. She had already admitted that.

I pressed harder. "Who's Jay? Where do you know him from?"

Her hands came up to support her head as she tried to focus. Why would the guy she was thinking of resort to kidnapping or worse, and why wouldn't she identify him? It made no sense.

"I don't know his last name. I think I met him one time when I was with Tyler. His name was Jay, and before you ask, I have no clue what his last name is."

"How does Tyler know him?" I asked. "Where did you see him?"

"We were getting coffee, and he walked by and they said hello. No biggie. She told me she thought he was cute . . . for a ginger."

I mulled it over quickly as there was still very little to go by. There were still so many unanswered questions. "Did Jay and Tyler go to school together or something?"

"No way, he's old. Like thirty. He works at one of the residential houses Tyler was hoping to move to if she could."

I asked the question just to hear the answer. But I already knew it. "Which house?"

"The big one. Bradford."

My heart sank. I hadn't wanted to believe any members of the staff from the residential homes could be involved in the girls' disappearances, but at least two of them were. Alan, the supervisor from Lennon's house, and Jay, aka Jordan Myers, from Bradford.

I needed to notify Dennis and Jennifer immediately. It started to pour in earnest as I tapped in a text message to the two detectives.

```
Jordan Myers from Bradford def a suspect. Overheard
discussing transactions with staff from Caroline St. Call me
when you get this. MQ
```

I sat back, my heart pounding with the rush of adrenaline. This could be the first step in solving the mystery of the disappearing girls. But clearly Jay/Jordan wasn't acting alone. Could they press him to name names?

"I filled in the detectives. Good information," I announced. Horrifying for sure, but Lennon had just identified a couple of the players. I squeezed her hand, and she leaned her head against my shoulder.

It was quiet for a moment; the only sound other than the *slap, slap* of the windshield wipers was a stomach growling with hunger. Mine. I looked over at Eric and in that way some couples do; we had an entire conversation without saying a word.

Me: I'm hungry. Can we stop?

Eric: I could eat. Let's do it.

Aloud, he said to Lennon, "We're stopping for breakfast. Any preferences?"

Lennon grinned at him, clearly pleased with the chance for a hot meal. "You mean am I like a vegan or something?"

Now Eric was grinning back at her. "Yeah, like that," he confirmed.

"Nope, as long as it's better than this sad-ass bagel, I'll go anywhere you want to go."

"Sunshine?" I suggested, referring to a cozy breakfast place only a mile or so from where we lived. The idea of walking there came up a few times a year but was unlikely to ever happen. I loved to walk on a beach or maybe around the mall, but that was it.

"Sunshine," Eric agreed, and I heard Lennon murmur "sunshine" as well.

We drove in comfortable silence for another fifteen minutes before exiting the highway and making our way through the sleepy streets of Old Lyme. Lennon was suddenly curious, carefully studying the houses and commercial establishments we passed.

"This is where my mom used to live," she said, and I nodded.

"Do you want to take a spin by her old house?" I asked, trying to recall if any of the Gallagher clan still lived there. No, probably not in years, I decided.

"Is that okay? Can we?" she asked.

"Sure thing. Quinn, what's the address?" Eric asked, and I scrambled to remember. When you're young, addresses really didn't mean all that much. You just walked down the sidewalk and cut through neighbors' yards until you arrived at your destination. But now . . .

"Turn right at the stop sign. Yes, right here. Now it's the second street on the left—nope, it's the third. Yes, Cherry Avenue. This is it. Um, maybe four or five houses down on the right. Stop. Yes, that's it. The yellow one. Yes," I said, and Eric stopped in front of a dilapidated ranch that had clearly seen better days.

I stared in shock at the peeling paint, the crumbling foundation, and the small yard with its brown coating of dead grass dotted with overgrown clumps of weeds and pools of rainwater. What a dump! I half expected to see signage noting

53 Cherry Avenue as marked for demolishment. I looked over at Lennon and tried to gauge her reaction to her family's former abode.

"That explains a lot," Lennon said with a frown. "Well, thanks, I guess. Can we go eat now?"

"Sunshine?" Eric asked, and Lennon and I nodded in agreement. Next stop? The Sunshine Café!

I waved Eric over to our booth as soon as I saw him enter the restaurant. He had let us out at the entrance to secure a table while he slowly circled the crammed-full parking lot as rain continued falling.

"I hope you're hungry, Lennon," he said as he slid into the booth next to me, giving me a quick peck on the cheek. I gave his hand a squeeze and turned my attention back to the menu.

"Yeah, I am, thanks, Eric," she said, smiling for the first time that morning. We sat in companionable silence for a few moments as we reviewed the huge menus.

"So what sounds good?" our server asked, materializing out of thin air carrying a pad and paper and a full pot of coffee. I gestured toward the coffee, and she poured me a mug. She repeated the process with Eric and then Lennon too. Seeing us all looking content with our coffees, she gave us a smile. "I'll let you marinate for a bit, but I'll be back in a jiffy to take your food order." I nodded and, as soon as she left, started flipping pages, staring at the dozens of options.

Eric motioned at me but directed his conversation to Lennon. "You might not have experienced it yet, but one of my favorite things about my wife is how she will look at every single item on the menu, even ask questions of the server, like 'How are those prepared?' or 'Can you make it without the onions but with extra bacon?'"

Lennon grew animated as she guessed where he was going with his commentary. "But then she'll order the same thing she always does?" she said, and Eric high-fived her. An enthusiastic one this time.

"Exactly. But only at breakfast when we eat out. Lunch and dinner, she's up for almost anything. But the most important meal of the day, no way; it's always the same." They laughed together, and I stifled a grin of my own.

"I'm glad my dietary preferences are so entertaining," I told them. "Excuse me for a moment, won't you?" I placed my menu down with a satisfying smack, and as soon as Eric stood to let me out, I hightailed it to the ladies' room. How awesome they seemed to have really hit it off. And were ganging up on me. Life was good.

I returned a few minutes later to find the two of them deep in conversation. Eric moved farther in, and I sat down to find our mugs had been refilled. Delightful.

"We ordered for you," Lennon announced, and the two of them grinned at each other.

"Little old me?" I asked, trying and failing to not look amused. Minutes later, our server placed a heaping platter of scrambled eggs topped with cheddar cheese alongside three strips of crisp turkey bacon in front of me. As I watched, the exact same meals were deposited in front of Lennon and Eric as well. He pushed the bottle of ketchup toward me.

"I don't imagine you want to defile your eggs with any of this?" he asked Lennon, gesturing to me as I doused my meal. Her eyes brightened, and I handed her the bottle.

"Oh yeah, I love ketchup on eggs," she said and proceeded to prove it.

"What about hot dogs?" Eric asked. "Not on hot dogs, right?"

"Do you mean those links of beefy goodness just begging for a generous squirt of ketchup?" she asked innocently, and I burst out laughing.

"You see," I told Lennon seriously as she attacked her meal, "you may look at the two of us and think, 'Yeah, those two have really got it together.' You probably think we agree on just about everything. Well, I'm sorry to say, but you would be wrong. Actually," I gazed sadly at Eric, who was enjoying his own meal, "we live in a house divided." I frowned in Eric's direction before continuing. "Ours is a union, fraught, I say fraught, with in-fighting and divisiveness over ketchup, the queen of condiments."

Eric hung his head in mock shame. "Now you know our dirty little secret," he admitted.

"I get the whole 'house divided' thing," she assured us both. "But at chez Gallagher, it was over missing drugs or stolen disability checks, so . . . I win," she added cheerfully and crunched happily on an extra crispy piece of bacon.

"We could swing by the old high school," I offered as we pushed back our plates and waited for the check.

"You mean the one where my mom *wasn't* a stoner and you *weren't* a nerd?" she said with a chuckle that sounded more like a cackle.

Eric snorted in laughter, and I frowned at them both.

"It was just a suggestion," I said. "I thought you might be interested. No need to be mean-spirited about it."

Lennon apologized immediately. "I'm sorry. That came out wrong. I didn't mean anything by it."

"I know, just dial the snark down a bit, especially when someone is trying to be nice. Okay?"

Lennon yawned in response but nodded quickly in agreement. "I will, I promise," she managed to say before yawning again. "I'm just beat. I haven't been sleeping well, I guess."

I studied her face. Paler than usual, purple crescent moons under her eyes. Yeah, she was most definitely in need of a nap. I looked at Eric, and he shrugged his agreement. Another couple's convo without a single word exchanged.

"Come home with us. You can take a nap, I'll make us some lunch, and we'll get you back in time to go to work. How's that?" I offered.

Nonchalant Lennon was once again making her appearance. "I guess so. I mean otherwise there'll be a lot of traffic on the highway at this time in the morning, and all those school busses, so it probably makes sense, you know?"

I nodded. *Yeah, sure thing, kid.* The ability to get want you wanted while letting the other person think you were doing them a favor was a valuable skill, and my young friend here was clearly a master.

CHAPTER 26

It was just past 2:00 in the afternoon when I determined it was time Lennon got up. I had spoken with both Dennis and Jennifer at length, and they thought the new information would be sufficient to bring both Alan and "Jay" in for questioning. I wanted to share the news with Lennon, so I knocked lightly on the guestroom door and waited. I thought I heard a "c'mon in" response, but when I peeked in, I saw only the top of Lennon's head, swaddled as she was in blankets and a quilt. I hated to wake her as she was sleeping so soundly, but I wanted her to eat something before I drove her back to New London. I sat on the edge of the bed and spoke softly.

"Lennon? You really need to get up. I don't want you to be late for work."

Her head moved slightly as she struggled to wake up. "Mom?" she called drowsily, and I froze.

"No, it's me. Randi," I said half-apologetically. The poor girl just wanted her—

"Duh, Randi, I knew it was you." She sat up in bed, yawned, and stretched her arms out. "I haven't slept that well since, well, I guess I've never slept that well," she said, shaking her head in amazement.

"It's the mattress," I told her. "We got a new—"

"Great mattress," Lennon assured me, cutting me off. "But I'm pretty sure it was because I didn't have to be on the lookout for one of mom's or Kelly's pervy boyfriends to try and slip under the covers with me," she said. "Or hold my breath when Alan came sniffing around."

Was this more snark, or had she really experienced that type of assault? But I knew she was telling the truth. I had seen it before, and the signs were all there, right in front of me. The anxiety, the trouble sleeping, the way she used sarcasm to deflect attention.

"We do have people you can talk to," I told her. "Or if you're more comfortable, you can always talk to me."

She studied me with a curious half smile on her face. "About?"

"The assaults. The men. What they did to you was unthinkable." I shook my head and wiped at my leaking eyes. "Do you remember any names?" I asked, and Lennon shook her head vigorously.

"Nah, just a string of randos with beer bellies, mullets, and tats galore. Charlene and Kelly sure knew how to pick 'em," she said. "Anyway, I'm fairly certain neither of them actually knew most of their names."

I shuddered as I recalled my years with Charlene and the depths to which she had clearly sunk. It was difficult to reconcile this troubled woman with my old friend.

"Hey, Randi?"

"What is it, sweetheart?" I asked gently. Her brown eyes swam with unshed tears.

"Thank you," she said softly. "For all of this." She motioned around the room. "Picking me up this morning. Breakfast. Welcoming me into your nice house." She smiled, but it didn't quite reach her eyes.

I squeezed her hand in mine. Toasty warm!

"It's been our pleasure," I assured her. "Are you hungry? I could heat up some leftovers from last night. Or whip you up a grilled cheese." Her eyes lit up, and I smiled. "Grilled cheese coming right up," I said. "Get yourself ready and join me."

I went to the kitchen, expecting to find Hobie standing by his dish, expecting a midafternoon snack, but he wasn't perched on his cat tree, surveilling the squirrels in the yard, and he wasn't even on the counter. I made Lennon two sandwiches on whole wheat, looked at the plate, and added a handful of chips. I checked the fridge for Coke but didn't find any. On impulse, I poured a glass of milk for her and stirred in a healthy serving of chocolate syrup. Tracey's twins always enjoyed it, and I thought she might too. It wasn't oat milk, but still.

I listened for sounds coming from down the hall. Maybe a sink running or a toilet flushing? Nothing. I waited another moment before retracing my steps and entering the guestroom. One glance confirmed what I had started to suspect. Lennon was once again sound asleep, snug and warm under the covers, this time with a big gray tiger cat curled under the crook of her arm. Hobie looked at me and blinked lazily before closing his eyes and resuming his catnap. "Nothing to see here," he was clearly communicating, so I took the hint and tiptoed to the kitchen. It was nearly 3:00. Even if we left here within the next half hour, we would barely make it in time for Lennon to change and hightail it to work. I made an executive decision.

I looked up the phone number for the Point and placed the call. After a few rings, a woman answered, and I explained the situation to her. How Lennon wasn't feeling well and how important it was for her to rest and get her strength back before returning to work tomorrow.

"Oh, for sure," the woman agreed. "We love your daughter, Ms. Gallagher. She's such a hard worker and always so responsible. I'm Celeste, the dining room manager, and you tell her to make sure and get plenty of rest and drink lots of fluids.

We'll see her when she's feeling better." I agreed and ended the call. Better the boss thinks I'm her mother than her attorney or parole officer, I thought with a smile.

I wrapped the sandwiches and put everything in the fridge. I thought about drinking the chocolate milk but made a cup of hot tea instead. I brought it into the family room and settled on the couch with a cozy throw around my legs. I considered grabbing the paperback I had been reading but chose to sit quietly and be in the moment. I took a sip of my tea before I closed my eyes and, lulled by the quiet and the knowledge that Lennon was safe, quickly fell asleep.

I woke with a start; the room had gone dark, and I looked around, feeling totally disoriented. The doorbell rang, and I realized that was what had woken me so suddenly. As I struggled to get up, I watched Eric bound to the door before opening it and greeting . . . pizza! I heard him thank the driver and shut the door behind him. He started to walk past the family room but stopped when he saw me.

"Hey, sleepyhead," he called. "C'mon. Pizza's here."

I got to my feet and followed him into the kitchen. The table was set with our best plates and silverware, and as I watched, Lennon poured sparkling seltzer into three crystal goblets. She looked up as we entered.

"He asked me to set the table," she said with a shrug. "I hope this is okay."

I looked at the heavy cloth napkins at each place setting, wondering if they were even ours. To say we rarely got out the "good stuff," as my mom used to refer to fine china and linens, was an understatement.

"It's terrific. Anyone for grated cheese or crushed red pepper?" I asked as I plunked down containers of both on the table.

"We have meat lover's and, um, meat lover's, I guess," Eric announced as he studied the contents of the two large boxes. "I'm pretty sure I asked for a plain cheese," he said apologetically. We helped ourselves to large gooey triangles loaded with toppings and started to eat.

I glanced at the wall clock and was shocked to find it was nearly 8:00 p.m. Had I really slept for almost five hours? Eric saw my look of surprise.

"I got home just before six," he said. "I saw you crashed out on the couch. And this one was sleeping with Hobes. I tried to get some work done until—"

"I bugged him to play cards with me," said Lennon. "I didn't want to wake you, Randi."

"I called your boss," I told her, and she nodded.

"Yeah, the first thing I did when I woke up was call the restaurant. Celeste told me how 'my mom' had already called to explain how I was um, 'under the weather.'" She gave me a knowing grin. "I guess I should say thanks, Mom," she drawled.

"No worries," I assured her with a wink. "So let me bring you up to speed." I quickly summarized my earlier conversations with Dennis and Jennifer.

"Will I have to testify in court?" Lennon asked and nodded happily when I told her she probably would. "Tell me where and when, and I'll do it. Anything to get Tyler and the other girls back."

I didn't want to get her hopes up, so I was relieved when Eric spoke up.

"Our friend here is quite the card shark," he told me. "She beat me at poker three out of four games."

Lennon blushed, looking pleased with herself, and suggested they play a couple more hands after dinner. While I cleaned up and stored the leftover pizza in the fridge, Lennon and Eric returned to their game at the kitchen island. I enjoyed listening to them. Teasing, gentle ribbing and shouts of victory (Lennon) and of defeat (Eric). It appeared our guest was nearly unbeatable.

Eric turned in early, as was his custom, to take a shower and read for a bit before falling asleep. Having had a lengthy nap, I was wide awake, as was Lennon, who had basically slept the entire day.

"Want to watch a movie?" I asked, and she nodded in agreement. "Ice cream?" Another nod. I offered to fix us bowls while Lennon searched for a movie to watch. I didn't really care what she chose as she was the guest, but I was surprised by the choices she presented when I joined her in front of the TV.

Between spoonfuls of mocha chip and fudge ripple, she motioned toward the set. "I was thinking *Mamma Mia* or maybe *The Princess Bride*," she said shyly.

"Either works for me," I told her. "But why was I thinking you would choose something like *Deadpool 2*?"

She shrugged in response. "I just thought one of these would be fun to watch together, you know?"

"Good choices. Let's do it," I said.

So we watched *Mamma Mia*, and when the ending credits rolled, we both decided we were still not ready for sleep, so we ended up starting *The Princess Bride* as well.

Nearly two hours later, we dragged ourselves off the couch, and after I left our bowls soaking in the sink, I said good night. I was going to settle for a pat on the shoulder or a quick hug but was surprised when Lennon pulled me into an embrace.

"Thank you, Randi," she whispered. "This has been the best day of my life." With a wave, she entered the guestroom and closed the door partway. "In case Hobie wants to join me," she added with a sleepy grin.

"Have fun storming the castle," I told her. "G'night."

I decided to forego my usual brushing, flossing, and moisturizing routine, so after discarding most of my clothing, I slipped into bed beside my sleeping husband.

He stirred and asked, "That you, Quinn?"

"It's me. Good night, my love," I whispered.

I lay awake for a while, thinking about the day and how much I had enjoyed spending time with Lennon. And Eric had as well. She was a special young woman and smart as a whip. Could we work something out to assist her in getting an education so she could really flourish? After things settled down and we found the missing girls, I would need to figure out a solution, even if it was from my new home in England. Her mind needed to be stimulated, not squashed. I wanted to see her thrive, not just survive. Anything was possible.

CHAPTER 27

The next morning, after Eric and Lennon wolfed down cold pizza and I ate a toaster waffle doused liberally with maple syrup, Lennon got herself ready to go back home. While she was taking a shower, I called Dennis. If he was surprised Lennon was still at my house, he didn't say a word. I couldn't wait to hear how the questioning of Dumb and Dumber had gone.

"We brought the two of them in separately," he told me. "Alan basically broke down into tears, but he denied knowing anything about girls going missing."

"If he's so innocent, why was he crying?" I asked, in full prosecutor mode. In my experience, innocent people might be nervous about being questioned, but they rarely sobbed.

"He was a hot mess," said Dennis, "but he swore up and down he had not been threatened by anyone at any time."

Oh great, now we had a classic "he said, she said." "What about Jordan Myers?" I asked. "Did you make him cry too?"

Dennis chuckled. He actually chuckled. "Jen is the one who handled the interrogation. I was strictly set decoration."

"I'll bet Jen can be intimidating when she needs to be," I said. "So what's her story?" I sensed a personal connection between the two of them, but Dennis was clearly not in the mood to share any details with me.

"Indeed," he agreed smoothly. "Mr. Myers denied having any sort of confrontation with Alan Newton. Claims they communicate strictly by phone on a weekly or as-needed basis and that Alan's work record is beyond reproach."

"But Lennon said she and her roommate clearly saw Myers illuminated under the streetlight from their window," I reminded him.

"Yes, I realize that. We would like to have a conversation with both young women, today if possible. Do you think you can arrange that for us?" I was conflicted, wanting to see Myers arrested but feeling protective of my new friend.

"You want her to identify him in a lineup?" I asked. "That could—"

"No, not right now," said Dennis. "We let them both go while we collect more evidence. We didn't have enough to hold either of them. That's why we need to talk to the girls."

I groaned, disappointed in the delay. "I'm not sure. What do you think?" I asked him. "Is it safe to bring Lennon back there?"

"We can't force the issue," replied Dennis quickly. "But the sooner we make a move, the safer it will be for both of them."

"I'll talk to Lennon," I told him. "I'll call you back shortly." I ended the call and turned to find I was not alone in the kitchen.

"Talk to me about what?" she asked, and I updated her on the latest. After a short conversation, we decided to drive to the house, pick up Carmen, and go to the police station. Depending on how that meeting went, we would decide on our next steps.

"I'm ready when you are," Lennon said, and minutes later we were in the car heading to New London. "I'll text Carmen. I'll tell her we're going to pick her up and go out for lunch. Is that okay?"

"Of course," I agreed and focused my attention on the heavy midday traffic. We parked in front of the house at 177 Caroline Street, and Lennon said she would run in and let her roommate know we were here.

"Weird," she said before she got out of the car. "Carmen still hasn't responded, and I don't think she's even read my text. It's Thursday, right?" I nodded. "She's off on Thursdays. I thought she would have jumped at the chance to go out for lunch. Maybe she's still sleeping."

Alarm bells started to go off in my head, but Lennon was already racing up the stairs and entering the house. Stop being paranoid, I told myself, but I knew I wouldn't draw an easy breath until I had both girls safely in the car.

I fiddled with my phone, sending a string of smiley-faced emojis and tiny hearts to Eric and immediately got a thumbs-up response from him. I was about to text Tracey to say hello when the car door opened and Lennon slid into the passenger seat. I watched her as she buckled her seat belt and tried to slow her breathing.

Before I could ask her about Carmen, she turned to me, her eyes swimming with tears and her mouth a thin line of pain.

"She's gone," she said flatly. "Gone, baby gone." My heart sank. I tried to grasp her hands to comfort her, but she pulled away, leaning against the car door, and staring miserably out the window. "It's my fault," she whispered. "If I had turned off the freaking light, Jay wouldn't have seen her in the window. Hell, if I had stayed in bed, she probably would have too."

I was about to protest none of this was her fault, but Lennon wasn't having it. "Can we go to the police?" she asked. "This has gone way too far."

I started the car and drove in the direction of the police station.

Alan was crying as he tied Carmen's wrists. "I'm sorry," he sobbed. "I don't want to do this, but you'll see. It's the only way I can keep you safe."

Carmen struggled against the ties binding her to a rickety wooden chair. "I promise, Alan. I didn't see nothin', and even if I did, I sure wouldn't tell the cops."

"That's what I told Jay," he said. "But he doesn't like to leave any loose ends. As soon as everything settles down and that nosy bitch lawyer finds something else to sink her teeth into, you'll be free to go. I p-p-promise."

Carmen shivered miserably in her thin robe. She had been tricked into thinking he needed help with something down here. She didn't particularly like Alan, but at least he had never come on to her like he had with some of the girls. She had followed him to the basement when he had suddenly gone postal on her, restraining her and tying her to a chair. She tried once again to reason with him.

"Please, Alan, I need—" He cut her off by stuffing a rag into her mouth. Her eyes wide with terror, she watched as he climbed the stairs and closed the door behind him, never looking back for a second. Too stunned to cry, she closed her eyes and tried not to panic.

CHAPTER 28

Lennon was a real trooper, I decided as I watched her being questioned, actually more like interrogated, by Jen from the Sex Crimes division. A couple of times I started to protest on behalf of my client when I thought the tone of the questions was more accusatory than was totally necessary. But Lennon handled it with a level of patience and maturity that floored me. Where had she learned to be so forthcoming and calm? Not from Charlene, of that I was certain.

When it appeared she had everything she needed to know from Lennon, Jen asked if she had anything else to add. Lennon's eyes filled with tears. The fine shell of her composure shattered in a million tiny pieces as she pleaded with the detective.

"Please find Carmen and Tyler. They can't be gone," she begged. "They're out there, and they're scared. You need to find them."

Jen's cool professional exterior cracked a tiny bit as well, and for an instant I could see she cared deeply about this case and the safety of the young women in danger. But like most of us in this line of work, she had to keep it buttoned up and hold her emotions in check.

"We'll do our best," she told Lennon. "I promise."

I quickly brought Jen up to date with the good news that Rose had been making significant progress on the list of names and updated contact information. I didn't share that all Rose had asked for in exchange for the increased workload was a letter for her personnel file. If she'd asked, I probably would have bought her a pony. I stood and began to gather my things when Lennon approached me, looking concerned.

"You did great," I assured her. "I was so proud—"

"Now what?" Lennon asked, sounding totally exasperated. I studied her closely while I formulated a response. I didn't want to present the plan as a done deal, but after speaking with both Dennis and Eric, there really didn't seem to be a whole lot of options.

"What would you like to see happen?" I asked to stall for time. Lennon did not hesitate.

"I would like to go back to my room and take a nap. Then I would like to go get a coffee with Tyler before I go to work, so I can make rent and see Seth. That's what I would like," she said, sounding both angry and exhausted. At the mention of a man's name, I looked at her with surprise. I started to ask who Seth was when Lennon held up a hand to stop me. "We are not going there," she said firmly, and I nodded.

"Well, we were thinking, I mean, Eric and Dennis and I talked and . . ."

"You think I should call in sick," said Lennon. "And what? Move in with you guys?" she asked with a smirk and a raised eyebrow.

Nailed it. "Yes," I said. "Exactly. At least for now."

She narrowed her eyes and pulled her parka tight around her. I could see her busy brain working overtime as she considered my offer. "Then let's do it," she said as she turned and led the way toward the exit. We walked to the car in silence, but as we were exiting the parking lot, she turned toward me, looking anxious. "Can we swing by the house again?" she asked. "I need, you know, my stuff."

I told her it was no problem and turned left at the next light. We pulled up in front of the house, the same space we'd vacated maybe an hour and a half ago, but the house looked totally different. Foreign, even vaguely menacing, I thought as I studied the wide sagging porch and the chipped paint with a critical eye. It was supposed to serve as a haven for young women in flux, but it was feeling anything *but* safe right now.

Lennon unbuckled and started to get out of the car. "I'm coming with," I told her and silenced her efforts to protest. "We'll be in and out, I promise. But there's no way I'm letting you go in there alone."

Lennon shrugged, knowing it would do no good to argue with me. I followed her up the stairs, across the porch, and watched as she let us in with her key. I was strangely glad to see the place was locked tight but wondered how much it really mattered if all the threats to the residents' safety carried keys of their own. We made our way through the small lobby and climbed two flights of stairs. Lennon again used her key to open the first door on the left, which allowed our entry into a small, dark room crammed with two twin beds, two dressers, and a desk.

She swiped at her eyes, seeming embarrassed to be once again in tears. "I know it's so stupid," she said softly. "As much as Carm bugs the hell out of me, always asking stupid questions and never knowing when I need to be alone with my thoughts, I m-miss her. And part of me hoped she would be here, lying across her bed, reading *Teen People* and asking if I thought the musical remake of *Mean Girls* would be better than the original or which Taylor Swift song would be the best one to get married to."

"The original is always better in my humble opinion, and 'Lover' from 2019. No contest," I told her, and she forced a smile as she retrieved the bags from our shopping trip last week and began emptying her drawers into them.

"Don't worry," she said. "I don't expect I'll be staying with you all that long. I'm just grabbing stuff before the goblins get in here and start scrounging around. If I'm gone two nights in a row, all my things will disappear."

I couldn't imagine not having a safe place to store my possessions, but I kept my thoughts to myself. There was nothing I could say to make any of this easier on Lennon right now.

She reached into the tiny closet and pulled out the sparkly emerald-green dress. "In case we get invited to any swanky parties," she said with a smirk. She added the dress to the growing pile, made up mostly of our recent purchases. A few dog-eared paperbacks followed. Looking around at the few items left behind, she shrugged. "Let's go," she said and started for the door.

"What about Carmen's clothes?" I asked. "Or her magazines?"

Lennon shook her head. "Nah, that wouldn't be cool. If—I mean, when she comes back, she'll need to know her stuff is still here." I stopped myself from pointing out the likelihood of everything being stolen. My young friend had more than enough on her plate right now.

"Need help?" I asked, but Lennon pushed past me and started for the stairs, locking the door behind her. She moved quickly despite balancing the shopping bags and her ever-present backpack. I was following her when I caught sight of a young man standing in the vestibule, shaking a finger at Lennon as she approached him. This must be the pervy Alan.

"Now, now, missy. Where do you think you're going?" he asked, managing to sound both curious and peeved at the same time. "And you forgot to sign in, again," he said with a frown. "And your guest too," he added. "What am I going to do with you, Lennon?" he asked playfully. He seemed chipper for someone who'd been recently questioned by the police. For a second, I worried she was going to lose her cool and let him know she had been the one to rat on him. But not Lennon.

She drew herself up to her full height, standing nearly nose to nose with the diminutive fellow, and leaned in close. "I'm heading out, my man. Just for a little vacay, I swear. I'm paid through November, so don't try to get someone else in here, you feel me?" The confidence she exuded combined with her no-nonsense tone clearly left no doubt in Alan's mind she was both ready and willing to kick his ass if need be.

He tried to save face by turning his attention to me, holding out his hand in welcome. "Alan Newton, den mother, haha," he said by way of greeting. Not wanting to reveal exactly how big a wrecking ball I could let loose on his miserable life, I shook his hand, immediately nauseated by his clammy handshake and his stained teeth.

"Randi," I said. "Family friend."

He forced a smile and asked me how he might be of service. My skin crawling, I assured him if he were able to grab the door, we would be on our way.

"Don't forget who your friends are, Lennon," he called out, and this time I had to stop Lennon from dropping her things and rushing at him. I shook my head and rolled my eyes at her. She turned and marched to the car, and I was proud of her for reining in her anger.

"Nice to meet you, Alan," I called out with a wave. "I'm sure we'll be seeing more of you," I added. *Yeah, first in the courtroom and finally behind bars, you sleazy little prick.* Adopting a behavior of Tracey's, I wiggled my fingers at him. "Byeeeee!"

I started the car as Lennon stowed her bags on the backseat. As she buckled up, I noticed her eyes were wet. I had thought she was angry, but now it appeared she was sad. And with plenty of good reasons.

"You okay?" I asked, and she nodded bravely before admitting she really wasn't.

"I miss Tyler," she said simply. "When you rolled your eyes back there, I realized that's what I was missing."

I thought about what she'd said for a moment before nodding. "I know exactly what you mean. It's like you're looking at a person who gets you. Really gets you—what you mean and what you say."

"And how you say it," she added. "When you rolled your eyes at me, I knew you knew what I wanted to say and I didn't have to say it out loud. Because you heard me." She was smiling again, looking brave and more certain of herself.

I squeezed her hand and pulled out into the street. "I'm glad you have that with Tyler," I said, careful to use the present tense. "It's a special bond."

"Do you have that with anyone besides me?" she asked, and I smiled.

"Yes, with Tracey. You'll have to meet her. She and your mom—"

"I know. The three of you were best friends. Now it's the two of you, and that's great." She was quiet for a bit, but I could tell there was more she wanted to say. "Um, what about Eric?" she asked.

I shook my head. "He's in training, but between you and me, I don't think he's really getting it," I said. "He's been a work in progress for over five years, and honestly I haven't been seeing any signs of real improvement. I am afraid he's maxed out when it comes to the eye-roll."

"At least he's cute," quipped Lennon, and I laughed along with her.

Yeah, Eric was cute all right. Downright adorable when he'd quickly agreed we had to take her in, at least until we left for London. I didn't know how long she might want to stay, but her safety and well-being had become of paramount importance to both of us this past week. I was so grateful he and I were on the same page and looking in the same general direction. Even if he couldn't roll his eyes at key moments, he was a keeper.

CHAPTER 29

Dennis called first thing the following morning. His greeting sounded jubilant, excited. I quickly learned why.

"We caught a break," he said. "The residents directly across from Bradford House have a Ring doorbell, and you'll never believe what it picked up." Before I could attempt a guess, he continued. "Clear as day footage of Jordan Myers carrying a nearly comatose young woman though the yard before stuffing her into the trunk of a car registered to him. We haven't positively ID'd the woman yet, but it looked enough like Chloe Anderson to get a warrant issued for his arrest." I was dumbfounded at the news. Finally, something to get that bastard off the streets and behind bars.

"So what happens next?" I asked.

"He was arrested without incident and is being held pending formal arraignment later today," replied Dennis before explaining the charges were still being tallied, but sex trafficking and kidnapping were certain, with prison sentences of twenty years or more for each conviction. Uniformed officers were going door to door throughout the neighborhood to see if anyone else had captured any additional footage. He promised to keep me in the loop, and I rushed to share the good news with Lennon.

She had adapted quickly to life in the Quinn-Hansen household. Not a morning person, she never joined me on my early morning beach walks, but on days when I didn't go in to work, she generally came stumbling into the kitchen around 9:00, always joined by her devoted companion, Hobie. I swear he followed her everywhere most days. I made sure there was coffee for her but otherwise left her to pull together something for breakfast on her own. Often, she would join me in my home office, slurping cereal and asking me about my pending cases. She was extremely bright and articulate, always able to identify the weak points in a case or poke holes in even the strongest of defense arguments.

I'd told her one day she should consider a career in law, and she had scoffed. "Wrong side of the courtroom for a Gallagher to be on," she'd said. But why not?

As far as houseguests went, Lennon was a dream. She kept her room neat-ish, made her bed, and when she did her laundry, she always checked to see if I had anything to throw in with hers. Without ever being asked, she took out the trash and recycling, emptied the dishwasher, and always tidied up after preparing food for herself. We planned dinners together for the nights when all three of us were home, and it was fun having her around.

After calling out from work for a few days in a row, she asked me if I would bring her to the Point so she could speak with her manager. She had decided it was too far away, and it wasn't fair to expect me or Eric to pick her up late at night. On the way to New London, I asked her what she planned to say, and she shrugged.

"I dunno. Sorry, I guess. I can't work here anymore, so I need to quit. Bye."

"What do you hope to get out of it? The meeting?" At her blank look, I continued. "What I mean is, what do you want to achieve by meeting face-to-face?"

"Um, I guess I want to tell her how much the job meant to me. How much I enjoyed the pre-shift dinners and the lively atmosphere. Maybe when I move back here in a few weeks or whenever, they could hire me back. I really care about the people I worked with . . ." She blushed, and I wondered if this was an opportunity to ask her about her mysterious co-worker Seth.

"What else?" I pressed. "What do you want to walk away with?"

She squirmed in her seat, her forehead scrunched in confusion. "My last paycheck, of course, maybe a letter of recommendation, and . . . Seth's phone number," she added, seeming pleased with her admission.

"That's my girl." A short while later, we pulled into the nearly empty parking lot. Lennon didn't want to get caught up in the busy dinner rush, and it was just after 4:00 p.m. "Go get 'em, tiger," I told her, and for once she responded with only a slight shake of her head. Maybe she was getting used to my corny expressions.

I watched her cross the lot and let herself in through the back door marked "employees only." I knew she hadn't wanted to quit or take a leave, but without any reliable transportation, it made no sense to continue working here. We would have to figure something out before our move, which we were thinking would take place in mid-January at the latest. That gave us just over two months, including the holidays, so a lot could happen.

I scrolled through my phone, hoping for some update on the Jordan Myers trial. So far, he hadn't cracked, maintaining his innocence and unwilling to provide names of the higher-ups in his dreadful network of sexual predators. I wished I could interrogate the smug little bastard myself, but Rick had not requested any assistance on the case from yours truly. It appeared my only role would be getting Lennon prepped and ready to testify.

"Speak of the devil," I said as the door opened and Lennon slid into the passenger's seat.

"First I'm a tiger, now I'm a devil?" she asked. "Make up your mind, woman."

"So how'd it go?" I asked, and she smiled, probably the biggest I had seen on her.

"Terrific," she said, patting her backpack happily. "I got my last paycheck, and they even paid me for this past week when I was 'sick,'" she added with air quotes. "Plus Celeste says I can use them for references if I need any work in the meantime, and they want me to come back as soon as I move back here. They are gonna train me to wait tables. I'll be making bank," she crowed.

Why did this last bit of news cause such a sinking sensation in my chest? Lennon had been living with us for barely a week, and we were moving to freaking London in a couple of months. Get over yourself, I thought as I pulled out of the parking lot. "That all sounds great," I told her, hoping I sounded sincere. And it really was great. But what about . . . ? "Any other good news?"

She let out a squeal of pure delight and waved her phone excitedly. "Seth gave me his number. And I gave him mine. He wants to take me out . . . on a date. Can you imagine?"

This time I did not need to fake my sense of joy. Was this her very first real date? "Oh, sweetheart," I said. "I am so happy for you. I can't wait to meet your, um . . ." I had to stop myself from saying "your young man." Who was I? There was no way I could play the cool parental figure if this kept up.

"He's real smart. And super cute. I have no clue why he would want to spend time with me."

I quickly moved into defense mode. "You're smart and super cute too. What are you going to wear?"

Her mood turned somber. "I don't know." She frowned. "I've got those nice sweaters you got me, but he's already seen a couple of them at work. My new jeans are good, but . . ."

"When the going gets tough, the tough go shopping," I informed her. "Let's hit the mall tomorrow and—"

"He probably won't even call," she said, sounding like an age-appropriate petulant teenager.

"Not with that attitude he won't. And who's to say you can't call him?" I asked, and she blushed, but she was smiling at the same time. Was I getting good at this parental advice thing or what?

"Meanwhile, I have to find a part-time job, get ready to testify, and find another place to live when I move back," she said, starting to sound stressed again. "And who am I to be going on a date when my best friend is missing?"

"All in due time," I assured her. "Everything that can be done to find Tyler is being done, and you need a break. For tonight, let's have a nice evening, play some board games or whatever. Eric is going to grill burgers, and you and I can whip up a salad. How's that sound?"

The smile she gave me in return was all the answer I needed.

It was several hours later, and Eric and I were curled up on the couch, the show we had been watching long forgotten. We were catching up on what had been a busy week for the two of us. Lennon had gone to bed a half hour ago, joking how the hectic pace of Old Lyme nightlife had worn her out. I had the sense she wanted a little private time to text with Seth. He had reached out shortly after we had eaten, and they had been back and forth ever since. The date was set for this coming Saturday. Plans were being made for a walk on the beach, weather permitting, followed by an early dinner at the Shrimp Shack here in town.

"We went there on our first date," I reminded Eric. "Remember?"

"Of course I do. But do you know anything about this kid?" Eric asked, a hint of suspicion in his voice. I supported myself on my elbow and studied him closely.

"Well, *Dad*, I actually don't know much. He goes to UCONN on a scholarship, I want to say his major is Engineering, he's smart, and oh yeah, *super cute*," I trilled.

"Don't you think we need to vet him a bit before we let him take our, um, Lennon out?"

Awww. He was already feeling paternal toward our houseguest. I chose not to remind him the young woman in question was an adult at eighteen, had street smarts galore, and other than the lobster incident had never once been in trouble. I knew what he meant, though, and I shared his concerns.

"I'll ask Lennon to invite him in to meet us before they head out. How's that?"

Eric nodded. "Okay, I guess that'll work. His Facebook page hasn't been updated recently, and the photos he posts on Insta are mostly related to sports and college life. He seems legit, I guess."

I shook my head in amazement. "Do you want me to see if Pop can ask one of his cronies from the department to run him through the system to see if he has a record?" I teased.

"Would he do that?" he asked, clearly taking my suggestion to heart.

"No, of course not," I told him. "I had him check you out before our first date, and he got into trouble with the department. Violations, privacy, blah, blah. Let's trust Lennon on this, okay?"

He studied me closely and, realizing I was just having a go with him, conceded defeat.

"Okay, I hear you. But it's better to be safe—"

"What do you think about Jake and Meg's offer to hire Lennon as a father's helper during the day?" I asked, and Eric agreed it seemed like a great opportunity. My stepbrother, Jake, ran a successful accounting firm from home, and ever since Meg had gone back to work part-time as a dental assistant, they were having a difficult time juggling two-year-old Teddy's naptimes and five-year-old Clementine's kindergarten schedule. Earlier this evening, I had told Sally how Lennon would be staying with us for a while, and less than a half hour later Meg had called me. After a brief conversation, Lennon called Meg back, and they were planning to meet tomorrow.

"I hope it works out," added Eric. "And it doesn't conflict with our driving lessons."

I had been thrilled during dinner when Eric had offered to teach Lennon to drive. They would be using my car for the lessons as Eric's huge four-wheel drive pickup truck was a) his baby and b) too massive for a beginner. I had never even backed it out of the driveway. Maybe after we left for England, she could . . . Don't get ahead of yourself, I thought. One step at a time.

"Do you think we're doing the right thing?" I asked.

Eric considered his response before speaking. He was such an adult like that.

"Yes, Quinn. I really do. We can provide a safe space for her while the trial is going on, and honestly, I know he's being held pending the trial, but until that psycho is locked up for good, it's the only way we can protect her. She's a good kid, you feel like you owe her mother, and I'm not going there with you tonight," he protested, holding up a hand to stop me from denying it. "She can help out your brother and his family, Hobes loves her, so yeah, definitely the right thing." He hugged me closer to him.

Definitely the right thing, I repeated to myself. I couldn't help but wonder if her mother would agree allowing her daughter to live with her old frenemy was the right thing. *Doubtful.*

CHAPTER 30

As we waited to hear more about the pending charges against Myers, I was frequently at loose ends, worrying about the upcoming trial. What if it got pushed forward into the new year? Could I leave for London before he was convicted and the girls were found? And was the latter even a likely scenario in this case? I tried to stay positive for Lennon's sake, but inwardly I struggled to envision a happy ending for the missing young women. We set up a meeting with state's attorney Rick Cooper to discuss the upcoming trial strategy. I doubted I would get any further involved in the court proceedings, but I relished the opportunity to sit in on a criminal case of this magnitude. Rick had been my mentor, and the chance to witness another of his courtroom performances was not one I would pass up.

As promised, I had developed an orientation session for the police personnel who would be interviewing past and current residents of the group homes across New London, along with critical talking points and a list of carefully worded questions. Chris had offered to help, and I'd added in the changes he had recommended. I would have liked to include role-playing exercises, but there was no time. The attendees to date had seemed grateful for the support, and the training had been well received. It was a first step toward creating a more reasonable climate of less blaming and more support for victims of sex crimes. Last week, I had attended several of the sessions as an observer and felt reasonably comfortable the tone of the interviews was one of caring and empathy, and the information gathered was being carefully recorded. Although I was still working at the office and had scheduled court dates, attendance at our Monday sessions had fallen off. Word had spread about the missing girls, and everyone was laying low, so I decided to cancel the sessions until after the trial. I wondered if I could convince Sandi to take over the group when I was gone. Meanwhile, most of the girls had been texting me with regular updates or just to say hello. No new names of missing girls had been reported to me since Jordan's arrest.

One morning after Eric had left for work, dropping Lennon at Jake's on the way, I began the daunting process of packing for London. We had determined we would not seek renters at this point. If after six months it felt right to do so, we would. So I wasn't worried about leaving valuables laying around necessarily. It was deciding what to take that had captured my full attention. Well, that and the knowledge that despite the fact we had only moved here four short years ago, we were already running out of storage space.

I called Eric at the office. "Hey, Quinn," he began, and I jumped right in.

"When is the last time you went skiing?" I demanded.

"Um, it's been a while," he admitted. "Do I dare ask why the sudden interest? Do you want to go ski—"

"How about golf? I'm going through the basement, and I'm seeing a whole load of sports equipment that never gets used, and there are like five pairs of ski pants. Shouldn't we donate it or sell it even? It seems ridiculous that—"

I heard a loud groan, and Eric protested. "We've already had the talk. You know, the one when we decided we were both allowed a little wriggle room, a handful of keepers that weren't up for debate. Or in the case of your TV show wardrobe that you can't fit into anymore . . ."

"Ack, don't get me started. I'm just saying it's nuts to hold on to all this stuff. Think of the children, the people who need..."

"Babe, I've got to run. I'm about to go into a meeting. We're doing a Zoom call with the crew in London, and I have a few things to prepare. Tell you what. I know you're probably chomping at the bit to clear the decks. Here's my take: Toss the clothing, but save the sports equipment, okay? Keep the golf clubs and donate the ski pants. How's that sound?"

"You got it, babe." That was way more than I had hoped for. Perhaps I hadn't lost my touch after all when it came to negotiating. My next call was to Tracey. She answered immediately, sounding out of breath.

"Hey, Randi. What's up? Ruth had to dash out, and my little humans are waiting for their snack."

"I won't keep you," I promised. "But do you remember when you said you wanted to go through the twins' stuff when they were heading off to college and maybe we should have a tag sale?"

"Um, yeah. And you said you would rather be dragged naked down—"

"It's London," I interjected, and I could clearly picture her reaction, much like it had been when I broke the news to her last week. Sad, anxious, disappointed. "Sorry, sore subject. But we have all this stuff, and it just seems like the time is right to purge, you know?"

"Aw, crap, you can't let me be mad, even for a minute? You know there's nothing I like better than organizing a sale. My place or yours? Hmm. Probably yours since we turned our garage into a playroom. One day only? Saturday for sure, but it's kind of late to post anything in the weekly flyer. It comes out tomorrow. But online, no problem. Are you thinking of starting at 7:00 a.m.? The early birds will show regardless, so you might as well be ready for them. Oh man, this is really short notice. I'll come over tonight about 6:00 for an initial assessment. Then Friday night we can start tagging. I've got markers and stickers. How're you fixed for tables? Whoops, sorry, the natives are getting restless. See you tonight. Byeeee." She ended the call and I stared at my phone.

Somehow during the brief one-way phone conversation, I had lost all my restless energy along with any thoughts of cleaning or organizing a single thing. The great cleanout would need to be scheduled for a later date. I hadn't even shared the news with Pop and Sally yet. I poured another cup of coffee and plotted my next move. Yard work? No, it was drizzling out and looked cold. It was an inside day for sure, and as much as I wanted to avoid it, my messy abode needed me. Soon, I was culling through the junk drawer, where all good things go to die. I had started with the rarely used potato masher that kept it from closing properly. Gone-zo! Used and mismatched birthday cake candles were next, then paper clips, bread bag ties, and rubber bands. I was making progress. At the rate I was going, we would be ready to move just in time for Eric to retire.

I looked up in surprise when Eric walked into the kitchen. No greeting, no hug. Hours earlier than I would have expected to see him. What was up?

"It's over. Done," he announced with no preamble, and I knew. Of course I did. One look at his face and it was obvious. But why? I came around the counter and pulled him into a hug.

"What happened?" I asked, drawing back to gauge his expression. Crestfallen, disappointed, angry. Yup, I knew the signs well. "Eric, talk to me," I begged. He pulled away gently and told me he needed a drink.

"Join me?" he asked, and I nodded. *Sure, why not?* He retrieved the pair of large glass mugs chilling in the freezer and set them on the counter. A bottle of root beer was next, followed by a quart of vanilla ice cream and a scooper. I watched as he concocted root beer floats, the longtime drink of choice in his family while he was growing up. Everything from scraped knees to report cards full of A's—this was how the Hansen clan responded to news, both good and bad. I pulled two tattered paper-covered straws from the newly organized junk drawer and placed them in front of him. I did try to contribute a bit here and there.

Wordlessly, he stuck a straw in each glass. "Outside?" he asked, and again I nodded. It was probably forty degrees today, but when your dream explodes in your face, sometimes drinking a root beer float while sitting on a cold, damp patio is the only thing to help you to feel better. I followed him outside and plunked myself on the chaise lounge next to him. I waited patiently as he took a long pull on his drink, wiped at his mouth with the back of his hand, and let out a long sigh.

"Eric," I began, but he cut me off.

"It's Cleve. You know my colleague in London?"

I nodded mutely. Of course I did. Cleveland Amory. Founder and president of Parametric, the wildly successful architectural enterprise that had been courting Eric's firm for months. The person Eric would take over for in London. "He was arrested this morning. Embezzlement of company funds," he said flatly. "Money-laundering, tax evasion, and that's just for starters. He has defrauded his investors, overstated his annual rates of return, new investor funds were used to cover margin calls . . . Can I pick 'em or what?" Eric shook his head, clearly still in shock.

This was the worst news ever. My heart ached for him. He had worked so hard to create this opportunity for himself and his partners, and with one phone call, it had all disappeared. I hesitated to bring it up, but I was a lawyer and had to ask.

"Are you or your firm implicated in these alleged crimes in any way?" I spoke softly but got an immediate reaction. He looked at me, wild-eyed and tense, but instantly understood the reason for my question.

"No, I mean, the folks in our legal department are going over everything, but no earnest money has changed hands. No payments of any kind."

I felt a sense of relief wash over me. That would be the worst possible outcome, if Eric were found liable somehow. I hugged him close to me and felt his shoulders droop. What a crap sandwich! After a while, Eric sat back and drained what was left of his soda.

"Can I get you a refill?" I asked before enjoying a couple of sips of my own drink. He smiled, just a ghost of a smile, but still.

"Better not, I'm driving." He stood to leave. "I had to get out of the office after that call. All those pairs of eyes," he said with a shudder. "Everyone pitying me or judging me. Blaming me. Awww, crap. But I need to head back for a meeting with the other partners to begin damage control. Something that won't tarnish my sterling reputation forever. Or the firm's," he added grimly.

I followed him into the kitchen. The warmer inside air felt wonderful on my chilled skin.

"Do you want anything?" I asked him. "A sandwich or some soup? I can whip something up really fast."

He shook his head and, noticing the cluttered kitchen countertops for the first time, asked, "What happened here?"

"Oh, you know me. Junk drawer be gone," I said, brandishing an imaginary magic wand. I received a knowing grin in response.

"I won't be late," he promised as he grabbed his jacket from the back of the chair. "Should I pick up dinner?"

"Leave it to me," I said. "You have more than enough going on."

He kissed my cheek and left the house. A minute later, I heard him start up his truck and back out of the driveway. I drained the last dregs of my drink, trying to make sense of all of this. No deal. No move. No London. A sense of relief coursed through me, and I let out a long breath. I felt terrible that I felt so, so wonderful, I realized. What kind of woman was I?

"The kind of woman willing to uproot her whole life so Eric could fulfill his dream," said Tracey a couple of minutes later after I posed the question to her. I nodded, still in a daze over this latest development. "Don't beat yourself up, Ran," she whispered, and I smiled, picturing her circling the large play area where her small charges napped on cots and blankets. "You agreed to go, and you would have gone, but the deal fell through, and that's it. An un-done deal. Don't make me come over there," she said, and I wondered briefly if she were still addressing me. "You heard me, Travis. Crayons are for coloring, not for sticking up your nose. Okay, that's it. Sorry, Ran, got to go. So no tag sale? Bummer. I'm sorry, not sorry you're stuck with me. Byeeee."

This was even more good news, I realized. No move to London *and* no need to hold a tag sale! But I still had a very disappointed husband to console. I wondered if he could get some time off sooner rather than later. A getaway sounded like a good idea, at least until I consulted my calendar. In addition to the trial, which would require Lennon to testify, I had several court dates lined up for a variety of active cases, and then there were the month-end reports. *Let's see . . .* It was the 31st. Oh crap, it was freaking Halloween. With all the crazy that life had thrown at us lately, it had completely slipped my mind, and apparently Eric's as well.

I grabbed my things and dashed out to the car, intent on arriving at the store in time to stock up on candy and rush home and make a stab at decorating. Does everyone wait until the last minute to buy their treats? I wondered as I perused the mostly empty shelves. I was certain that as early as this morning they had probably been overflowing with every type of confection you might imagine. Now all that remained were some neon-colored sour balls just screaming "choking hazard," a few dusty-looking boxes of generic chocolate witches left over from last year, and an economy-sized bag of a whitish fluffy cotton candy confection aptly labeled "ghost poop." *Ugh.* Hard pass. What would Sally do? I wondered. She was easily the least flappable woman I knew. And very crafty. She would probably hand-dip caramel candy apples or concoct something deserving of a centerspread in a woman's magazine for the little ones lucky enough to knock on her door tonight.

I debated going to another couple of stores but decided to give up the ghost, as it were. I joined the long line at the self-checkout completely empty-handed, and when it was my turn, I reached over and grabbed an open box of Hershey bars from the display. One by one, I scanned each bar while the waiting customers grumbled and complained at how long I was taking. Forty-seven candy bars and ninety or so dollars later, I was shoving everything into thin-as-tissue plastic bags when I heard a wolfish whistle behind me.

I turned to find an older gentleman surveying me and my haul and smiling broadly. "Whoo-eee," he said. "Full-size." I smiled faintly at him, hoping like hell he was referring to my choice of candy.

The rain began to fall in sheets, and I arrived home barely in time to unearth my gallon-sized orange-and-black-striped candy bowl from the top shelf of the pantry and turn on the porch lights before the children started to arrive. There would be no relaxing evening sitting out on the driveway for Eric and me. Lennon texted, asking if she could have dinner with the Colby clan and go trick-or-treating with the kids. I responded immediately.

Of course. Have fun!

For the next hour or so, I oohed and aahed and asked the "And who are you supposed to be?" question old folks like me had been asking small children since the beginning of time. While their parents huddled under umbrellas, their little ninja warriors and fairy princesses selected a chocolate bar and raced off to the next house. By the time Eric got home, my bowl was empty and the stream of trick-or-treaters had dwindled to nothing. After he toweled off and changed into dry clothes, he joined me on the couch.

"Sharesies?" I said, offering him half of the last candy bar. I made it appear like I had saved it especially for him, but honestly, I just hadn't had the chance to finish it yet.

"Thanks, babe," he said and ate it slowly, chewing reflexively and staring at nothing. I suddenly remembered I had offered to take responsibility for dinner. *Whoops!*

"Can I make you a sandwich?" I offered weakly, not at all certain there was any bread in the house.

He shook his head. "Nah. I'm good. Just sit here with me, will you?" he asked, and I snuggled into his warmth.

"Always," I told him, and seconds later Hobie joined us on the couch. Despite the disappointing news about London, I felt content. Our next chapter wouldn't include a transatlantic move, but I knew we would figure out something amazing for the two of us. Or possibly the three of us? Was being able to help Lennon the silver lining to the dark cloud that was Cleveland Amory and London?

CHAPTER 31

The next morning, Eric left for an emergency Saturday session with his partners to craft a plan to distance themselves from the scandal refusing to die across the pond. He told me a public relations firm had been hired to rebuild his company's tarnished reputation.

"I'll bet you a bag of half-priced Halloween candy the first recommendation those spin doctors make will be to fire my sorry ass," he said, grabbing his coat and heading toward the door.

"*Au contraire,*" I corrected him. "Yours is a fine ass. Nothing in the least bit sorry about it."

He tried to smile, but the grim reality of what he was facing was too much, even for a cockeyed optimist like him. "Thanks. I'll give them that feedback," he promised. "I'm sure that will do the trick."

I wanted to ask him if being fired was really the worst thing that could happen. I knew how proud he had been making senior partner status at forty, but he had always been frugal, had invested well and if needed, I could go back to work full-time in the private sector. We would be fine. I wanted to tell him all that and more, but that was not what he needed to hear right now.

"You've got this, babe," I said, giving him a playful swat on his fine ass.

He blew me a kiss and walked to his truck. As he settled in, he looked right at me and mouthed, "I love you."

Then he was backing out of the driveway, and I sagged against the door. "Love you more," I silently messaged him.

To take my mind off Eric's dilemma, I decided to straighten my office, and I busied myself organizing folders and filing. Shortly after I came back upstairs, Lennon emerged from her room. Her hair shot straight up, and her pale face was lined with pillow creases. She looked lovely.

"That must have been some sleep," I told her.

"It was epic," she agreed. While I poured us both a cup of coffee, she foraged around in the fridge before standing at the kitchen island with a tired looking slice of veggie pizza in front of her. Ugh, this practice of eating cold pizza. Was I the only one immune to its charms? She sipped and chewed happily, and I watched her with a smile on my face. Should we be talking about her upcoming testimony? I didn't want her words to appear to be memorized or practiced, but surely a discussion of what did and didn't work well in the courtroom couldn't hurt.

Turned out we were of like minds again this morning. With increasing regularity, Lennon and I had been finding we were having similar thoughts, and we had begun to finish each other's sentences.

"Can we look at calendars for the next few days?" she asked. "I want to talk with you about testifying. Get your thoughts if I can. And I know how busy you are, and I'm starting to get busy too." She spoke the last words with a clear sense of pride and some excitement as well.

"Sure thing," I told her. "I am going to make my work schedule based on when Jake and Meg need you to babysit, so I can either drop you off in the morning or pick you up in the afternoon. Saves Jake from having to run you both ways," I added.

"And Eric promised me to take me driving tomorrow. It would be great if I could get my road hours in before it snows in a few weeks."

I nodded in agreement. "Sounds like a plan. But the question of the day remains."

Lennon looked up from her pizza. "What's that?"

"What you're going to wear on your date today with Seth. Duh," I reminded her.

Her eyes grew wide as she visualized her choices in her head. "Will you help me?" she asked, and I smiled in agreement. With everything we'd had to deal with, we had neglected to go shopping this week, so we only had a handful of choices to consider. Who was I, and what had I done with my inner retail muse? Figuring a pre-dinner walk on the beach was out of the question as the rain was now coming down in sheets on the verge of turning to hail, Lennon ended up with a cute mustard-colored cropped sweater, dark wash jeans, and, to really tie everything together, a pair of ankle boots in a deep chestnut. The boots were supplied by Tracey, who had arrived shortly after I called her asking for help. Okay, begging for help.

"It's cool we wear the same size, Tracey," Lennon said as she twirled in front of the full- length mirror in my bedroom.

Tracey agreed. "Those look amazing on you, and they're a little tight on me, so keep 'em, okay? You'll be doing me a favor. Now I won't need an excuse to buy a new pair. Hey, maybe we could go shopping next week if you're free."

Lennon agreed happily, and I watched the two of them, delighted at how well they were getting along. Of course, the twelve-year-old girl who still resided in me was not nearly as pleased. "Middle school me" felt jealous and threatened. And totally left out. And embarrassed by my abnormally sized clown feet.

I heard an impossibly young sounding adolescent voice say, "I like to shop." Both women turned toward me. So I *had* said it aloud.

"Of course you'll join us, silly," said Tracey.

"We'll even take your car, and I can drive," Lennon added as she twirled again, delighted by her stylish outfit.

"Adult me" smiled happily. But there was no way in hell I would allow her to drive without several more lessons with Eric under her belt.

By the time I heard from Eric, telling me he was on his way home, Lennon and Seth had already left for their dinner date. I had been thoroughly charmed by her "young man," and the smile on Lennon's face had been nothing short of radiant. I called Tracey as I chopped peppers, mushrooms, and onions and shredded a chunk of aged cheddar. Breakfast for dinner, I thought as I imagined placing a fluffy omelet in front of my darling husband. His text had been spare and concise, giving me no clue how his emergency meeting had gone.

"Tell me everything," demanded Tracey. "How did her hair look?" She had given Lennon a few suggestions while wielding my ancient curling wand, and Lennon had promised to try it herself when she got out of the shower.

"Really great. Flipped it up a bit, and she let me do her makeup," I added excitedly. Silence on the other end. What the . . . ? "Oh, come on, T, I can do makeup," I whined. "Maybe not on myself, and not the one time for prom when I tried to do yours, but honestly she looked beautiful, so give me a break, would you?"

Tracey chuckled, then burst out laughing. It wasn't really all that funny, was it?

"Sorry," came her muffled reply. "Chase is trying to describe a girl he met at a party off campus last night. She was walking around with a parrot on her shoulder, a LIVE parrot, and she referred to herself in the third person all night long . . . Oh, Chase, not really. Was her name Polly?" She dissolved into laughter again.

"I'll fill you in on Seth tomorrow," I told her as I heard Eric's truck in our driveway. "Hey, Chase. How's it going, boyo?" I shouted and ended the call after I heard him return my greeting. I turned as Eric entered the kitchen through the mudroom, drenched and exhausted and sadder than I could ever recall seeing him. He shrugged off his wet coat and slipped off his shoes before leaning into my open arms.

I held him close until I could feel his racing heart slow down, matching my own steady breath.

"Babe," I said. "Can I fix you a Hansen special?"

He shook his head. "I think I might need something a little stronger tonight."

Crap. This couldn't be good.

CHAPTER 32

It was a couple of hours later as the three of us stood in silence, observing a nearly comatose Eric passed out on the couch. "He doesn't usually drink like this," I assured Lennon and Seth. "He's just had a really bad day." I glanced over at Lennon, hoping she wouldn't make a crack about how often she'd seen her mom sprawled on the couch, drunk as a skunk, and to my relief she only nodded.

"He's such a great guy," she told Seth. "I can't wait for you to really, um, meet him."

I studied my sleeping husband, who had started to snore softly, and wait, was that . . . ? Yes, drool was running down his chin. There was no dignity to be found here this evening.

"Let's leave him for now and go into the kitchen, okay?" I led the way, sneaking a look over my shoulder to see the two of them following me closely, their hands clutched tightly together. What an adorable couple, I thought. What a crappy night to meet this lovely young man.

They turned down my offer of coffee or a soft drink, claiming they were full from dinner. We sat at the island, and I listened to Lennon describing the food, the atmosphere, and the rain lashing against the window where they had sat in a quiet corner of one of my favorite dining spots.

"Did I tell you Randi and Eric went there on their first date?" she asked Seth, and he smiled at her and nodded. I was listening to Lennon but found myself watching Seth watching her. I knew that look. That "How did I get so lucky?" and "Pinch me, please. I think I just won the lottery of love" look. Eric had worn it, and so had Pop. Come to think of it, they both still did.

My poor, sweet man, I thought, suddenly feeling disloyal that while I was in here laughing and chatting away, he was a room away, feeling crushed. The meeting had not gone well. Just as he had suspected, the first piece of advice the spin doctors had offered his partners was to get rid of him. "You need a scapegoat, someone to take the fall, and he's clearly a liability." Apparently, it had taken most of the day to clearly communicate the firm's "new direction" after spending several hours discussing optics and different strategies to "move the needle." That is what you get when you pay consultants by the hour, I thought bitterly. Blah, blah, blah, and oh, by the way, you're fired.

What a bunch of bullshit, I thought. He had helped to grow that freaking firm, worked hard to get it to the point where a company like Parametric would approach them and seek them out as partners. If he hadn't done such a great job, he wouldn't have been let go. How crazy was that? As he'd talked, he'd sipped whiskey neat from a glass, after unearthing a bottle I hadn't known we even owned. A light drinker, it hadn't taken long for him to start slurring his words shortly before passing out where he sat. Not long before the two lovebirds had returned home from their date.

I rejoined the conversation as Seth was saying good night. "I'll get out of your hair," he told me. "I'll come back and hang with you guys again, if you'll have me." He gave me a quick hug. *What a sweetheart!*

Lennon piped up, offering to walk him to the door, and off they went. I returned to the family room and studied the love of my life. I pulled a woolen throw over him and propped a pillow under his head, then turned out the lights and padded down the hall to our room. I could still hear Lennon and Seth talking softly at the front door and decided I had talked enough and listened enough for one night. I slipped out of my clothes and slipped between the chilly sheets. Flannel sheets tomorrow, I vowed and pulled the covers up around me. I was sad and cold and exhausted, and I hoped like hell I would find the strength to support Eric in whatever he chose to do next.

Hobie hopped on the bed next to me and, after making a couple dozen blanket biscuits, curled onto Eric's pillow, purring loudly. I stroked his soft fur and told him I loved him. That he was the best boy ever. And eventually, I fell into a troubled sleep with visions of talking parrots clouding my dreams.

CHAPTER 33

On Monday morning, Lennon was alone in the house and thoroughly enjoying the quiet. Despite having canceled the Monday morning meet and greet with her "minions," Randi had gone into work. She had asked Lennon to join her, but she said she needed to catch up on laundry. Eric had left to meet his brother for an early lunch to talk about his current employment situation. Poor guy, she thought. She could tell he was a hard worker and was certain a bigger and better opportunity would present itself soon. She had heard him and Randi talking last night. At least they didn't appear to have any immediate financial concerns. The loss of a paycheck would have spelled immediate disaster for anyone in her family. The Gallaghers seemed almost proud of their hand-to-mouth approach to life. Not me, thought Lennon. With Randi's help, she planned to go to college and make something of herself. Maybe she could live here a little longer since they wouldn't be moving to London after all. With a spring in her step, she rinsed out her coffee mug and returned to her room. She stripped her bed, planning to wash the sheets and—her phone buzzed from the nightstand, where she had left it.

She picked up the phone and saw she had an incoming text from an unknown number. She scanned it quickly. It was from Carmen!

Hey Len, I want to explain about the last time u were here. Can u meet for lunch? My treat. Carm

Carmen was back! The first thought that crossed Lennon's mind was why she wasn't texting from her own phone, then she recalled how often her roommate had to change phone carriers whenever she stopped paying her bill. The second thought was how to get to New London.

Where? She texted Carmen. What time? U had me scared.

Carmen texted back immediately.

Can u come here? Like noon?

Lennon thought for a minute. It was nearly eleven. Jake didn't need her today, and Randi would be gone all day. Maybe Eric would too. She was dying to find out why Carmen had disappeared and to hear any new gossip about the girls in the house as well as those who were missing. She could use the rideshare app to travel to New London, and maybe Randi could pick her up on her way home.

Ok. See u in an hour. L

She would need to hurry, she realized, but taking a quick look around her room, she decided to spend a few precious minutes straightening up. She prided herself on keeping her surroundings neat. After everything Randi and Eric had done for her, it was the least she could do. She gathered the pile of sheets from the floor and carried it, along with the contents of the full hamper, and dumped everything in the super-capacity washing machine in the laundry room. She would run it as soon as she got home later today. She hurried back to her room and shoved her cosmetics from the vanity into her backpack. The time spent riding to New London could be spent applying some much-needed blush and maybe even a touch of mascara. After pulling on a pair of jeans and a sweater, she grabbed her phone, the book she had been reading, and her backpack. Taking a last look around the room, she noted it barely looked like anyone lived there. Neat and tidy!

She opened the rideshare app and was pleased to see that Suzy, driving a white Camry, would be out front in five minutes. Her luck was holding, she decided. She grabbed her parka, mittens, and Doc Martens from the hall closet, gave Hobie a quick snuggle, and kissed the top of his dear little gray head. She was lacing her boots when she heard a car pull up out front. No time to leave a note, but she would reach out to Randi after lunch to arrange for a ride home. She locked the door and pulled it shut behind her and hurried down the walkway. Time to find out what had happened to Carmen, look for her art supplies in the room that was still hers at least on paper, grab a bite to eat, and get out of there.

Her tiny room on the third floor of the residence on Caroline Street had been such a godsend when she'd first been sent to live there. It was a marked improvement over a couple of the foster homes, group homes, and especially her alcove at her aunt Kelly's. The plastic shower curtain nailed to the ceiling provided the only hint of privacy during the years she had stayed there. What a dump that had been. But now even the Caroline Street residence seemed sketchy, foreboding. She climbed into the backseat of a car smelling like wet dog and confirmed the address with Suzy. She was probably about Randi's age, fresh-faced and smiling. She turned back to Lennon.

"Woman goin' crazy on Caroline Street," she sang cheerfully. Noting Lennon's blank expression, she clarified. "It's a song title. Jimmy Buffett? Oh, to be so young," she added and pulled a U-turn and headed toward the highway. She started to hum softly, and Lennon closed her eyes, grateful she had not gone crazy. She needed to start spending more time with kids her own age, she decided. None of them would know that song either.

When I arrived home just after 5:00, the house was dark and empty. The minute I entered the kitchen from the back door, Hobie started to meow and wind his way around my legs. I turned on some lights and saw he was out of food and water.

"Poor fella," I said and set out to remedy the situation. "Where's Lennon? Why didn't she feed you?" A minute later, I hung my coat in the front hall closet and started toward Lennon's room. "Lennon," I called out. "All the lights are off, and your pal was starving." I stopped short outside her door. Even in the dim light, I could see the room was nearly empty. The bed had been stripped; no books were on the nightstand, no socks on the floor. Mystified, I peeked into the adjoining bathroom. The usual collection of cosmetics was gone from the counter. What the hell? When I saw the closet only contained a few items and several empty hangers, I realized Lennon had left and taken most of what she owned with her. I dug my phone out of my pocket and called her, but it went directly to voicemail, so I left a message.

"Lennon. It's Randi. I just got home, and most of your things are gone. I'm kind of concerned. Can you please call me and let me know you're okay?" I ended the call and sat on the edge of the bare mattress, trying to recall our last conversation. It was last night after dinner. I had asked if she wanted to come to the legal aid office with me, but Lennon had said she planned to sleep in and do some laundry since Jake didn't need her to help with the kids. Soon after, she had gone to her room, where she had probably spent time texting back and forth with Seth before reading half the night. But where was her book? And the other half of her wardrobe? I regretted not asking for Seth's phone number when I'd had a chance. I studied my phone again. Still no word from Lennon. I would send her a text in the off chance she was somewhere she couldn't talk freely. Like where? A movie theater? A church?

Lennon, please call me or let me know you're okay. A thumbs-up emoji would be fine. I'm getting worried. R

Hobie came into the room, looking well pleased with himself and licking his chops. Seeing me, he jumped onto my lap, made half a dozen biscuits, and fell sound asleep. I sat like that until Eric came home just before 9:00 p.m. He had called me earlier at work, letting me know he and John were heading to Newport to check on a sailboat someone had for sale. They planned to spend the afternoon and stop for dinner on the way home.

He walked in and took one look at me, knowing immediately something was wrong. I told him Lennon wasn't answering her phone.

"Half her clothes are gone, no makeup on the counter, and she stripped her bed. She's . . . gone." The tears I had been holding back for hours finally surfaced, and Eric sat with me, stroking my back while I sobbed into his shoulder. "Why would she leave us? Everything was going so well. I don't understand . . ."

"C'mon, Quinn. You've been sitting in here for hours. Let me make you something to eat. C'mon now. Cheesy scrambled eggs? How's that sound?"

I nodded and let him lead me toward the kitchen, Hobie following closely behind us with the hopes of a second dinner. After I had eaten a plate of eggs doused with ketchup, I realized how exhausted I was. I stripped down and slid into bed, glad I had put flannel sheets on that morning.

Eric noticed the full laundry basket in the corner of the room and told me he would bring it to the laundry area. A minute later, he returned looking concerned.

"What's up?" I asked him.

"You said you thought half of Lennon's clothes were missing, right?" I nodded, and he hurried on. "The washer is full of her clothes, but she never ran it. If she did leave, she left all her things behind."

I sat up, and the deep sadness I had been feeling turned into fear. She would not have left her clothes. Wherever she had gone, she clearly had planned to come back. So she either went out and got delayed or someone had taken her.

Eric read my mind. "I'll contact the OLPD. And the area hospitals," he added and went to grab his phone.

"Good. I'll check with the Point and see if Seth is working tonight," I called after him. "And the walk-in clinics too." We met to compare notes a short while later. There was nothing the police could do as Lennon had been missing less than a day. None of the hospitals or clinics had any record of her, and the Point was closed on Mondays. I sent texts to Dennis and Jen letting them know their witness had vanished, and I left a message for Chief Brody at the NLPD. Dennis called me just seconds later and promised to get the word out on Lennon. I heard a female voice in the background and recognized it immediately. It was Jen, and they were together somewhere at nearly 11:00 p.m., so my suspicions they were an item had been correct. If only all my instincts were as reliable.

Where was she? Who had taken Lennon?

CHAPTER 34

Neither of us got much sleep, so rather than continuing to toss and turn, I stumbled to the kitchen to make a pot of coffee just before 5:00 a.m. Eric joined me, and we sat at the island in silence watching the sun rise. After a while, we moved into the family room and turned on the news, flipping back and forth between networks. The morning dragged on until my phone buzzed with an incoming call shortly after 8:00. I answered without even looking to see who was calling.

"Hello?" I all but shouted.

"Ms. Quinn, it's Ed Brody here in New London. I understand you have a young woman gone missing."

"Yes, Ed. She's the daughter of an old friend and a witness in the upcoming Myers trial. Do you have any news for me?"

"Well, it appears we got lucky. I put her name out on the scanner for patrol to be on the lookout, and I recalled you said she was living on Caroline Street."

"Yes. The corner of Caroline and Alden. Did someone spot her?"

"Well, not today, but a rideshare driver must have been monitoring the traffic because she called in to say she picked up a young woman matching the description out your way yesterday late morning. And dropped her off at the home on Caroline."

I felt a sense of short-lived relief turn to dread as I imagined the unsavory characters who may have been waiting for her there.

"Ed, I'm really concerned about her welfare. Can you send a patrol car out to check and see if—"

"Already done," he responded quickly. "Two of my officers arrived there at 7:30. They knocked and rang the bell, but there was no answer. One of them went around the back, but no sign of anyone inside."

"That makes no sense," I told him. "By my count, there are six or seven young women living there as well as the resident supervisor, a man named, um . . . Alan Newton. This time in the morning, someone's got to be home."

The chief's voice took on an even more serious tone. "Are you fairly certain Miss Gallagher would not willingly remain in the house of her own accord?" he asked.

"I can tell you with one hundred percent certainty she would never stay there unless she was being held against her will. Someone must have tricked her to get her there yesterday, and I'll put on money on her roommate, Carmen." My voice cracked a bit as I imagined Lennon restrained, scared, and possibly hurt.

"Your word is all I need, Miranda. We'll review the situation, and I'll be in touch when I know more," he said and ended the call. I turned to see Eric dressed and ready to go.

"Get dressed," he said. "Let's go find our girl."

By the time we turned onto Caroline Street forty minutes later, the whole neighborhood had erupted. A half dozen squad cars, ambulances, and other emergency vehicles blocked the street, and a restless crowd of curious onlookers spilled over onto neighboring yards. As we inched closer, a uniformed officer waved Eric away. "Turn around, sir," he called out. "This here's a crime scene."

"Our daughter is being held in there against her will, Officer. We need to get to her," Eric told him.

The officer shook his head. "I'm sorry, sir. Emergency personnel only. You need to turn around. I'm sure your daughter will contact you shortly."

Eric turned to me, looking more panicked than I had ever seen him. "Call the chief, babe."

I did and listened as the call went directly to voicemail. I felt so helpless, not to mention scared shitless. I knew there was no point in leaving a message. He was up to his eyeballs in an emerging hostage situation. The officer rapped his knuckles on the driver's side window and once again told Eric to turn around and leave the area. I had a sudden thought and decided to act on it.

"Don't worry," I told Eric as I unbuckled my seat belt and opened the door of the truck. "I love you," I said and dashed down the street. I heard him call out to me and the officer shouting for someone to stop me. But everyone's attention was drawn elsewhere, and I managed to get within fifty or so feet of the crowd of first responders clustered in front of the house. I pulled the hood of my jacket over my head and tried to keep a low profile while I searched for the chief. I spotted him and started to make my way toward him when a beefy uniformed patrolman stopped me in my tracks. I had been about to duck under the yellow crime scene tape marking the outer perimeter.

"This is a restricted area, ma'am," he said. "You can't be here. You need to—" Before he could finish, I started to holler for the chief.

"Ed," I called out. "Chief Brody!" His head whipped around, and when he saw me, he waved me through.

"It's okay, Officer Kearns. She's with me."

I wriggled myself past the patrolman and rushed to Ed's side.

"What's happening?" I begged. "I saw the ambulances, and I . . ." I was trying to slow my breathing, but the panic I was feeling nearly doubled me over. "Tell me, please."

Ed's words were clipped, but his eyes were kind and full of compassion. "Shortly before 0900 hours, my squad attempted to gain entry to the home. Repeated requests to come out with hands raised were ignored and my guys were in the process of breaking down the door when Newton appeared in the doorway. He was pointing a gun at a young woman who appeared to be intoxicated or drugged. He told our officers he would kill her if they came any closer and said he had six more residents tied up in the basement. He closed the door and . . ."

The panic I was feeling left me weak, almost unable to speak. But I managed to get out my only question. "The woman. Was it Lennon?" He nodded sadly, and I sagged against him. Lennon had been drugged and was being held at gunpoint. Literally, the worst-case scenario. My phone was buzzing in my pocket. I looked at the screen. Eric!

"Jesus, Quinn. You had me scared shitless. Are you okay? Have you found Lennon?" he asked, sounding nearly as scared as I was feeling. I turned away from Ed and shared what I knew. His breathing was ragged as he peppered me with questions, none of which I had answers to. I decided to keep him on the open line as I tried to find out more.

"Is there a hostage negotiator on-site?" I asked. At Ed's nod, I continued. "What does Newton want? Is he willing to let any of the girls go?"

Ed shook his head, looking really pissed off. "The kid's a total amateur. He's got no clue what he's dealing with here. We have snipers waiting to take him out, but he's at least clever enough to hide behind his hostages. They can't get a clear shot."

"They'd kill him?" I asked, and the chief nodded vehemently.

"Of course," he replied. "Think of the optics. Seven young women housed in a state facility run by an approved agency held at gunpoint by a deranged employee. The governor wants this taken care of pronto."

There was a loud commotion on the porch of the big house. I looked up and almost couldn't believe my eyes. A man I recognized as Alan Newton was being dragged from the house by several young women. He was not struggling, at least in part due to the gun pointed at his head. A gun yielded by none other than Lennon Gallagher. Several officers were shouting at her to put down the weapon, and she did, holding up her hands for all to see.

"There are no bullets," she called out. "The gun isn't loaded, dumbass," she added, primarily for Alan's benefit. His look of fear changed to one of confusion.

"But Jay gave it to me in case anyone got out of hand," he complained. He was about to continue when he was pulled out of reach of the girls, handcuffed, and read his Miranda rights. The emergency medical technicians swarmed the porch, and though I could no longer hear anything being said, it was obvious they were getting vitals on the freed hostages. Lennon was listening to one of them and nodding when she looked out at the crowd, searching for something or someone. She caught sight of me, and her face lit up. She waved to me, beaming, grateful someone had shown up for her. It didn't appear she had been drugged, but even from a distance I could see she looked drawn, exhausted. I hoped it wouldn't be long before we could take her home for rest, food, and kitty snuggles.

Nearly two hours later, we arrived home with Lennon firmly in tow. After being examined by the medics on the scene and being told she was good to go, she had been questioned at length by a couple of plain-clothed detectives at the station. As her attorney, I sat beside her, nodding when I felt the question being asked was one she could answer. We left feeling relieved Alan would remain behind bars for the time being. During the drive, Lennon told us how she had received a text she had thought was from Carmen, but after she arrived at her former residence, she had been confronted by Alan, who had pointed a gun at her head. He had forced her to the basement, where she found Carmen and five more girls from the house. They were huddled against the moldy cement walls, spread around the space, probably to keep them from whispering and brainstorming ways to escape. Alan had restrained each of them, and Lennon could make out their muffled cries from behind the duct tape covering their mouths. Lennon swung around in an effort to wrestle the gun away from Alan, but he pushed her away, and she fell to the floor. He quickly approached her and tied her hands behind her back.

"Sit still and be quiet," Alan warned, but Lennon could see he was nearly as frightened as his captives. She pulled herself into a sitting position before studying her environment more closely. There was an exit door, but even in the gloomy light of the basement, she could see the new-looking locks would prevent a quick escape. The windows were not only small and high up on the walls, but most were boarded over with plywood. The only light in the space came from a solitary bulb dangling from the ceiling. The stairs leading to the main floor were narrow and poorly lit.

She looked up to see Alan approaching with a bottle of water in his outstretched hand. He tried to force her to drink it, but suspecting it contained drugs meant to keep her compliant, she took a big swallow, and as soon as he turned away, she spat most of it out. Whatever she had consumed left her drowsy, and she half dozed until the sound of fire engines and ambulances woke her. Seconds after the police pounded on the front door, Alan grabbed her and dragged her up the stairs. With a gun pointed at her head, he opened the door enough for them to be warned to back off. Knowing Alan expected her to be highly incapacitated by now, she slumped against him, studying the gun he was brandishing. After slamming the door, they headed back to the staircase. Halfway down, she made her move. Turning toward him and leaning in close, she pursed her lips into what she hoped was a sexy grin.

"Hey baby," she whispered, and he reacted as she hoped he would. Despite the tense, potentially deadly situation he was in, he shoved the gun into his waistband and lunged for her. Lennon grabbed the gun and kicked him, watching him tumble down the last few steps and land in a heap on the floor.

She blushed furiously as she described her attempts at seduction, and I congratulated her on her bravery. "You did what you needed to do, sweetheart. You survived," I told her and watched as tears streamed down her dirt-smeared cheeks.

We returned home, and while Lennon took a shower, Eric made sandwiches and I read over the emails and calls I had missed. There were several from Dennis, so I called him first. He answered right away, sounding breathless.

"We found them," he said. "The girls. We found them." I must have screamed really loudly because seconds later a puzzled Eric and a dripping, towel-clad Lennon joined me.

"Putting you on speaker," I told Dennis. "Eric and Lennon are here. Tell us. Who was found? Everyone? How did this happen?"

"Myers finally cracked," he said. "He gave us the name of his contact. Some thug who's been trolling the coastline for years. Name's Augustus Jones."

"Did you find Tyler?" Lennon asked, her eyes wild with excitement and fear.

"Yes, Lennon," said Dennis. "Allison Tyler was one of the girls we identified. She's had a rough time of it, but it looks like she's gonna be fine." After Lennon finished shrieking, he added, "Say, Miranda, maybe you can take me off speaker, okay?"

"Of course," I told him, and seconds later it was just the two of us. "Talk to me, Dennis. What are we dealing with here?"

He told me Jones had been under surveillance since yesterday and several hours earlier had been followed to a high-priced condo complex in White Plains, New York, where he let himself into a unit on the third floor. Seconds later, a young woman exited the unit screaming that she was being held against her will. The plainclothes detectives rushed to her aid and apprehended Jones as he ran into the hallway to grab the girl. A search of the unit was conducted by uniformed officers from the local precinct, and two more young women were found, along with a hefty amount of drug paraphernalia. When I asked about the identities of the women, he told me that in addition to Tyler, Chloe Anderson and Riley Jackson had been identified.

I felt relief tinged with sadness; while it was wonderful three young women were now safe, there were many others still unaccounted for.

"Where are they now?" I asked, and Dennis told me they were being held overnight in New York, undergoing physical exams, and answering questions about their captors.

"They'll probably be released in the morning, barring any unforeseen circumstances, and brought to Yale New Haven Hospital for further treatment."

I knew the drill, that "treatment" was code for detox. They had been held long enough to have developed drug habits, not to mention the psychological effects of being kidnapped and forced to have sex with strangers. Dennis promised to keep me in the loop, and I went to find Eric and Lennon to tell them what I'd just learned.

CHAPTER 35

While we waited to hear any updates on the three young women, I decided to go and see my dad. We barely talked anymore, at least that was how it had felt to me. Ignoring Eric's claim I was "finding mysteries everywhere," I called and invited myself over for a visit. I knocked once before letting myself in. "Hey, guys, it's Randi," I called out, glancing around the familiar open concept kitchen/family room with stainless appliances, sleek quartz countertops, and glass-front cabinets. Nothing like the kitchen in the home I had grown up in with its scuffed linoleum floors and avocado fridge.

I watched as my dad entered the room. Bathrobe tied tightly around his spare frame, he peered at me from behind the spacious breakfast bar. "You're early," he said. "Coffee?"

I set my bag on the floor, swung myself into one of the padded leather barstools, and turned to face him. "Yes to coffee. And as far as being early, every time I see you lately, you're rushing off to do this or that. Always so busy. I figured if I wanted to have a conversation, I would show up early and make you talk to me." My voice caught on the last words, and I forced myself not to cry. Pop didn't make eye contact with me as he scooped coffee into the machine.

"Nothing? Seriously, old man? What's going on?"

Pop pressed a button, and the coffeemaker came to life, resulting in the hiss and slightly bitter aroma of freshly brewed coffee. He finally faced me, looking sad and deflated . . . and possibly scared? My dad was scared? Of what? Had Sal lied to me when she said he wasn't sick? Maybe she was sick? There'd been a health scare a couple of years back with her, but I'd thought everything had been resolved. Maybe . . .

"It's the move, my girl," he said, and my whole body froze. How on earth had he heard about the move? The one that was no longer going to happen?

"It was a false alarm, Pop. The guy got arrested for embezzlement and a whole boatload of other charges. That's why I never told you about London. It was never actually a done deal." I stopped as my father stared at me, open-mouthed.

"Randi, what the hell are you jabbering on about? Who said anything about London? We're moving south, to Florida. Why would we go to London, of all places?" he asked.

Relief it wasn't his health was quickly replaced with shock. I had never lived more than an hour away from this man. One of the main reasons I had resisted moving to London was standing right in front of me. Pop in Florida?

"You're moving to Florida? When were you going to tell me?"

"I thought you knew," he said sheepishly. "Like, maybe your sister told you. So what's the deal with London? Are you moving there?"

"No. Wait, are you telling me Jules knew? You told her before you told me? I can't believe you."

He threw up his hands in disgust before grabbing two mugs and filling them each with coffee. "We need to talk about this," he said evenly. "Sounds like we have a failure to communicate," he added, forcing a grin. I loved trading movie quotes as much as the next gal, but I was not in the mood today.

"As much as I appreciate the cinematic reference, *Cool Hand Luke*, I'm more interested in hearing about Florida." I took a long bracing sip, then motioned to him. "Tell me what's going on, would you?" I asked. So he did.

The cold weather had been getting to them, he admitted. Sally's health issues a couple of years ago had gotten them thinking she could get more exercise if they lived in a warmer climate. A number of their friends had moved south recently, and it was beginning to feel as if they should give it a try. "We love the beach, and we can go out walking every day year-round," he said.

"I understand," I told him. "I really do. But what about . . . us?"

He frowned, shaking his head. "You kids are all grown up and have your own lives," he said, "and hell, you were ready to move to London, which basically proves my point. And before you bring up the grandkids, we'll visit a couple times a year, and if Jake and Meg need a babysitter, we can head back up here and they can take off. Or they can bring the kids to us and we'll take 'em to Disney World or what have you. But we have our own lives to live too. It took us years to find each other, Sal and me. We deserve to have this time together, and I don't want to leave this world with a single regret." Pop watched me closely for my reaction.

I shrugged and hopped up from my stool, crossing around the island to embrace my dad. My wonderful, amazing dad. "I want you to live your best life, Pop," I told him as he wrapped his arms around me. We stood eye to eye, but to me? He had always seemed larger than life. I snuffled into the shoulder of his bathrobe. "I love you," I told him and started to cry when he responded as I'd known he would.

"I love you more, my girl."

We stood in silence for another moment or two before Sally came breezing into the room, clutching a box of tissues. Despite a runny nose, she was her usual cheerful self.

"Good morning, Randi," she called out. "Can I get you a muffin or some fruit?"

Wiping away happy tears, I assured her I was fine and splashed more coffee into my cup.

"Well, cholesterol be damned. I'm making scrambled eggs. Who's with me?" Pop asked.

"Sounds good," I agreed, and Sally began bustling about the kitchen, grabbing plates and placemats. I watched the two of them with a lump in my throat.

My folks are moving to Florida, I thought. Look out, Sunshine State!

CHAPTER 36

Thanksgiving Day started off with a bang . . . literally. There was a multi-car pileup on I-95 caused by a freak ice storm at dawn. So much for one of the busiest travel days of the year. Surface streets were clogged and fender-benders were reported by the dozens. Eric, Lennon, and I had made pancakes earlier and had a roaring fire going, so we were snug and comfortable. Even the promise of a turkey dinner with all the requisite sides at my brother Jake's house couldn't motivate me to leave the house. At least that's what I had told Meg when I called after my first cup of coffee. I heard myself promise if the weather conditions improved during the day, I would circle back with her.

Tracey called to report one of the twins had been in one of those fender-benders. Kind of. Flynn had been walking to the mini-mart to pick up a pint of heavy cream for her when two cars had crashed into each other, barely missing him. The near impact had caused him to slip on the icy parking lot, and he'd sprained his wrist and whacked his knee. He had limped back home after going inside and buying the cream, and Dale was now driving him to the emergency clinic in town.

"Are you sure they're open?" I asked, and she mumbled something about why I thought Dale, being a guy, would have called first to check.

"It's like asking for directions," she said. "You can't see me right now, but I'm literally throwing my hands up in surrender. His mother is expecting us, and the only thing I was asked to provide for the Ryan feast was a bowl of freaking whipped cream. But as far as I know, it's still in Flynn's backpack, which is on its way to the clinic, and if they're not open, Dale says he's gonna drive him to New London. To the emergency room. Today. In an ice storm. On Thanksgiving. He thinks Chase and I should go to his mom's house without them. And without the whipped cream. 'No way, Jose,' I told him. Not happening. So Chase went back to bed, and I'm sitting here with my two new best friends." She was now slurring her words.

"Ben and Jerry?" I asked but was sure it was more likely to be Martini & Rossi. Tracey thoroughly enjoyed her martinis from time to time. "Gotta go, T," I told her. "Promise me you won't drive anywhere and keep me posted about Flynn. I love that kid." I waited until she wished me a 'Happy Shanksgiving" and ended the call. I sent a quick text to Dale, asking about Flynn and letting him know his wife was feeling no pain and would be waiting for him at home. He sent back a smiley-face emoji, which seemed like an odd response, but honestly? The holidays always bring out the weird in people.

Pop called to say he and Sal would not be going to Jake's either. Sal's cold had gotten worse, and it was probably best to skip a large gathering.

"It looks like it's all melting now," I said, "but the roads are still going to be a mess."

"Well, you stay safe, my girl," he said.

"Love to Sal," I told him. At least he wasn't being a total grouch now that the secrets we had been keeping were out in the open. No more secrets, I vowed. It was close to the end of the year. New year, time for a fresh start!

Eric was tuned to the Weather Channel, and I perched on the chair next to him.

"What do you think?" he asked me.

"About?"

"Going to Jake and Meg's for dinner. Should we head over there?"

Hmmm . . . I had been looking forward to an afternoon by the fire with a book and this darling man and maybe a few hands of poker with the resident card shark who lived down the hall. I shrugged. Maybe?

"This might sway your opinion," said Eric. "Remember we were talking about how we were out of just about everything and you said, 'It's the day before Turkey Day and the stores will be mobbed, and we'll be at Meg's on Thursday and you know how much she always makes, and she'll send us home with leftovers so we wouldn't need to shop till next week.' Remember that?"

Oh yeah. It was settled. I looked at the clock on the end table. They had planned to sit down to eat at 1:00. "We should be ready to leave in a half hour. I'll call Meg; you tell Lennon."

I was toweling off after the world's fastest shower when I heard my phone buzzing. It was a text from Dennis.

Time to give thanks. D

Say what now? I wiped the steam off the mirror over the sink and studied my hair. A messy bun would have to do. I applied moisturizer, under eye concealer, and a dash of blush and studied the results. Ack! I should schedule a haircut and a facial next week. Maybe a mani/pedi too. And Lennon could join me. Maybe Tracey too. Girl's day at the spa!

I headed into my closet to find something warm to wear when I saw my phone still on the nightstand. Another text from Dennis. Seriously?

Pull up some extra chairs. D

Chairs for unexpected guests? I decided to call him, figuring this could go on forever and I was running out of time. He answered on the first ring.

"Miranda, I need to see you," he said by way of a greeting.

"You know it's Thanksgiving, right?" I asked.

"Can I swing by in about an hour?" This being Dennis, I figured it had to be important, something about the case.

"We'll be at my brother's house," I told him. "I'll text you the address."

"See you in an hour," he replied and ended the call. I texted Jake's address, then grabbed a pair of gray slacks and a light blue cashmere V-neck and dressed quickly. I ran to the kitchen, where Eric was waiting, as was Lennon, ready and raring to go. She had on a burgundy sweater and a pair of jeans with Tracey's ankle boots, and she handed me my coat before pulling on her parka.

We made our way out to the truck, and as I buckled myself in, I remembered. "I got a couple of weird texts from Dennis," I said. "He wants to meet me at Jake's. Says he needs to talk."

Eric shrugged. "Knowing Meg, she'll have enough to feed an army. Poor guy's probably alone. You should ask him to stay for dinner." I nodded in agreement.

It was the usual bedlam at Jake and Meg's, thanks to a couple of siblings who had significantly more energy than could be expended on a day inside. Lennon got them busy coloring, and after I explained the situation to Meg, an extra chair had been added for Dennis.

A couple of minutes later, we heard a car pulling into the driveway, followed by doors opening and closing.

"He's here," said Meg, and we began the process of transporting all the food into the dining room. Jake went to the door and let out a long, low whistle.

"What the hell?" he said and opened the door. I watched as Dennis came trooping in, carefully wiping his feet on the mat. He was followed closely by a trio of young women who looked, well, shell-shocked. They stood there awkwardly, looking cold and scared. Then I recognized one of them. It was Riley Jackson, which could only mean the others were Chloe and . . .

I headed toward Dennis, but Lennon came barreling past me and flung herself into the open arms of the tallest of the three girls. "Tyler, you're back," she cried, and the two girls hugged and jumped up and down. Meg, Jake, and Eric stood by as I greeted Riley. I was less effusive in my approach and received a warm smile. Dennis gestured to the third girl as he introduced us.

"Chloe, this is Ms. Quinn, the lawyer I told you about. She's going to help get all of you settled over the next few weeks."

The round-cheeked girl brushed her hair out of her eyes and smiled shyly.

"I'm so glad to finally meet you," I told her. "You've been through quite an ordeal."

"Yes, ma'am," she murmured. "It's nice to meet you." I shook the hand she extended. Small and ice cold. None of the girls were dressed appropriately for the weather, and all three looked like they hadn't eaten in days. My sister-in-law came to the rescue. Leave it to Meg, I thought proudly.

"Come in," she told them. "We've got plenty of turkey and stuffing, and well, just about anything you want. How does that sound?" All three nodded happily. "Go to my closet," she instructed Lennon. "Grab three hoodies and three pairs of sweats." She turned to the girls. "Follow her and get rid of these damp clothes. Then c'mon back and we'll eat." Lennon led the way, and the girls disappeared up the stairs, Clem trailing along behind them.

Eric and Jake went into the kitchen with Meg to get plates ready for the newest arrivals, and by unspoken agreement

Dennis and I settled ourselves in the den. Dennis looked haggard, totally exhausted, but happy as well. Dinner might be a bit delayed, and that was fine by me. I was on the edge of my seat while I waited for him to fill me in.

CHAPTER 37

"They asked me to escort the girls back to New London following their release from Yale New Haven Hospital. I can't reveal the exact nature of their injuries, but I'm sure you can imagine they were scared, dehydrated, and they complained of fatigue and vaginal tears and bruising," said Dennis. "The findings were consistent with repeated forced contact of a sexual nature."

I shook my head sadly. "What about drugs? What kind of drugs were they given?"

Dennis shook his head in disgust. "Just what you would expect. Signs of intravenous drug use, and blood and urine samples were positive for heroin and one of the girls' labs showed traces of a synthetic opioid, probably fentanyl. Two of the girls were already showing signs of withdrawal when they were admitted. Detox procedures were followed, and all three responded well to treatment this past week." He looked at me then, his eyes bloodshot and his normally dark complexion almost gray. I squeezed his hand and thanked him for bringing the girls here.

I knew it was a common practice to get trafficked victims hooked as quickly as possible, to make them compliant and dependent on their captors. This was bad, but it could have been even worse. Then a thought came to me.

"Have any more girls been found?" I asked. "What about . . . ?"

Dennis shook his head. "No sign of the others," he confirmed. "Chloe told me she had been watching for her friend Lyndsey Wilson ever since she was brought to the city. The girls have been moved around quite a bit. Every few days apparently." He shook his head, angered by what he had seen. "Despite all they have experienced, they are communicating openly with us, and Jen plans to keep them safe and under police protection. They'll need to testify against—"

We were interrupted by the sounds of four teenage girls approaching. I knew they would require counseling and a good amount of support to process all they had gone through, and I would make certain whatever resources they needed would be made available. But for today, I was grateful to see them laughing together and teasing each other. Riley was carrying Clem piggyback style as they took their seats at the re-set table. Soon everyone was enjoying heaping plates of turkey and every side you could imagine. I was still too keyed up to sit still and eat, so I busied myself in the kitchen arranging three kinds of pies as well as a half gallon of Friendly's vanilla ice cream and a can of whipped topping. I briefly considered texting Tracey to see if Flynn was home or if they had gone to her in-laws but decided we had already more than enough moving parts under this roof.

I returned to the dining room and caught the tail end of what had to be a description of Seth by a giddy Lennon, which resulted in shouts of "you go, girl" and "get some" from the other girls. Clem picked up on it as well and started zigzagging around the room, mimicking what she had just heard. Her little brother joined her, and the two of them were quickly singing "go girl" and "get some" at the top of their lungs. It was hard not to laugh when little kids parroted suggestive phrases with no idea what they meant. I glanced over at Lennon and earned an eye-roll and a big smile. You go, girl, I thought. Get some, but only if you really want to, and if you do, be sure to use protection. I returned a smile to Eric, thinking how much I loved my family. Dennis had been reading a text when he stood and beckoned me to follow him.

We went back to the den, and I waited while he scrolled though messages on his phone. Finally, he gave me his full attention.

"We got him," he said with more enthusiasm than I'd ever seen from him. My eyes widened as I considered what he had meant. Unable to wait for me to ask, he rushed on. "Gus, the guy who's been moving girls around like chess pieces? He finally gave us a name. You're not going to believe who's been pulling all the strings."

"Tell me," I begged. "Who is it?"

"None other than Edward C. Westerhaus, more commonly known as Dr. Chris, the highest paid radio host in the country," he said, not even trying to hide a wide smile of satisfaction.

I stared in horror at Dennis, stunned into silence at this shocking news. I wanted to demand he take it back, tell me it was some kind of sick joke, that it was someone else, not my Chris. My friend. I wanted to scream, to cry, but mostly I wanted to go back in time and never have to hear this horrible, overwhelming news. But I was too numb, paralyzed. How could this possibly be true? I forced words out, but it sounded nothing like me.

"Was he taken into custody?" I asked, haunted by the image of this man I had cared for in handcuffs, behind bars.

Dennis shook his head. "He must have been tipped off," he admitted. "Warrants were to be served at his Manhattan penthouse as well as his estate in Long Island, but no sign of him or his wife, um . . ."

"Susan," I supplied. "His recently renovated estate," I clarified.

Dennis studied me closely. "I'm just putting two and two together. You worked at Sterling a few years back. Did you know the doctor well?" That was the million-dollar question, I thought sadly.

"I thought I did," I admitted, "but I guess not." I brushed away the angry tears threatening to fall. "So are you telling me he was involved in the abductions?" I asked, my mind racing as I tried to connect the dots. Had I inadvertently warned him when I told him of the ongoing investigation?

"Yes, he was. Jen did a little more digging and discovered the holding company EWE, LLC is owned by Mr. Westerhaus. Edward Westerhaus Enterprises: E-W-E. According to her sources at the Department of Justice, Dr. Chris and two of his associates were each charged with a dozen counts of conspiracy to coerce and entice to travel for the purpose of illegal sexual activity. He was running an interstate prostitution network that included multiple brothels in Connecticut, Manhattan, Brooklyn, and White Plains as well as one in Albany. They've allegedly been operational since July 2020."

"A dozen counts?" I asked. "Does that mean they located more girls?"

Dennis nodded. "Yes, but none from your list. There were two or three women working at each of the sites I mentioned, but other than our three, none were from Connecticut."

I shook my head in amazement. "What happens next?" I asked. "More arrests?"

"Yes, they're securing warrants as we speak. The sex buyers identified so far include professional athletes, politicians, and government contractors with sky-high security clearances, and Westerhaus was at the center of it all. He did his best to keep his hands clean, leaving it to his associates to hire guys like Gus, Jordan, and others, collecting girls like they were subway tokens and putting them to work in private homes and luxury condos. And it looks like he was blackmailing some of his clients as well."

And the hits just kept on coming, I thought.

"I might have warned him," I said softly. Dennis looked surprised and leaned toward me.

"What are you saying? You told him?" His tone was gentle, but his dark eyes were watching me closely.

I tried to recall my last conversation with Chris and nodded slowly.

"I mentioned that there was an ongoing investigation about missing girls . . ."

"When was this?" Dennis asked, and I closed my eyes, trying to remember. We had spoken a couple times since, but that particular conversation was a while ago.

"It's been a month, maybe five weeks," I admitted.

Dennis was frowning as he texted a message. Probably to Jen, informing her I had screwed up big-time. He read the response and nodded.

"Westerhaus appeared at a shareholder's meeting for Sterling Broadcasting three nights ago," he told me. "So it's unlikely that what you told him sent him running."

I let out a sigh, relieved my careless words probably hadn't impacted the case.

"What now?" I asked.

"This will be all over the news tomorrow," Dennis promised. "I should probably thank your family for welcoming us into their home today. I need to get the girls back to New London. Jen has arranged temporary lodging for them until we can figure next steps."

I followed him toward the dining room, drawn by the sounds of laughter. But I wasn't ready for that, not yet. Eric looked over at me, and I shook my head sadly before I turned away.

I checked my phone and saw I already had voicemail messages from several of my former Sterling colleagues. "Damn it," I mumbled before realizing my niece Clem was crouched nearby.

"Damn it," she started to sing. "Get some, damn it."

"Sorry," I mouthed to Meg as I rejoined the party.

"Pumpkin, pecan, or apple?" Jake asked me as he dug into the pies, cutting slices for everyone.

"Yes, please," I told him, holding out my plate. It wouldn't be Thanksgiving without stuffing yourself full of pie, I reminded myself. And giving thanks for all the blessings and special people in your life. And praying that degenerate criminals get their own just deserts. Having missed the main course, I was studying my plate, thin-ish wedges of all three pies topped with ice cream, when Jake's phone rang.

"Who has a house phone anymore?" I asked Eric as I pushed the plate aside, certain I wouldn't be able to swallow a single bite. He had a mouthful of pumpkin pie and shrugged in response. Jake came back from the kitchen, his face etched in concern.

"What is it?" I asked him, and he shook his head, looking dazed.

"That was Julie," he said. "Mom's in the hospital."

CHAPTER 38

Minutes later, we were racing north on I-95, heading to the regional hospital serving several of the shore communities. Eric drove, and I sat wedged into the front between him and my brother. Lennon had insisted on joining us at the last minute and was sprawled across the backseat. Trying to quash any thoughts of the deceitful, disgusting scumbag I'd considered my friend, my focus was on my stepmother. I peppered my brother with questions, as I still didn't understand what we would be facing upon arrival.

"Did Jules say they brought her in an ambulance? Is it her heart?" I pressed, and Jake shrugged again.

"I told you, Ran, it was a bad connection, and Jules was crying and—" he began.

"Like crying, crying?" I asked. "More upset or more scared?"

In response, Jake and Eric shared a look, and by unspoken agreement, Eric took the lead.

"He's already told you what he heard, babe. 'Hospital, Mom, and soup.' That's all we know, so let's not panic until we know more, okay? We'll be there in less than five minutes."

I mulled over what little I knew and checked my phone again. I had texted Pop as we were leaving, letting him know we were on our way. No response. I could feel my heart pounding as we pulled in and parked in the last emergency room parking space. The four of us raced into the small lobby, and I caught sight of a familiar face almost immediately.

"Sally," I cried out and hurried toward her. She was sitting in the corner, sipping a cup of hot tea and thumbing through a tattered issue of *Woman's Day* magazine. She looked up in surprise as she saw me approaching, and her eyes widened even further when she caught sight of her son.

"What on earth?" she asked as I hugged her tightly. "What are the two of you doing here?" Jake and I stared at her as she coughed into a tissue.

"Jules said you were rushed to the hospital," Jake said.

"That's silly," she said. "I'm fine. Just a simple cold."

That's when it hit me. "It's Pop. What happened to Pop?" I begged.

"I'm right here," said Pop. "Why are you here, and what's with all the yelling?"

I stared at him in amazement before I hugged him close to me.

"We're waiting on Julie," Sally told us. She glanced at an incoming text and smiled up at us, slipping her phone into her pocket. "It's from Brad," she said with a smile. "She's doing fine. They'll be down in a bit. A minor accident," Sally told me. "Don't look so worried."

She turned to Pop. "We need to go eat something, Dez. Anyone else want to join us?"

We made our way toward the nearly empty cafeteria. Pop and Sally snared the last two turkey dinner specials which, in my near starving state, looked amazing. Lennon and Jake each got chocolate pudding, Eric ordered a coffee, and pulling up the rear, I surveyed my choices before accepting a tightly wrapped egg salad sandwich from the counter and grabbing the last dessert: lime freaking Jell-O.

We took over a large table in the center of the room, talking and catching up on what had been quite a momentous holiday. It turned out the inciting incident bringing us all here was a commonplace slip and fall.

It all started when Julie and Brad arranged to bring takeout to Pop and Sally's earlier today. The chicken soup they had picked up from Katz's Deli had leaked from the container, and Jules had slipped in the puddle formed on the lobby floor at the condo complex. Brad had buzzed up to Sally, and she and Pop had come rushing down. Her fall had caused her to smack her head on the console table and twist her ankle. Not wanting to wait for an ambulance, they carried Jules out to Pop's Jeep, and the four of them had been here at the hospital all afternoon. The emergency room doctor had given Jules a mild sedative for the pain, and somehow, she had butt-dialed her brother, speaking nonsense to him as the meds took effect.

I wrapped up half of my uneaten sandwich and started to put my Jell-O back on the tray. Eric grabbed it from me and all but licked the dish clean, scraping the tiny green remnants with an intensity that frankly troubled me.

"There's always room for Jell-O," he said with a goofy grin on his face, and for a split second I could plainly see a very young Eric enjoying the same treat.

"You have green teeth," I told him and kissed the top of his head before dumping my trash in the receptacle. Coffee, I thought, but the glass partition had gone up and the staff had left. Clearly, there would be no further delicacies served here today. *Crap.*

Eric appeared by my side and offered his coffee to me. I thanked him gratefully and swigged down the cold remains from his gigantic Styrofoam cup. If the caffeine didn't hit my bloodstream stat, I would be the next one on the floor.

"Jules," Sally called out, and we turned to see our sister being pushed toward us in a wheelchair. She looked sleepy but greeted us happily. She was higher than a kite.

"Hello, hello. Did you all come out today on account of little old me? My brother, Jake . . . I love you, man. And, Randi, my big sister. You're so cool, and I love you to pieces. And Eric, you stud muffin. Hi, Eric," she called out, smiling adoringly and wiggling her fingers in a flirty wave. "And you," she said, sizing up Lennon, "I have no clue who you are. Do you suppose they have any Jell-O around here?"

"Looks like the place is closed, honey," Brad told her. "Remember what we said about using our inside voices, okay? Let's get you home and tuck you into bed." He gestured to our parents, who were standing nearby taking it all in. "Let's take her home, okay?"

"Sure thing," agreed Pop. "You ready, Sal?" After a flurry of quick hugs and goodbyes, the four of them made their way toward the exit, Jules singing something nonsensical, but at least it was in her inside voice.

Eric and Lennon went to retrieve the truck, leaving my brother and I behind. I turned to him, a question burning in my mind.

"Did we miss out on a perfect opportunity to blackmail our sister?" I asked. "Like getting her to admit to an obsession with K-pop or having a girl crush on Kate McKinnon?"

Jake nodded slowly. "Yeah, I believe we did," he said with a grin. "Go Jules."

"Get some," I murmured as we walked out to the truck and my waiting stud muffin.

It was a few hours later, after Eric and I had talked, both of us struggling to unpack all we had learned about the monster we had admired and considered our friend, when I allowed myself to cry. Great, gasping ugly tears of outrage, sadness, and disgust. I knew Chris was considered innocent until proven guilty, but I also knew innocent people didn't run and hide. I hoped he was found, and soon, because with resources and connections like his, he could be halfway around the world by now. *Bastard.*

CHAPTER 39

"I'm sorry you weren't able to meet Cruella," I told Lennon as we waited for state's attorney Rick Cooper to join us in his office. I was referring to the haughty administrative assistant with a white streak through her black bob, who generally served as a sentry blocking admission inside these hallowed halls. Lennon nodded absently. "It will be fine, you'll see. You're helping to build a stronger case against these lowlifes. You have nothing to worry about." I knew Rick could be a real hard-ass at times, having been on the receiving end of his dogged determination and innate belief he was the smartest person in the room more than once. But surely, he would go easy on Lennon.

"Speak of the devil," Lennon whispered to me with a wink as Rick came striding in with a gait more suited to a much taller man. His too-large-for-his-face dark-rimmed glasses did nothing to hide eyes nearly sparkling with excitement. I felt relieved, almost joyful myself. A happy Rick, this close to trial, was a confident Rick.

"Ladies, I'm so sorry I got held up. I hope you've not been waiting too long. Miranda, so good to see you. It's been too long," he said, grasping my hand in his. Turning to Lennon, he introduced himself. "I am Richard Cooper, state's attorney for the New London District. And you must be Lennon Gallagher. It is a pleasure to meet you. I appreciate your coming in today."

Don't call him Rick, I silently begged Lennon. It was how I had been referring to him, but it wasn't appro—

"Good morning, sir. Thank you for having us," Lennon responded smoothly. This young woman never failed to surprise me.

"Yes, well. Let's get started, shall we? We have a lot to cover before the trial. The court date is set for this Tuesday, December 4th, and I believe we'll be able to settle things quickly. It's a traightforward case," he added. "Barring any surprises, of course." He emphasized the word "surprises" as if it were a curse word, and to a prosecutor in the courtroom, that was precisely what they were.

Rick outlined the highlights of the case against Jordan Myers. Clear and concise. He had always had the ability to say more with less, another one of his superpowers. I was pleased to see Lennon listening carefully, nodding as appropriate and asking questions if a legal term or strategy needed to be clarified in her mind. In a nutshell, the State's claim was the defendant had repeatedly used his position as a manager overseeing half a dozen group homes for young women in New London to target at least three of the residents and restrain, threaten, render incapacitated, or by some other means coerce them into the repeated performance of commercial sex acts.

If convicted, he would serve between forty and fifty years in prison for the recruitment, harboring, and transportation of the women whose disappearances could be in whole or in part attributed to him: Riley Jackson, Chloe Anderson, and Allison Tyler.

"What will you be asking me when I'm called to testify?" said Lennon, sounding less nervous the longer our discussion lasted. Grace under pressure, that was Lennon Gallagher.

"I don't want to appear to coach you in any way," replied Rick, "but I'm certain your attorney here will have a good idea as to the nature of the questions," he added with a knowing glance in my direction.

You bet I do, I thought.

"But generally, I will ask you about the disappearance of your friend Ms. Allison Tyler and what you heard and saw the morning of the argument between Mr. Newton and the defendant."

Lennon nodded her understanding. "And I should only answer the specific questions you put forth. Don't embellish or get carried away. Keep my responses succinct and to the point. Right?"

Rick's eyes lit up behind his thick spectacles. She done good, I thought.

"Yes, that's it exactly," he said with a smile, a rarity I had witnessed on only a handful of occasions. "Are there any more questions either of you have for me?"

Lennon and I looked at each other, and she shrugged.

"Can you give us a minute?" I asked Lennon, gesturing toward the door. She took the hint and left, and I turned to Rick.

"What can you tell me about the Westerhaus case? Please, Rick," I added. "It's important."

He studied me for a minute before relenting. "It looks like he has left the country," he said. "But if he's found, the case against him is solid. Receipts, emails, text messages, video . . . From what I understand, there is enough evidence to put him away for the rest of his sick, twisted, miserable life."

Despite my grief, I had to smile at the out-of-character emotional display from my former boss. "Don't sugarcoat it, Counselor. Tell me how you really feel," I said. Behind his oversized spectacles, his dark eyes shone bright.

"You didn't hear it from me, but I hope they fry the son of a bitch," he said.

Yeah, me too.

A short while later, we were driving back to Old Lyme. I glanced over at Lennon to see her eyes were closed and there was a smile on her face. She had put on a few much-needed pounds since coming to stay with us, and it suited her nicely. From a professional perspective, she would make a credible witness. Personally, it delighted me to watch her transformation from street urchin to confident, charming young woman. I focused my attention back to the road before trying and failing to visualize the current contents of the fridge. I was about to ask Lennon what she thought about accompanying me to the grocery store when she spoke up.

"Can I cook for you guys tonight?" she asked. "You've both been so good to me and made me feel so welcome. Would that be okay?"

I told her it sounded great, and she asked if we could stop at the store before heading home. A short while later, I found street parking in front of a shop we frequented for its array of fresh produce and excellent butcher department.

"I'll be right back," she promised and scooted into the store.

It was my turn to close my eyes for a moment, and I did, realizing I too was smiling. While Lennon prepared dinner, I would return emails and relax in the hot tub before we ate. And maybe again with Eric after dinner, I thought, my smile widening at the image in my mind.

Lennon returned shortly with a full bag, the contents of which she refused to disclose, and we drove home. Dinner would be a surprise, she informed me, so there would be no peeking. I agreed, and after a quick snuggle with Hobie, I collected today's mail and went to my office.

Over the next couple of hours, I thought I could hear the occasional clatter of pots and pans from above, but as my office had been built as a virtually soundproof studio, I knew it was only my imagination. I knew Lennon would reach out if she needed any help, so I kept my focus on the task at hand.

Just after five, Eric stuck his head in. "Hey you," he called out and crossed the room to give me a quick kiss. I returned the kiss, lingering a bit, my lips barely grazing his as I recalled my plans for a couple's soak in the hot tub tonight.

"Have you been in the kitchen lately?" he asked me, and I shook my head.

"All I know is Lennon offered to make dinner for us, so I am giving her space. What do you suppose she's making?" I asked, realizing I was getting hungry.

Eric shook his head. "No clue. She shooed me out and said she would let us know when dinner was ready."

"She's a bossy little thing," I said, and he agreed.

We chatted for a bit about our respective days, both agreeing the updates on the Myers trial sounded encouraging. On the other hand, Parametric's announcement that they were filing for bankruptcy was more bad news. Our phones buzzed with texts from upstairs.

Dinner's ready!

"Be ready to speed dial for a pizza," he warned me. "I have a feeling."

I swatted his butt gently as we went up the stairs. "Oh, come on, how bad could it be?"

Pretty freaking bad, I decided several minutes later. The table had been set, again with our finest china, silver, and crystal, and we had clinked our glasses filled to the brim with sparkling water topped with a thin wedge of lime.

"Be right back," Lennon promised, all bright-eyed as she dashed over to the stove.

Eric sniffed the air. "Some kind of beef?" he ventured. "It's kind of hard to tell."

Lennon bustled back to the table, proudly bearing a large fancy-looking casserole dish I didn't recall ever seeing. She placed it gently on a pair of pewter trivets and, after removing the cover, announced, "It's lamb stew á la Gallagher. Let's eat." Taking the large soup bowls from each of our place settings, she set about scooping enormous servings of brown chunks of meat, brightly colored carrots, and large wedges of potatoes.

"Mmm, looks delicious," I said, and Eric agreed.

"Dig in," ordered Lennon, looking pleased with herself. So we did. It would be nearly impossible to describe the complexities of the dish to anyone not present at our dinner table. How might one convey the unlikelihood of mushy carrots resting alongside potatoes rock-like in their un-doneness? Or the charred taste of meat burned to a crisp on the outside and yet somehow blood-red in the center? We spooned up mouthfuls of gravy tasting more like beer, and I wondered how we were going to make it through the meal without hurting Lennon's feelings.

Suddenly, she hopped up and headed back to the oven. "I can't believe I forgot the biscuits," she called to us, and she jerked open the oven door, releasing a plume of dark smoke and the unmistakable aroma of burned bread. "Damn," she cried as she surveyed the small black discs of dough dotting the ruined cookie sheet. "I'm sorry," she wailed. "I'll replace it, I swear," she promised as she upended the contents into the trash.

She returned to the table and watched us as we gamely attacked our bowls of stew, trying to pick around the raw potatoes and the still bloody pieces of lamb. I scrambled to think of something positive to say but came up blank. Not Eric.

"The celery is really nicely chopped," Eric assured Lennon gravely. "Sometimes you find all different-sized pieces of celery in homemade soups or stews, but this is fairly uniform, I think.

It's good." He looked at his bowl and nodded again. "Good celery," he repeated.

I tried to keep myself from cracking up, but it was a losing battle. "Good celery," I said, bursting out laughing. The stresses of the last few weeks melted away as I looked at my husband and my newest friend through eyes now brimming with tears. Happy ones. Lennon was the next to lose it. She put down her fork and raised her arms to the heavens.

"Thank the Goddess for the good celery," she intoned.

We laughed and teased each other, reminiscing about past dinners gone bad, and naturally I brought up my mother's propensity to overcook and underbake everything. Lennon shared the highlights of the last Gallagher Thanksgiving from a few years earlier. It had featured a deep-fried turkey, which had been delicious. It had been served with a weed-infused cranberry sauce, the consumption of which resulted in the police and fire departments being called when several stoned family members got the munchies and set the front porch on fire attempting to deep fry Oreos and slabs of pumpkin pie.

"Gotta love the holidays," said Eric with a rueful grin.

"Worst stew ever," Lennon pronounced, and Eric and I agreed. She wouldn't let us help her clean the kitchen, so while we waited for the pizza delivery, Eric and I took a soak outdoors in the tub. The night air was bitterly cold, but the moon and stars were clearly visible, and the hot water was soothing. While not the romantic soak I had been envisioning, it was relaxing and enjoyable. As we toweled off, Eric whispered his plans for me and my body later in bed, and I shivered not with cold, but delight. Who said having kids put a crimp in your sex life? I wondered. Certainly not me.

CHAPTER 40

The State of Connecticut vs. Jordan Myers trial was proceeding as planned. Rick was pleased with the twelve jurors and two alternates that had been chosen, and despite the media attention the case had attracted, the courtroom was relatively quiet with no outbursts or distractions.

I almost felt sorry for the young lawyer Myers had hired to represent him. The charges against her client were difficult to refute, and the defendant himself did nothing to generate sympathy or understanding from the members of the jury. Her opening argument had been brief and to the point, but she was more than a bit outclassed having to follow Rick, who excelled in the courtroom.

He had outlined the State's case against the defendant, relating how he had come to be a suspect and thoroughly describing the various charges. He played the doorbell videos which captured Myers in the commission of his crimes. The jury gasped aloud at the final video, which showed him dragging an unconscious woman toward his car and allowing her head to rest briefly in the gutter while he struggled to open his trunk. Myers stared at the screen, but his blank expression made it impossible to know what he was thinking. He had sat still as a stone since the trial had begun, not a flicker of emotion crossing his freckled face. Thinking about how his actions had led to the girls going missing, not to mention Lennon's recent scare, made me want to scratch his eyes out or beat him senseless. But I too sat still, trying to appear cool, calm, and collected. It was a struggle to say the least.

The next witnesses called to testify were two of the young women who had been rescued from the White Plains condo. Allison Tyler was first, and she proved quite credible, detailing her first meeting with the defendant and his subsequent use of drugs and physical restraints to prepare her for transport. Myers' attorney attempted to challenge her credibility and trip her up on specific dates and timeframes, and Rick objected several times. But Allison was steadfast in her claims that it had been the defendant who had approached her, drugged her, and forced her into the back of a van heading to New York. Lennon sobbed openly as her friend described the harsh treatment she had been subjected to during her days as a sex worker and the drugs she had been forced to take. When she told of the challenges she was facing since she had been freed, it was clear to everyone that for these young women the nightmare was far from over. Riley Jackson's testimony was very similar to Allison's, but it did not have quite the same emotional impact. I was just as glad that Chloe Anderson was not testifying as I'd seen jurors so overwhelmed with stories like these become almost numb to the horrors as it quickly became almost commonplace. It had been determined that Chloe would not have made a credible witness due to recurring health problems and her difficulty reacclimating following her release.

I felt Lennon stiffen beside me when the next witness, Alan Newton, was called. Alternately stuttering and sobbing, Lennon's creepy former "den mother" told the jury how he had been approached by his supervisor, Mr. Myers, several months earlier. He admitted he had agreed to identify young women who might be looking for a change of scenery and new job opportunities. He stated he'd had no idea the women would be harmed in any way and described himself as "shocked and outraged" when he learned of their fate. Last week, Newton had pled guilty to lesser charges in exchange for his testimony today, a point Rick made clear up front in case the defense tried to use it to weaken his testimony. Newton would still serve up to a year for each of seven counts of unlawful restraint in the second degree and pay a fine of roughly ten thousand dollars. After Alan was escorted back to the holding cell, Rick called Lennon to the stand.

She approached the witness stand with her head held high. We had finally managed a trip to the mall, and the simple blouse and dark skirt she wore were the result. Her hair was styled and shiny, and her face was scrubbed clean of makeup, making her appear even younger than eighteen. Only the pair of Doc Martens she sported gave any hint to the determined badass she was. She responded in a clear and confident manner that the evidence she was about to give to the court was indeed the truth, the whole truth, and nothing but the truth.

Rick approached her, smiling broadly, as if their conversation was of a social nature. After quickly dispensing with introductions, his tone became brisk. "Miss Gallagher, can you please tell the court how you came to be acquainted with the defendant, Mr. Jordan Myers?" he asked.

Lennon sat forward in her seat. Don't be too eager, I thought. Restraint, I had cautioned her.

"Certainly," she began. "I met Jordan, although I knew him as Jay, on the street one day when I was out for a walk with my best friend. Her name is Allison Tyler, and you just heard her testimony. She met him where he worked at the Bradford House before he was arrested, the same location where the other three missing girls once resided before they each disappeared. Allison called him a ginger and told me she thought he was cute," she wrinkled her nose and spoke even more clearly into the microphone, "but I pegged him as a douchebag right from the start."

"Language," the judge cautioned, and Lennon appeared chastened.

"I'm sorry, Your Honor. Please excuse my choice of words. I should have said something less offensive, like creep or lowlife." She sat back, and although her expression was neutral, I could tell she was smiling on the inside. Several members of the jury were as well. I covered my mouth to hide my own joy at her skillful testimony. She had managed to place the defendant squarely in the middle of this case, establishing his relationships with all three young women and describing her initial reaction to the defendant and even using his nickname, which could be construed as an alias. If I had been Ms. Calder, I would have objected several times. Hearsay, character assassination, facts not in evidence and more, but Rick continued without being challenged.

"And, Miss Gallagher, was that the only time you saw the defendant?" he asked. Lennon wasted no time recounting the argument between Myers and Alan Newton. She never stated she actually saw the heated discussion take place, nor did she claim she had not. But her testimony matched word for word the account of the incident she had previously made to Rick. She recounted the parts of the argument she had clearly heard. In a voice tinged with fear, she spoke slowly and clearly.

"My roommate, Carmen, and I saw him leave our house that morning, and it was apparent to me he saw both of us watching him. I moved out the next day, and I tried to warn Carmen to be careful, but she disappeared later that morning. The poor girl," she added after a dramatic pause. She shook her head sadly.

Quit while you're ahead, I counseled her wordlessly from my seat in the stands, and she did. Smiling and moving about energetically, Rick smoothly confirmed the facts Lennon had presented. He concluded by asking her how she felt when she saw the defendant staring up at her in the window that morning.

"Were you frightened?" he asked, and with no objection of "leading the witness" from the defense, he waited for her response.

"Mr. Cooper, sir. I wasn't frightened. I was positively terrified for my life and that of my roommate," she said, her eyes glistening with unshed tears.

Brava, Lennon, I thought. Game. Set. Match.

The judge asked Ms. Calder if she had any questions for the witness, and to her credit the young lawyer approached Lennon and attempted to poke holes in her testimony. Anything was better than to let Lennon's admission of fear for her life be the last thing the members of the jury heard. A couple of times Lennon came dangerously close to losing her cool, but she managed to respond politely as Calder picked away, trying to rattle the witness to no avail.

After consultations with both attorneys, the judge declared closing arguments would be heard following a brief recess. I told Lennon I wanted to check my messages and stepped out into the hallway. Nothing too critical it appeared, but I called Rose at the office to check in. I debated a quick trip to the restroom but decided against it as the doors opened and people started to file back in.

Following closing arguments nearly anticlimactic in their brevity, the jury heard instructions from the judge before beginning deliberations. It might not have set an actual record for the fastest jury decision ever in returning a unanimous verdict of guilty on all counts, but I can attest to the fact I had barely returned to the courtroom after tucking into the restroom, placing a quick call to Eric, and giving a radiant Lennon the biggest hug, when it was announced the jury had reached a verdict. Lennon and I stood silently, squeezing hands as the verdict that was no surprise to anyone in the room was read aloud.

It was a victory, that was for certain. A bittersweet victory, but you took what you could get in situations like these. But I knew I wouldn't do any celebrating until Edward Westerhaus was located, tried, and convicted.

CHAPTER 41

The following Monday, I drove slowly through the busy side streets of New London until we got to the ramp to I-95. As I accelerated to merge with the traffic heading north, I glanced over at my passenger. Lennon was pulling off her new parka and fuzzy mittens. She placed them carefully on the backseat, sat back, and sighed.

"You too warm?" I asked, and she shrugged.

"Nope, but I figured I should ditch the new threads so Charlene doesn't pitch a hissy fit," she said with a smirk. "She has a sixth sense about these things. It's like she would know if I got undressed in the parking lot right before I saw her."

Knowing full well how little things could always set Charlene off that way, I nodded in agreement. "Probably wise," I said. "Want me to turn up the heat on your side?"

"Yes, please," she said and closed her eyes, letting the warm air from the vents blow on her face. "Hey, Randi?"

"Yes, sweetheart. What is it?"

"Yeah, so down in that basement. You know I was only a little bit buzzed. I wanted Alan to think I was, you know, out of it so maybe I could get the gun away from him."

"That was so smart. You really can think on your feet." We had already discussed this, and I wondered where the conversation was headed.

"What I'm trying to say is, the minute I got the gun, I checked and saw it wasn't loaded. One of Aunt Kelly's loser boyfriends used to take me to shoot cans and shit. Anyway, what I'm trying to tell you is when I saw there were no bullets, I should have felt relieved, yeah?"

I shrugged. "There are no guidelines on how you're supposed to feel at a time like that. So do you want to tell me how you did feel?"

She looked away, trying to seem interested in the laces of her boots, but spoke clearly. "Yeah, I felt disappointed cuz now I couldn't shoot the motherfucker. Does that mean I'm a terrible person?"

We had pulled into the visitors' lot at the York facility. I turned to look at her, and she watched me closely, tears forming in her sad brown eyes.

"No, dear girl," I told her as I drew her in for a hug. "It means you're human." As we walked toward the entrance, I murmured, "You got this," to Lennon, and she nodded, eyes straight ahead. I felt her hand seek out mine, and she gave me a quick squeeze.

"You've got it too," she whispered. We entered the large overheated lobby and joined the short line. We emptied our pockets and walked through the metal detector without incident and waited until the doors to the visitors' lounge opened. We made our way inside, and the first thing I noticed was a small gray-haired woman sitting by herself at a table in the far corner. I had thought I was prepared for the sight of my old friend, but I felt both sadness and shock as she looked up at us and gave a half wave. It had been nearly twenty years since I'd laid eyes on Charlene, and I fought to maintain a neutral expression as we approached her.

"Quick one," she murmured to her daughter, who leaned in to receive a brief hug.

"No touching," came the warning from one of the guards, but we were already seated around the small round table. Charlene's dark eyes darted back and forth between Lennon and me, looking for something . . . possibly some sign of weakness to exploit or a closeness between her daughter and me she could get upset about. Lennon had warned me her mother could smell fear from a mile away, so I crossed my legs and folded my hands in front of me. Stay calm, I told myself.

"Well, this ain't exactly a high school reunion," she said with a low chuckle. "But it's sure good to see the two of you together, thick as thieves. You're looking good, old pal," she said, giving me the once-over. I flushed, knowing I couldn't honestly say the same about her.

"It's good to see you, Char—" I began, but she had continued speaking.

"And what do you think of my little girl? My pride and joy, that's what she is," Charlene said proudly. "Shame you couldn't have a kid of your own. I'll tell you there's nothing like it. But I guess you'll hafta take my word on that."

I felt Lennon stiffen, and I tried to communicate what we had practiced earlier. *Don't engage. Don't let her push your buttons. Show no fear.*

"She's delightful. The first time I met her, I told her she reminded me of you at her age," I said. "And that's what we wanted to talk to you about today." Charlene's ears pricked up with interest. During their weekly phone call last evening, Lennon had told her mother she and I would be visiting today, but as far as I knew, she hadn't explained the reason for my tagging along.

"Don't tell me, let me guess," said Charlene. "You want to take her on an all-expense paid trip around the world, and you need me to sign a permission slip, or I dunno, maybe you're gonna enlist her in the navy or some shit and you need a copy of her birth certificate, or maybe—"

Lennon cut her off. "I am going to live with Randi and her husband in Old Lyme, Mom. I'm eighteen, and I don't need your permission or even your blessing. But I wanted you to hear it from me. Eric taught me how to drive and is helping me get my driver's license. They have the coolest cat named Hobie. You know I always wanted one. And Randi's helping with all the paperwork for me to enroll at the community college for the upcoming semester next month. What do you think? Isn't that great?" Lennon watched her mother closely for her reaction.

Charlene sat back and folded her arms across her sunken chest. She nodded sagely.

"Well, well, ain't that grand. My little girl—driving a car and going to college and living with my best friend out in East Bumfuck. Why that may be the greatest news I've heard in my whole entire life. If you're lucky, maybe she'll buy you a pony," she jeered and shook her head. "And you, former friend. Fake friend. First you take my boyfriend, and then you steal my life. And now you're coming after my own flesh and blood. You're really something, girlfriend."

She glared at me, but instead of feeling anger at her cruel words and twisted perspective, I felt . . . sad. A deep and abiding sadness for this pitiful person sitting next to me. I leaned closer, motioning for her to do the same. Looking like she was hoping to initiate some sort of fight to include any combination of slaps, punches, or hair pulling, she leaned in, her dark eyes glowing with mischief. "Give me a reason to smack you upside the head, bitch," her body language and facial expression virtually screamed. I spoke in a low voice.

"Char, it pains me to see you in here. It really does. I understand you're up for parole, and I want you to contact me. I'll see if I can help get you out of here. But if that occurs, you need to promise you'll stay away from Lennon. She'll be in touch if and when she wants to talk to you, but until she does, don't try to call her. Your daughter is smart, really smart. I wish you could see it, and I hope someday you will. She's going to work her way through community college and then get her bachelor's degree and maybe head to law school if that's what she still wants in a few years. She is going to live with us right now but maybe go to UCONN next year. Or Smith College or Mt. Holyoke or wherever the hell she wants. You need to be okay with this, do you understand? She's got the chance to be successful, to be happy. I know you, Char. And I know deep down that's what you want for her." Charlene didn't respond, and I sat back feeling frustrated. What would it take to get through to her?

Lennon stood to leave. "We should go," she told me before turning to face her mother. "I'll still call you every week, Mom. There will always be money in your commissary, and I'll make sure Aunt Kelly has my new phone number and address for emergencies. But I won't be coming to see you for a while cuz I'm going to be working hard to get good grades. And you'll see, you'll be proud of me someday." She started to tear up, but as Charlene continued to sit there stone-faced, Lennon wiped her eyes angrily. "Let's go," she said to me right before Charlene finally stood and walked toward her.

"Quick one," she whispered, and Lennon automatically leaned in to her mother. Charlene murmured into her daughter's ear. "Don't go messin' with her husband, you hear? And, girl? From the moment you were born, I've always been proud of you." Lennon pulled back in surprise, staring at her mother. For once, Charlene didn't get the "no touching" warning, and, emboldened, she turned to face me next. "You take care of my girl, Randi Quinn. Don't let nothing bad happen to her, or when I get out, you and me's gonna have words. Got it?"

I nodded and forced a smile. "Got it. And let me know when your parole hearing gets scheduled. I really do want to try and help you, okay?" I studied my old friend's face closely, but her expression had changed. She was once more closed off, on emotional lockdown. No one could get to her now. With a half wave, she turned and shuffled over toward the guard who would escort her back to G block. Lennon and I stood silently, waiting for her to turn and wave or smile before she disappeared from our view. But nothing. The door closed behind her, and that was that.

Lennon and I arrived back at home to find Eric staring transfixed at the television. There on our sixty-five-inch widescreen, we watched together as FBI agents arrested a surprisingly frail Edward "Dr. Chris" Westerhaus as he exited a private plane that had just landed in the Bahamas. The crawl at the bottom of the screen said it all:

Dr. Chris Under "Haus" Arrest. Radio Host Could Serve Fifty Years to Life.

CHAPTER 42

Two weeks later . . .

Everyone looked up, and conversation came to a halt when Sally clinked her fork against her juice glass. We had gathered at our house on Christmas Day for brunch. It was the last time we would all be together for a while, and I, for one, was glad we had managed to pull it off. After another couple of clinks to make certain we were paying attention, Sally spoke up.

"I want to thank Randi and Eric for hosting us today," she began, and the sounds of "hear, hear" and "thanks, you guys" followed. Eric and I beamed at each other from across the table as she continued. "I was hoping we could go around the table and share what we are most grateful for this past year." To silence a couple of the groans her request had elicited, Sally raised a hand. "I know, I know, it's usually a Thanksgiving tradition, but if you'll recall, this Thanksgiving was anything *but* traditional." That was an understatement for sure. The ice storm, an emergency room visit, the missing girls reappearing, the secret life of Dr. Chris exposed . . . "So please indulge me. Who would like to begin?"

Jake stood and cleared his throat. "I'll go," he said. "Mom, I think this is an excellent idea, and I would like to say how grateful I am to be with my family today. My wife," he said as he motioned to Meg, who was smiling up at him, "and my kids," he added, gesturing at Clementine and Teddy, who were playing together at the kids' picnic blanket a few feet away. "I love you all, but I am also grateful for Eric," he said, which garnered a few looks of surprise. "My brother-in-law, who, if he hadn't bungled his big opportunity, would have up and moved my sister three thousand miles away from her family." Everyone chuckled at that, especially Eric.

He stood, grinning happily, and raised his mug of coffee. "I guess that makes me up next," he quipped. "Thanks, pal," he said to Jake. "Leave it to the bean counter to go straight to the bottom line. If you haven't heard the news yet, you're looking at the newest member of the faculty in UCONN's Architectural Design program. Classes begin in three weeks, and I have got some ground to cover before then. But moving on, I'm grateful for all of you, most of all my amazing wife. Quinn, you never cease to amaze me, delight me, and inspire me. You were ready to uproot your life and allow me to live my dream, but you knew I already was. To living the dream with you, babe." Sounds of agreement followed, and I blushed and waved away the attention. I blew a kiss to Eric, who sat down seconds before Julie hopped up.

"I'm next," she said. "I am excited for you guys," she said, indicating her mother and Pop. "We would love to come and visit you, but we are going to stay home and get busy. Like real busy. Trying for a baby busy," she added. Everyone cheered, and Brad hugged her close to him.

"No pressure," Brad said with a grin, and Pop stood next.

"I love my family," he said simply. "I never dreamed my life could be so full again. And soon maybe even fuller." He shook his head, seemingly amazed at his good fortune. "Sal and I will miss you while we're collecting seashells and soaking up the sunshine in Fort Myers, but like she said, we'll be back in the spring." I brushed away the tears filling my eyes. Not ready to make a permanent move right now, my folks had decided to rent a condo near the beach for three months. I was certain the warm sunshine and the lack of snow would suit them both and at some point they would move south permanently. "And don't forget, we are taking off at seven in the morning, so say your goodbyes today. I'll not be having all our neighbors gawking at us." We all laughed at that. Despite being a warm and affectionate man, Desmond Quinn drew the line at most public displays of affection.

Eric's brother went next and ended his short speech of gratitude with a special announcement. "And, Dez, you're not the only one with a growing family," he said, squeezing his wife's hand. "Trish and I got a call from Skip this morning. He and Becky are expecting a baby this summer. Little Jesse's gonna be a big brother." Everyone called out their congratulations, and John sat and hugged his wife. Becky had called me the other day to share the news, and Eric and I had been thrilled. Being sworn to secrecy these past couple of days had been challenging. But our family was growing and changing, and we couldn't have been happier.

Sally assured John and Trish they were planning to spend some time with Skip and Becky while they were in Florida. When no one stood to go next, the conversation continued and the food was passed around again. Trish's fruit salad, Eric's turkey sausages, and my French toast casserole were on the menu, and everyone was enjoying the meal.

I looked up in surprise when I heard the familiar sound of a fork clinking against glass and grinned at the image of the newest addition to our home, Ms. Lennon Gallagher. Her hair had grown out a bit, and she looked as fresh-faced and glowing as any eighteen-year-old I had even seen. The short green cocktail dress she wore positively sparkled and suited her petite frame perfectly. She grinned at all of us.

"As much as I love hanging out at the kids' blanket, I wanted to say something real quick. Thank you all for making me feel so welcome," she began, and I watched Sal and Meg grasp hands and tear up. Pop looked close to tears himself, still in shock a "good Gallagher" had finally materialized. I wiped away new tears of my own as I listened to this young woman I had come to adore. "Eric, thank you for teaching me how to drive," she said, "cuz your wife sure as hell wasn't up to the job." That brought some laughs, but I winced, recalling the one lesson I had given her; the one ending with lots of shouting (Lennon) and even more tears (both of us). Good times for sure. "And to Jake and Meg for hiring me to watch your kids. I love spending time with them, and it's nice to not have to ask for an allowance at my age. And thank you, Sally, for letting me drive your car for the next few months. I promise to keep it clean and to obey all posted speed limits," she added with a wink in Pop's direction. "And mainly to you, Randi. For believing in me, for supporting me, and for making me believe I had a right to a better life. Thanks to you, Tyler, Chloe, and Riley have a shot at much better lives too. Everything you did to bring them home and get them the help they needed to start over . . . You are amazing."

I smiled, thinking of all we had accomplished in the past month. It hadn't been easy, and Chloe in particular still had a long way to go, but all three young women had a safe place to live and were receiving counseling to deal with their trauma as well as vocational guidance to find work that suited them. I met with them weekly as a group to discuss their progress. As far as I knew, Joe hadn't assigned a nickname to them . . . yet.

Lennon was finishing her comments. "I will never understand how I got so lucky to have you in my life, Randi. I want to be a kick-ass lawyer like you someday." Cheers followed, along with Clem's high-pitched giggle.

"Mommy, Lenny said 'ass.'"

I looked around at this cobbled-together family we had created in the past five years. How had I gotten along without them all this time? These were my people, my favorite humans in the whole world. As I watched, Tracey, Dale, and the twins came bursting in carrying brightly wrapped gifts and more food. They had been at Dale's mom's house and had made me promise we would start brunch without them. Before I could get to my feet, Tracey drew me into a hug from behind.

"Merry Christmas, my friend. Look at you, all happy and shit," she whispered, but not quite softly enough.

"Mommy, Miss Tracey said a bad word," Clem giggled.

"No one likes a snitch, Clemmie," said Tracey with an eye-roll in my direction.

I couldn't argue with that.

The next day . . .

Eric and I arrived first. It was 6:40 in the morning, and we, well I, wanted to say goodbye to my folks in person. But Pop's Jeep wasn't in its usual parking spot, and no one had answered when we rang their doorbell. We stood on the sidewalk, confused, and I texted Sal with a question mark and a heart. We had both heard Pop say they were leaving at seven. As we watched, Jake and his family drove up. He pulled alongside of us and rolled down his window.

"What's up?" he asked sleepily. "Did we miss them?" Before either of us could answer, Julie drove into the lot and, seeing us all together, drove closer, waving excitedly.

"Do they know we're here?" she asked before studying our faces. "Guess not," she said.

We waited around for a few more minutes as the sky brightened and a handful of tenants passed by clutching towels, on their way to the early morning water aerobics class held in the center's Olympic-sized indoor swimming pool. Sally attended nearly every day. But clearly, not today.

"Well, this blows," said Jake, earning him a glare from his wife, while in the backseat Clem and Teddy started singing, "This blows, this blows," over and over.

I felt my phone buzz, and everyone else did too. There was a new message in our family group text chain.

Said goodbye yest. Got an early start.
See you in the Spring. Love, Sal & Dez

I shook my head, resigned to the fact we had been outsmarted by the master. Leave it to Pop.

"Anyone up for breakfast?" I asked, and we all agreed to meet at the pancake parlor near the center of town.

"Bacon and scrambled eggs for you?" Eric teased as we pulled into the parking lot a few minutes later.

"I'm having waffles," I told him with a grin. Eric's exciting new teaching career, Lennon starting college, Pop and Sal's big adventure . . . Life was changing for all of us, calling for new traditions, a different lens with which to view the world. Out with the old, but . . . "Bacon and eggs on the side," I mumbled. Not everything had to change all at once. Some things were pretty damn good just the way they were.

THE END

P.S. Want more Miranda?? Here's the first chapter of *Miranda Writes*. I hope you enjoy it!!

Miranda Writes

CHAPTER 1

Despite a brain still foggy from endless champagne toasts, I was feeling good. Yesterday had been a wonderful day. I finally had something to celebrate, following the demise of what had once promised to be a stellar legal career. My blog-turned-podcast, *Miranda Writes*, had recently garnered enough attention that the Sterling Broadcast Group had brought my closest supporters and me to New York in a limousine to sign a lucrative contract to host a daytime TV show. Things were looking up after a few tough years.

We had arrived back to Old Lyme, CT in the early evening and dropped off my dad and his girlfriend Sally, followed by my best friend Tracey and her husband Dale. Then, with help from the limo driver, I had carted all the floral arrangements and fruit baskets from future sponsors into my house. I was awestruck by the outpouring of support I had received. When I first started blogging, I had never imagined that it would lead to this. Honestly, back then I had been writing to maintain my sanity, nothing more.

The local network affiliate had already started airing promos of my upcoming show and I had stayed busy all night, fielding phone calls, texts and emails from friends, neighbors and former classmates. The calls stopped around 11:00 p.m., but I had lain awake for hours, my mind buzzing with topics for shows and names of legal experts I wanted to invite as guests. I had finally fallen asleep and was still in bed, debating the merits of a pot of home-brewed coffee and a slice of multigrain toast versus a drive-through latte and a cinnamon roll roughly the size of my head. My phone buzzed beside me. Probably a long-lost law school classmate or a childhood friend calling to congratulate me or to wish me well, I guessed. I checked the time as I found my phone. 5:45 a.m. Too early for a friendly call, I thought with a flicker of concern. *Hmmm*, unknown number.

"Hello."

"Um, hello. Is this Miss Quinn?" The voice was soft but familiar.

"Yes, this is Miranda. Can I help you?"

"Yes, ma'am. I need to talk to you, Miss Quinn. I don't know if you remember me—"

"Who is this?" I asked, barely masking my annoyance. I was rarely up for a game of twenty questions, and never before I had my coffee.

"It's, um. Becky. Becky Lewis." I sat bolt upright in bed, the chill I felt having nothing to do with the sudden loss of my down comforter. Becky Lewis? Yes, I certainly remembered her.

"Becky? Of course, I remember you. What's um, up?"

"I'm sorry, Miss Quinn. Really, I am. I saw you on TV last night and I thought I should get in touch with you about what happened." I was struggling to follow her. What had happened?

"What do you mean?"

"He did it again, Miss Quinn. He hurt that girl. Just like me and the other one." My heart sank. I knew who she meant. Of course, I did. Three years ago, I'd had the chance to put him away, and I had blown it. Now he had attacked another woman, and it was all my fault. This one was most definitely on me. But I still needed to ask. To be sure.

"Who, Becky? Who is *he*? What did he do?"

"Terry. Terry Kane. He raped another girl."

To keep reading, order your copy of *Miranda Writes* today!!

AUTHOR'S NOTE

Human trafficking is a form of modern-day slavery and a serious crime. Traffickers use force, fraud, or coercion to make victims engage in labor or commercial sexual exploitation. Everyone has the potential to discover a human trafficking situation. While victims may sometimes be kept behind locked doors, they are often hidden right in front of us, working at restaurants, elder care centers, nail salons, agricultural fields, and hotels. For urgent situations, notify local law enforcement immediately by calling 911. You can also call the National Human Trafficking Hotline so they can ensure response by law enforcement officials knowledgeable about human trafficking.

Call **1-888-373-7888** to report a tip, connect with anti-trafficking services in your area, or request training and technical assistance, general information, or specific anti-trafficking resources. The hotline is equipped to handle calls from all regions of the United States from a wide range of callers including, but not limited to: potential trafficking victims, community members, law enforcement, medical professionals, legal professionals, service providers, researchers, students, and policymakers.

Gail O

ABOUT THE AUTHOR

Gail Ward Olmsted was a marketing executive and a college professor before she began writing fiction on a full-time basis. A trip to Sedona, AZ inspired her first novel *Jeep Tour*. Three more novels followed before *Landscape of a Marriage*, a biographical fiction featuring landscape architect Frederick Law Olmsted, a distant cousin of her husband's, and his wife Mary.

Miranda Fights is the third book in the Miranda Quinn Legal Twist series. Olmsted enjoys writing about quirky, wonderful women in search of a second chance at a happy ever after. When not writing, she loves being on the water, especially in a kayak. She is well known for her blonde brownies, and coffee is her love language. For more, visit her on Facebook at gailolmstedauthor.

NOTE FROM
GAIL WARD OLMSTED

Word-of-mouth is crucial for any author to succeed. If you enjoyed *Miranda Fights*, please leave a review online—anywhere you are able. Even if it's just a sentence or two. It would make all the difference and would be very much appreciated.

Thanks!

We hope you enjoyed reading this title from:

BLACK ROSE
writing™

www.blackrosewriting.com

Subscribe to our mailing list – *The Rosevine* – and receive **FREE** books, daily deals, and stay current with news about upcoming releases and our hottest authors.
Scan the QR code below to sign up.

Already a subscriber? Please accept a sincere thank you for being a fan of Black Rose Writing authors.

View other Black Rose Writing titles at www.blackrosewriting.com/books and use promo code **PRINT** to receive a **20% discount** when purchasing.